D0930193

Dead by Dawn

Center Point
Large Print

Books are produced in the United States using U.S.-based materials

Books are printed using a revolutionary new process called THINKtech™ that lowers energy usage by 70% and increases overall quality

Books are durable and flexible because of Smyth-sewing

Paper is sourced using environmentally responsible foresting methods and the paper is acid-free

Also by Paul Doiron and available from Center Point Large Print:

Widowmaker
Knife Creek
Stay Hidden
Almost Midnight
One Last Lie

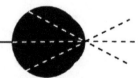

This Large Print Book carries the Seal of Approval of N.A.V.H.

Dead by Dawn

Paul Doiron

CENTER POINT LARGE PRINT
THORNDIKE, MAINE

This Center Point Large Print edition
is published in the year 2021 by arrangement with
St. Martin's Publishing Group.

This is a work of fiction.
All of the characters, organizations, and
events portrayed in this novel are either products
of the author's imagination or are used fictitiously.

The text of this Large Print edition is unabridged.
In other aspects, this book may vary
from the original edition.
Printed in the United States of America
on permanent paper.
Set in 16-point Times New Roman type.

ISBN: 978-1-64358-997-8

The Library of Congress has cataloged this record
under Library of Congress Control Number: 2021936920

For my uncle Augie

Tell me this is the future,
I won't believe you.
Tell me I'm living,
I won't believe you.

—LOUISE GLÜCK

1

The hill is steep here, and there is no guardrail above the river. I think I am being careful, keeping a light touch on the wheel, feathering the brakes. But then I come around the curve and see the spiked objects scattered across the asphalt in my headlights. They look like barbaric versions of children's jacks. Or medieval caltrops laid on battlefields to maim horses—except that these hunks of metal have been welded from box nails and placed here for the malign purpose of blowing out automobile tires.

The front wheels of the Jeep run over the first of them before I can react, and the sound is like two muskets being fired in tandem. The wolf dog in his enormous crate in the rear lets loose a strangled yelp. And now the back tires are bursting, too, and the steering wheel tugs one way, then the other, and when I pump the brake pedal nothing happens because I'm going too fast. I am over the edge before I can exhale.

I feel the drop in my stomach. The high beams touch the frozen river a microsecond before the vehicle itself does, crashing into and through the ice with such violence that the engine block lurches under the hood. The airbag bursts like an outsized puffball in my face. My lungs let go of their oxygen. And icy water rushes up around my legs to pierce my groin.

The cold delivers a body blow, the assault fiercest upon my heart. My breathing becomes rapid-fire, insufficient to my lungs' needs.

Because fear moves faster than thought, I experience the panicked recognition of what has happened—of what *is* happening—as scalding heat along my scalp. Then neurons flash inside my brain. And I am fully awake to my predicament.

My first thought is of Shadow, trapped inside his kennel.

The danger to me registers as a secondary concern—except as a scolding voice inside my head.

Bowditch, you idiot.

I'd taken the blind curve too fast. Should have known better than to pump the brakes when the tires detonated. Shouldn't have tried steering through the blowout. Not that my mistakes matter now.

Another nanosecond passes before I realize that the upended Compass hasn't broken entirely through the ice but is stuck, half in and half out of the Androscoggin River. I am staring down, past the bobbing airbag and the spiderweb cracks in the windshield, into shimmering brown water illuminated by halogen bulbs.

Cold crushes my chest. I slam my left fist on

the controls in the door to bring the windows down, but I am too late. The electrical system shorts out, and darkness floods in as absolute as the river.

Just sounds now: the water sloshing, the thrashing of Shadow in his cage, the crunch of ice, my own overloud heart.

At a course I took with the Michigan State Police—part of my continuing ed as a Maine game warden—the students practiced escaping a sinking vehicle. But I was surrounded by rescue divers that day, and the water was as warm as a bathtub. It surprises me that memories of that distant exercise still reside in my muscles. I'm not making decisions exactly. My hand finds the seat belt release button. The buckle snaps back, and I fall forward into the flood.

Half blind, I twist and turn, trying to get my legs out from under the airbag and steering wheel, and knock my kneecap on something hard. I find my face above the surface for the briefest of moments. Sinuses burning, I snort out water.

The Jeep is settling as the ice cracks beneath its weight. I glance overhead at the lift gate and see a grayish haze. I am looking through the back window into an unaccountably pale sky.

I grab the headrests and pull myself backward, halfway between the front seats, but something catches at my waist as I try to kick-swim through the gap.

The gun in its holster on my belt.

I use most of the muscles in my upper body to push against the seats, feel something give, and then I am through, the rising tide close behind.

High-pitched barks alternating with snarls—cries of fear and rage.

Shadow's enormous kennel is made of roto-molded plastic, double-walled and crushproof. I bought it on the strength of an internet video that showed the box resisting a shotgun blast from a distance of ten feet. It has lived up to its warranty. The walls are intact; the gate remains shut. Despite the violence of the fall and Shadow's desperate efforts to break free, the straps securing it to the frame haven't given an inch.

Climbing into the back, across the folded-down seats, requires awkward contortions. The same web belts that kept the crate from coming loose during the impact have become an actual web, blocking my passage. I reach for the folding knife in the front pocket of my jeans.

The Gerber 06 Auto is no gentleman's folder but a massive hunk of machined metal: an aluminum and steel bar containing a razor-sharp switchblade for use in combat. It weighs 7.1 ounces. The drop point blade, serrated at the hilt, is forged from S30V steel alloy and measures 3.6 inches from tip to finger guards. My friend

Billy Cronk carried this knife on his tours of duty in Iraq and Afghanistan and survived while thousands of his fellow warriors perished. Although Billy never said so, I believe the blade may have taken lives. He gave it to me as a gift on my thirtieth birthday. His nickname for it was "The Beast."

When I push the oversized button on the handle, the blade swings open. It doesn't spring from the tip like a switchblade from a 1950s movie. The serrations are sharper than wolf's teeth; I saw easily through the nylon straps.

But now the untethered box lurches. One hundred and forty pounds of drowning canine causes it to move. And at first I can't get past. Then the crate bucks again, creating an opening, and I seize my chance to swim through.

I reach down for my sidearm to blow out the back window. My fingers slap my side expecting to close around the grip of my SIG. But I find— nothing. Straining to squeeze between the seats, I have dislodged the paddle holster. It was designed to slide in and out of my waistband without my having to remove my belt.

The light inside the Jeep is all but gone. The last pocket of air is closing. I need to break the glass.

Then it hits me: I've been holding the tool I need the whole time. Opposite the blade of the tactical knife, at the end of the pommel, is a strike point, which is a fancy name for a window smasher.

Now I am completely underwater, and my lungs are burning like I've inhaled chlorine. I drive the strike point into the window. The glass explodes into shimmering bits that catch light as they drift past in the coffee-dark current.

As soon as I undo the latch, the wolf bursts through the door of the kennel. Swimming, a foot catches my hand, and I feel a searing pain as his curved claws rake my skin.

I let out a gasp and the last of my precious air bubbles away.

For an instant, I am paralyzed again, unable to think or act. The lack of oxygen is popping my eyeballs from my skull. I don't recognize the black ribbons before my eyes as the blood from my hand.

I manage a few lame kicks, and I am sucked through the broken window as if by the current, although it's just the weight of the Jeep descending to the rock-tumbled bottom.

Training to become a game warden, I learned that a corpse will sink before it rises, that the human body loses buoyancy after our last breath leaves us. Half-dead, I float. With almost no help from my dangling arms and legs, I rise toward the surface, only to knock my skull against the drifting ice. I have been carried past the hole made by the Jeep.

All day, I'd been following the half-frozen Androscoggin, observing the wide river with no expectation of having to rescue myself from it. I recall stretches of open water disappearing and reappearing from beneath vast silvery sheets of ice. I recall steam rising, because the air is so much colder, through the ragged gaps.

I'm trapped and out of oxygen and caught by the current.

Swept along by the river, I repeatedly bump my head against the impenetrable ceiling. Even if I had the strength to scramble along, feeling for a hole to admit me into the December night, I probably wouldn't find one.

This is the way it ends for me, I think.

Maybe Shadow found his way out. It makes it easier to believe he did.

My eyes close.

My bobbing skull strikes the ice again, bounces off, rises one last time. And somehow my face has found its way above the surface. I choke out river water, take the biggest breath I have ever taken, and look up at snowflakes blowing like feathers across the sky.

2

Early that morning, my best friend brought his daughter to my house to see the wolf.

Billy Cronk lived with his large family in a small house down the road from mine, in Ducktrap Village. I had asked him to help me load the crate into my Jeep because it was a two-man job. I had also wanted to ask his advice about a sensitive personal matter. He had surprised me by bringing along little Emma.

When I'd first met Billy years ago in the black forest of Down East Maine, I was convinced I'd run into a lost descendant of the Norsemen who had briefly invaded North America during the time of Leif Eriksson. He stood six feet five inches tall with a golden beard and blond braids. And he possessed some of the weirdest eyes I'd ever seen in a person—the disquieting ice blue of a sled dog. That day like most days, he'd worn a hunting knife in a sheath on his belt that could have served most people as a machete.

The uneasiness I'd felt in his presence was more than a reaction to his intimidating appearance. Billy had served as a light infantryman during some of the most brutal battles of the Iraq and Afghanistan wars and carried himself with the perpetual alertness of a professional soldier. He was a man who had killed other men, and violence followed him like a shadow. I'd once watched a barroom packed with drunk loggers and hunting guides—some of the meanest brawlers in the North Woods—fall silent when he stepped through the door. Some of these roughnecks even slipped out the rear exit rather than cross his path leaving.

Billy Cronk was no gentle giant.

The man was brutal against anyone who threatened his family or his friends. A year after we'd become close, I had occasion to witness the violence of which he was capable, and what I'd seen had chilled me to the marrow. Based in part on my testimony, he'd gone to prison for the crimes I'd watched him commit. He was only free thanks to a questionable pardon issued by our blowhard ex-governor.

Which wasn't to say that there was no kindness in the man.

He wrote heartfelt (if poorly composed) poems about summer sunrises and migrating monarch butterflies. He wept openly when he listened to Cape Breton fiddle music. He made a quiet practice of rescuing and rehabilitating injured animals. His current charge was a blue jay, blind in one eye, he'd nicknamed Racket.

Given this secret tenderness, it was hardly a surprise that his youngest child, his only daughter, had made him her slave.

Emma was even blonder than her father, platinum-white, with her mom's rosy complexion and thoughtful gaze. While her four brothers were all husky for their ages, Emma Cronk was almost elfin in her smallness. The fairy-like quality was reinforced by her current obsession with the Harry Potter books. This morning, she was wearing a black wizard's robe her mother had sewn for her out of fabric bought from one of the local dollar stores. Pink snow boots peeked out from beneath the salt-stained fringe.

Upon entering my drafty, unswept house, she announced, "You don't have a Christmas tree!"

She wasn't any blunter than other kids. It was just that as an unmarried man of thirty-one, I found most children to be discombobulating.

"I've been busy, Emma. I haven't had time."

"But you don't have any decorations at all, Uncle Mike." She emphasized her words with the wand Billy had carved for her. "How will Santa leave you presents if you don't have a Christmas tree?"

It was December 21, the winter solstice, the shortest day of the year. The holiday was less than a week away. It seemed too late for a tree, especially since I would be traveling for Christmas—although I wasn't yet sure of my destination. That particular conundrum was what I'd wanted to discuss with Emma's father.

"I don't want presents," I said, squatting down to her height. "I have everything I need."

Her eyes bugged out. "What?"

Emma Cronk delighted in gifts. She delighted in making lists of gifts she wanted. She delighted in tearing open gifts with puppylike eagerness. She delighted in unwrapping other people's gifts, not always with their permission.

"Uncle Mike will get a tree," said Billy in his bearish growl. "Don't you worry, Emma."

"Well, he'd better!"

I moved to ease her dismay by making a cup of hot chocolate.

"Your dad and I need to talk outside for a few minutes," I said. "Would you like me to put on the TV?"

Emma, in her tiny voice, said she'd prefer to write, thank you. She produced a little journal and pen from the pocket of her robe.

"What are you writing?"

"Spells."

Billy and I took our coffee mugs onto the porch, overlooking the wooded enclosure where the wolf lived.

"Do her spells work?" I asked him.

"The crazy thing is I think they do," he said, breathing steam from his mouth. "Aimee had the flu, and it went right away after Em cast one of her 'chantments. Now she's working on making it snow for Christmas."

The dawning sky was clear enough that I could see Venus. "There's none in the forecast."

"Those weathermen have no idea what they're up against in Emma."

It was past seven, but the sun hadn't cleared the treetops. The understory was a study in sepia: drab alders, gray maples, fossil birches. We'd scared a flock of pine siskins from the feeder tray, and the birds now chided us from the nearest branches, their calls hoarse and buzzing.

The morning air had a snap to it, but Billy didn't seem to feel the cold, any more than a grizzly would. He wore only a shawl-neck sweater over a flannel shirt, blue jeans, and his usual neoprene hunting boots. And that long knife on his belt, of course.

For my part, I've always subscribed to the maxim "There's no bad weather, only unsuitable clothing."

My outfit consisted of a hooded down-filled parka over a commando sweater, over my government-issue ballistic vest, over a merino wool base layer. Beneath my blue jeans (admittedly not a good choice for a day with a forecast high of twenty-five degrees), I wore merino long johns and heavy wool socks. My boots were specially designed by L.L.Bean for use by Maine game wardens in all weather: waterproof, hard-toed, insulated with PrimaLoft, and fashioned with the stickiest lug soles I'd ever worn.

On my belt I wore my badge on a clip and my service weapon, a SIG Sauer P239, in its paddle holster. I'd dropped a couple of magazines in the pockets of my parka almost without thinking. As always, I wore my father's Vietnam dog tags around my neck and carried the push-button knife Billy had given me.

I figured I would be spending the day in the Jeep and had little need for gear beyond what I carried in the government vehicle.

I leaned against the porch rail. "Maybe she can try bewitching my new neighbor."

"The lawyer who bought the land across the river? Mr. Purple Polo? I thought he was just a summer complaint."

It was an impolitic term for a second-home owner. The downside to living in Vacationland was that we year-rounders found ourselves outnumbered during the warmer months—and forced to reckon with the economic carrots and sticks wielded by our fair-weather neighbors.

"He claims no one told him when he bought the place that there was a wolf across the river," I said. "He and his wife came up for leaf season and heard Shadow howl, and it just about froze their blood. The sheriff explained the situation, but it didn't satisfy Mr. Purple Polo. He and his wife showed up here last week in their BMW X5 to have a look at the beast and threaten me with a lawsuit."

Billy scratched his beard, which might have been woven from gold and copper wires. "Shadow's not a beast. He's a dog."

"He's a *wolf* dog. Recently living in the wild."

A brave siskin returned to the feeder and cracked a sunflower seed with his sharp bill.

Billy lowered his voice to keep from scaring off the songbird. "Shadow doesn't budge when you go inside his pen. He lets you scratch his ears."

I didn't mention that every time I reached out to pet the wolf, I wondered if I would draw back a bleeding stump.

"He's not tame, Billy. Maybe he was once, but he won't ever be again. I made a commitment to take care of him, no matter what. I heard at the Lincolnville General Store that my neighbors have a history of suing people who irritate them. They know most of us locals can't afford the cost of hiring attorneys—"

My friend rested a hand on the hilt of his knife. "Do you want me to go see them for you?"

"No!" I said, frightening off the siskin.

"So what did you want to discuss with me if not your neighbors?"

"I don't know what to do about Christmas."

"You're having Christmas Eve supper at our house."

"I mean the day itself. I've got two invitations.

Usually I go up to Sixth Machias Lake and spend the evening with Charley and Ora. Their daughter Ann comes from Bath with her husband and kids. I think Charley likes having me there as a buffer against his son-in-law. The problem, this year, is Stacey will be there, too."

"Oh."

"Meanwhile Dani wants me to break from tradition and go to her mom's house in Pennacook."

"Oh."

"Exactly."

Stacey Stevens was Ora and Charley's younger daughter. She was a wildlife biologist, a bush pilot, a wilderness EMT, and my old flame. We had lived together for three years—almost gotten engaged—before things fell apart. She had recently returned to Maine after self-imposed exile in Florida.

As for Danielle "Dani" Tate, I was no longer sure what to call her. She was a former game warden, now a state trooper, and six months earlier I would have referred to her as my girlfriend. And yet since the summer, we spoke less and less and saw each other rarely.

I should've realized that Billy was the wrong person to ask for relationship advice. He and Aimee had been sweethearts at Machias Memorial High School. As a couple, they were an advertisement for wedded bliss.

"You're kind of running out of time to make a decision," he said.

"Tell me about it."

He scratched his bearded chin. "Isn't Pennacook where you're going today?"

"Shadow's vet, Dr. Holman, has her practice there."

"Two hours is a long drive for a check-up."

Elizabeth Holman had removed a crossbow bolt from the wolf's side—acquired in his last hours as an escapee in the wild—and nursed him to health. He had suffered ligament damage from the arrow, however. The injury prevented him from running at full speed, which meant he would never chase down prey again, if I had considered re-releasing him into the Maine woods, which I hadn't.

Now he lived behind my house in a compound roughly an acre and a half in size, with chain-link fences ten feet high, impossible to scale. The fence extended below ground into a concrete foundation so he couldn't escape by digging his way out, either. I had made sure he had bushes and trees where he could hide and an exposed ledge where he could sun himself, but there was no denying the fact that his pen was still a jail yard.

Dr. Holman had made house calls for her first exams. She'd brought along a dart gun with ketamine-filled projectiles to tranquilize the wolf, but Shadow had learned to find redoubts in the trees that made it impossible for Lizzie to get a shot at him.

"I still don't understand how you think you're getting Shadow into a crate," Billy said. "That animal is smarter than 80 percent of the guys in my prison quad and 90 percent of the guards."

Now it was my turn to smile. "You know me. I've always got a plan."

I pointed at the frozen ground where a snaking length of orange extension cord twisted and turned from the house all the way to Shadow's enclosure. I had positioned the kennel just inside the fence. The electrical cord led to the box and disappeared through one of the air holes on the side.

"Try not to make any noise," I whispered as we descended the stairs.

Billy could move through the underbrush as silently as a deer.

Of course, I was the one who stepped on a twig.

The sound didn't cause Shadow to bolt. His snoring continued from inside the crate.

I had tied a length of Kevlar cord to the open door of the kennel. Now I gave it a hard yank and the gate swung shut, and there was a click of the latch fastening. Shadow arose inside the box and growled, but he didn't fight against his sudden confinement. That had been my biggest worry— that he would injure himself trying to escape.

"I put an electric blanket in there last week. He started sleeping inside a couple of nights ago when that polar vortex came through."

Billy let out a laugh that frightened the remaining siskins from the trees. "Did Charley suggest this?"

"I'm capable of coming up with my own harebrained schemes without Charley Stevens's input," I said with false affront. "Besides, a scheme is only harebrained if it fails."

"This one worked."

"I can't take full credit for it, though. Shadow is smart. I think he remembers what this crate means—that he's going for a ride. Maybe he senses there'll be a chance to make a break for it."

"This place isn't a jail, Mike. I can say that from personal experience. You've given him a good life here."

I could easily have refuted Billy's assertion. How many tunnels had Shadow started over the past sixteen months? All those holes dug in vain.

"I need your help getting the kennel into the Jeep."

Nearly all wardens drove trucks, investigators included, but my superiors had leased the Compass Trailhawk for me so I could sneak down Maine's scofflaw peninsulas without word getting out that a game warden had been spotted.

Billy gestured toward my personal vehicle. "Why aren't you taking your Scout?"

"Because I have warden business, too. A woman in Stratford wants to meet with me. Her father-in-law drowned while duck hunting in the Androscoggin River four years ago. She doesn't think the case should have been closed so quickly and has issues with how the wardens treated her."

"And you're going to go listen to her whine?"

"What can I say? I'm a masochist."

Shadow growled a few times, but he didn't make the job of moving him impossible by shifting his weight. The vet had prescribed some medicine to put in his food—Gabapentin and Trazadone—to mellow him out.

I left Billy in the yard while I went inside to fetch my briefcase. Emma was still scrawling away in her little grimoire. She blinked foggily, as if returning from someplace deep.

"Wait!" she said. "Did I miss Shadow?"

"He's still here. Your dad and I put his crate in the back of my Jeep. You can go talk with him now."

The junior wizard snatched up her journal and her wand and was out the door with a whoosh of her handmade robe.

On my desk I found the note from the woman I'd told Billy about, three sheets of beautiful blue script, signed by a "Mariëtte Chamberlain (née Van Rooyen)."

Dear Warden Bowditch,

I have read about you in the *Sun Journal* and the successes you have enjoyed investigating cold cases, and for this reason, I wish to speak with you, in person, about my father-in-law, Professor Eben Chamberlain, whose name you must recognize, but if not, he is the eminent man who died under suspicious circumstances while duck hunting along the Androscoggin River in Stratford four years ago this month. Despite an "exhaustive" investigation, his demise was insufficiently explained by the members of your service about whose commitment, competence, and professionalism I continue to have doubts. I have written to the governor and the attorney general and your own colonel with no result. Because you did not participate in the failed examination of my father-in-law's death, your reputation remains unsullied in my estimation, and therefore you are my last remaining hope.

The rest of the document was written in the same florid style and provided details of her father-in-law's initial disappearance and the rescue mission that became a recovery mission, as happens in many such cases. I knew the story better than she thought—I'd followed the search from afar—and saw no way to help her. But she had reached out to me with such desperation, I felt I owed the grieving woman the courtesy of a meeting.

Billy Cronk, it seemed, wasn't the only softy in Ducktrap.

I dropped the letter along with the Warden Service's official report into my leather attaché.

Outside, I found Billy crouched with his arm around Emma, looking from a safe distance at the wolf in his crate. Shadow stared at them through the cage with his inscrutable sulfur eyes. The sight of father and daughter prompted an odd sensation: longing.

I was closing in on thirty-two. Children were not a near-term prospect in my life. Nor even a medium-term prospect. This vision of the Cronks filled me with a feeling of my life slipping away.

As I was reaching to close the lift gate, Emma said, "Stop!"

"What is it, Em?"

She produced her wand, directed it at the cage, and moved her lips soundlessly, while twirling the tip.

Billy had told me that she was insistent he find a rowan, or mountain ash, from which to carve her magic stick. The finished result resembled a unicorn's twisted horn.

"What spell did you cast?" Billy asked.

"Protection. So Shadow will be safe on his journey."

"What about Uncle Mike," said Billy with gruff affection. "Doesn't he deserve a spell, too?"

She nodded her blond, braided head. "Don't move!"

I stood in place as the little girl waved her rowan wand and mouthed the silent words to keep me safe against whatever dark forces I might encounter that day.

3

I float in the current until I am jostled by a miniature iceberg. The jolt reminds me to move my legs, heavy from the weight of my waterlogged boots. Amazingly, I am still gripping the knife in my stiff hand, a case of premature rigor mortis.

I give a few hard kicks trying to propel myself, dolphin like, above the surface. The thicker ice ahead is visible as a pale smudge, more gray than white. If I don't get on top of it fast, I'll be trapped underwater again.

The cliff is somewhere behind me to the right. Through the blowing snowflakes, I can't see land. No rocks, no trees, and no houses pouring light from their windows. Shouting for help would be a waste of breath and energy.

I reach up at the ice plate beside me, but as I feel for a grip, it rolls like something heavy falling off a shelf.

Something hard strikes me from behind. A dead tree fallen into the stream. I grasp for a branch with my left hand. The tree, which had been floating lengthwise in the current, begins to pinwheel. I have upset its course, and now I am turning with it, watching the trunk and roots swing past. Just as I am about to let go, it crashes

33

against the nearest sheet, cracking through the crust along the edge and catches on the thicker stuff.

I have only seconds before the current pushes the tree loose again. I "climb" shoreward along the weathered trunk, but already I can feel it shifting, sliding, its roots being pulled by the hydraulic force of the Androscoggin.

Once again it is the knife that saves me. I plunge the blade into the ice while the tree drifts away. The point scrapes, then sticks.

My legs swing downstream, the toes of my boots appear before me. For an instant, I am like a sea otter reclining on his back. I am terrified I will lose my grip. So I reach up and get two hands on the knife handle and begin kicking furiously. When my chest touches the edge of the ice, I do my best to pull myself up, hoping the blade sticks.

I manage to get my elbows onto the flat surface. I bring up one knee to get a purchase only to hear a sharp crack. The ice, which can't be more than three inches thick, is breaking like china under my weight.

I lift my other leg clear of the water and roll onto my back. My teeth chatter uncontrollably.

It seems I'm on another ice floe. This one is larger, the size of a barn door, but not buoyant enough to keep me afloat. Water streams over its opaque surface as it begins to sink beneath me. I lunge onto the adjoining sheet and, this time, keep moving. I crawl on hands and knees, listening for the cracks that foretell a collapse.

I am nearer to the eastern bank than the western bank where I plunged off the road. Forty-degree water moving at two thousand cubic feet per second separates me from safety. I have no choice but to continue on, to the unknown shore.

The snow, light and dry from the crispness of the night, flutters more than falls.

Movement downstream catches my eye. Amazingly, it is Shadow. The black wolf is bounding across the ice and in three leaps gains the eastern shore.

My wet face hardens into a mask as I climb to my feet. Now I hear the cracking sound familiar to any skater who's tested a frozen pond for the first time.

I leap forward, then leap again, somehow keeping my balance. My flash-frozen clothes make rubbing noises as I move. Suddenly the world lurches beneath me. I have stepped onto yet another floating plate.

I have no time to think. My foot goes through a soft, slushy spot and I nearly lose my boot in the hole, but I am inspired by the sight of the wolf and full of fresh resolve, and I keep going, until I find myself standing on something that feels like land. It is the laminated ice that has built up, over the course of subzero nights, along the river's edge.

A steep bank, lined with gnarled oaks, rises above me. It is undercut from frequent floods, but if I can get a grip on one of the exposed roots, I can pull myself to safety. Carefully, I put away my knife. My hands are quickly becoming bear paws, but I clench them to force blood into my fingers. The hard, smooth lattice of tree roots provides the handholds I need.

When I reach the top, I press my body face-first onto the powdery ground, like a child attempting a snow angel.

Then the joy of having escaped the river gives way to brutal reason.

Ten minutes. That is all the time I have before hypothermia sets in. From my training, I know the process is inexorable; if I can't rewarm my core, my heartbeat will slow, my brain will cloud, and I will die.

Ten minutes to get warm.

With no means of making a fire, nothing to use for a shelter, no way to signal for help.

All I have is a knife.

4

The road west of Ducktrap took me through a landscape of leafless forests and hayfields that had been mowed to a hard stubble after the harvest. The last time I'd come through, this countryside had been white with snow. Now it was tundra again, hoary brown in color and patched with ice, with ridges of rotting snowbanks along the roadsides.

I glanced at the thermometer in the dash. Nineteen degrees, cold enough for snow, but the barometer was rising. The online forecast had said there was only a sliver of a possibility the Midcoast would receive any precipitation before Christmas. It would take some powerful magic to change the weather.

Emma Cronk was a sweet, strange child. No wonder Billy doted on her. And with four older brothers and the most dangerous man in Maine for a father, I feared for the first boy who asked her on a date.

I felt again the longing I'd experienced watching Billy wrap his arm around his beloved child.

Then in my head I heard Dani say: *"I don't know how anyone can decide to bring children into this world, as fucked up as it is."*

To drive out the thought I turned my attention to the bleak land whipping past. The snow that hadn't melted before the latest cold snap had a dingy, aged appearance. But I knew there would be fresh, clean snow the farther I got from the coast. Up north, the ski mountains were doing a booming business, and it was to the mountain foothills that I was now headed. To Dani Tate's hometown of Pennacook.

It had been two days since she'd called to say she was applying for yet another new job. Having been a state trooper for less than four years, she was already thinking of jumping ship. The Portland Police had a flashy new chief who had been recruited from Gary, Indiana. At his first press conference, he had announced his intention to restructure the department from top to bottom and increase the diversity of his force.

"He's creating two new sergeant positions, one focused on domestic violence," Dani had said excitedly. "There's no way he's not hiring a woman for that position."

"I thought you were committed to the state police."

"It's the same boys' club as the Warden Service. Jemison is promising to make real changes. And the job would be a stepping-stone to something even bigger."

Dani had had a health scare six months earlier—she'd contracted encephalitis that was at first diagnosed as the often-fatal Powassan virus—and had come through with no lingering damage to her brain. But she had emerged from illness with a new ambition.

"I am not going to wait for the things I want to fall in my lap," she'd said. "Life's too short."

"Not if you learn to live in the moment."

Even now I remembered the silence with which she received this principle, so central to the way I lived my life.

Had she given up waiting for me, too?

I hadn't thought of myself being in a hurry to settle down. But recently, a detective friend had announced that his new wife was pregnant, and I'd been surprised by the stab of envy I'd felt.

As far as I knew, however, Dani and I hadn't officially broken up. In four days we were still scheduled to drive to her mother's house in the same derelict mill town where I was taking Shadow. I tried to give her the benefit of the doubt that she'd been too preoccupied with the possibility of a new job to confirm with me.

It would be the first time in six years that I missed celebrating Christmas with the Stevenses. But this year, Stacey would be there again.

In the town of Liberty I passed a farmhouse with an all-terrain vehicle in the dooryard and a life-sized dummy, sewn together from grain sacks and dressed like Santa, propped behind the

39

handlebars. A nearby spruce had been decorated with strings of Budweiser cans. It must have required some truly heroic drinking to provide the raw materials. Instead of a star at the top, the merrymakers had secured a naked, spread-eagled Barbie doll.

Shadow broke wind inside his kennel forcing me to roll down the windows. The air that came whipping in felt like it had blown all the way from Siberia. My eyes began to water from the intense coldness. I rolled the windows up.

The wolf didn't want me to forget about him, it seemed. The veterinarian would need to anesthetize Shadow before she began her exam; it was simply too dangerous to try using a muzzle and other restraints. My hope was that he'd sleep the whole way home, provided I didn't linger long in Stratford.

I slid my hand into my briefcase and pinched the letter I'd received from Mariëtte Chamberlain (née Van Rooyen). Her linen stationery included her phone number. I tried not to veer off the road as I keyed it into my cell phone.

"Yes?" came a woman's voice.

"Is this Mrs. Chamberlain?"

"I should think you'd know who it was since you're the one who rang me up." She had an accent I couldn't place. Australian? Zealander?

"With whom am I speaking, please?"

"Mike Bowditch. I'm an investigator with the

Maine Warden Service. You sent me a note about your father's case."

"Are you driving?" She pronounced the last word *drrroyving*.

"Yes, I am."

"Would you do me the courtesy of pulling over and calling when you are no longer a danger to other drivers."

"Ma'am?"

She had hung up.

I pulled into the boat launch at Lake Saint George. Ice extended in a silver ring from the shore, but most of the lake was open water. Some tiny ducks, buffleheads, bobbed in the blue chop. They disappeared beneath the surface for minutes at a time before popping up like corks.

I removed the folder from my briefcase and opened it across my lap. In addition to the official report, the file 14D, and the medical examiner's findings, I had printed dozens of other documents: transcribed interviews, maps showing search grids, river flow information, and hydraulic diagrams.

"Mrs. Chamberlain, I am no longer driving," I said into the phone.

"Thank you for responding to my letter, Warden Investigator Bowditch."

Definitely Australian, I decided.

"Mike is fine."

"I'd like to keep our relationship professional. Your colleagues presented themselves as advocates, but we discovered that it was just an act, or, in the case of the lead investigator, utter rubbish."

"To whom are you referring?" I asked, although I already knew.

"A shifty fellow by the name of Rivard."

Marc Rivard and I were old frenemies. At one time, he had been my sergeant, then briefly my lieutenant. In both roles he had made my life miserable. His career arc had been a sharp rise, followed by an even sharper fall. After he'd botched a case involving the slaughter of some moose on the land of the richest woman in Maine, he'd been "encouraged" to leave the service. It hardly surprised me that Mariëtte Chamberlain had reached the same conclusion about the man that I had.

"I am afraid I don't understand what you'd like me to do," I said into the phone.

"Reopen the case!"

Definitely a New Zealand accent.

"Your father-in-law's body was recovered. The medical examiner's report noted water in the lungs which indicated he drowned. Excuse me for being blunt, but what is there left to investigate?"

"His head was bashed in!"

"According to the autopsy, the damage to his skull occurred post-mortem."

"His body was in the water six days before he was found—how can the doctor be sure?"

I was no expert in forensic medicine, but I suspected she had a small point. Our longtime chief medical examiner had a history of blunders.

"Are you suggesting he was bludgeoned and then tossed into the river? I'm looking at a sworn affidavit by an eyewitness who saw him alone in his boat."

"This won't do!" Mariëtte Chamberlain said. "I refuse to have this conversation over the telephone. I require your presence."

"My presence?"

"What time can you meet me this afternoon? At two o'clock? Let's say two o'clock. I will see you at my father-in-law's farm in Stratford. The address is 2 Riverlands Road. I will expect you at two o'clock."

Mariëtte Chamberlain demanding my attendance annoyed me enough that I considered blowing her off. But I knew myself well enough to admit that I wouldn't. Curiosity would always trump my petty resentments, let alone my better judgment.

The tomcat who climbs to the top of a tree with no plan on returning safely to the ground—that would always be me.

An hour later, I got my first look at the Androscoggin River, the third longest in Maine.

The "Andro" has its headwaters in the Boundary Mountains that separate northern New England from Canada. Its watershed marks the border between Maine and Quebec. The river then tumbles 1,245 feet—the steepest drop of any comparable watercourse in the state—and flows east across 164 miles before it enters the vast, brackish estuary of Merrymeeting Bay.

For centuries, the hydraulic muscle of the Androscoggin had powered dozens of mills, making paper and shoes, textiles and electricity. Communities had grown up along its banks and prospered, until the end of the twentieth century, when seemingly overnight, the world had gone topsy-turvy. The factories had been closed and the pulp machines had been sold and shipped to third-world nations in the Global South. Capital flows like a river to the lowest level.

Livermore Falls was one of the casualties of globalization. Like my destination of Pennacook, the town had once been a capital of the American papermaking industry. Now there was a park where a factory had once stood, complete with baseball diamonds and tennis courts, none of which were in use on this blustery morning. There was actual snow here, a foot of it. I saw a couple of heavily bundled people walking their dogs across a well-trodden field. Their heads were wreathed in clouds of steam and their hands clutched plastic bags full of shit.

I entertained a perverse thought of giving Shadow the freedom of the park. Which of his fellow canines would he eat first, I wondered: the black-and-white mutt or the young boxer?

Maybe he would maximize his calorie intake and go for the owners.

It was necessary to have a sense of humor around the half-wild animal. Otherwise his captivity afflicted me with too much sadness and guilt.

"How're you doing back there, big guy?"

He answered with a grunt.

Professor Chamberlain had died on this same river, in this same month. Stratford was twenty or thirty miles downstream, above the man-made reservoir of Gulf Island Pond. I decided I needed a better look at the river that had killed him.

I followed Foundry Road to Mill Street, drove to the end, and parked above a dam that had outlived its reason for being. An off-white sheet of ice stretched across the pond above the impoundment, but only a suicidal fool would have ventured onto that eggshell surface.

Below the falls, there was a maw of open water. It was very dark, with a tea-brown tint from the conifer needles decomposing at its bottom. A mist rose from the plunge pool, and where the beige spray had splashed the concrete levee, it had frozen in translucent layers to form an almost-beautiful ice cliff. Downstream, the river bubbled in the fast-flowing channels before it disappeared again beneath a patchwork of ice.

I doubted a man could last five minutes in those lethal currents.

What a horrible way to go.

5

On the snowy bank of the river I pull the parka's hood over my wet head and empty my pockets. To avoid losing anything I might need, I lay everything onto a blaze orange bandanna that I'd tucked inside a pocket during deer-hunting season and forgotten. Now that square of bright cotton feels like a godsend.

It turns out I am better outfitted than I'd first imagined.

Just barely.

I have the Beast, of course, and that's already proven its worth twice.

"A man without a knife is a man without a life," Charley Stevens always says. I don't know if it's some old proverb or a rhyme of his own creation. But the wisdom behind the saying reminds me to keep a tight grip.

Somehow I didn't lose my pocket flashlight: a SureFire Tactical that fits in my palm. It has a maximum output of 1,500 lumens—roughly equivalent to a 100-watt incandescent light bulb—all of which I would need to get me out of this mess.

Also I have a pair of leather gloves with a layer of Thinsulate insulation. Soaked as they are, I wonder if they might incline me to frostbite more than no gloves at all. But I put them on nonetheless.

My kit includes other items for which I see no immediate use: a dead cell phone. Two magazines of .357 SIG cartridges but no means of discharging them. A waterlogged notebook with blurred notes from my interviews. A Bic ballpoint pen. My wallet and badge. My leather belt. My bootlaces.

No matches. No lighter.

No hat or scarf to warm my throat.

My gun lies at the bottom of the Androscoggin, forever in its holster.

But when I push the button on my SureFire, a white beam shimmers from the end. The gaskets prove to be as watertight as promised. I shine it at the river and see only shimmering curtains of snow between me and the far shore. As a means of signaling for help, it is useless—at least from this location.

I try the phone again. The water has bricked the damned thing, as the tech geeks say. Or maybe the cold did it. Or the impact from the crash.

I check my watch, a vintage Seiko Marine-master (fortunately still running) that is one of my stepfather's hand-me-downs. Since his recent remarriage, Neil has increased the value of his gifts to me while decreasing the time he's made himself available for phone calls and visits. The glow-in-the-dark indices tell me the time is 5:05, and I know that is correct because the watch is insanely accurate, despite my ill treatment of it.

Ten minutes before stage three hypothermia sets in: the kind that is irreversible outside a hospital. I am already shivering. It is my body's reflexive attempt to generate additional heat. The time to worry is when the shivering stops. I need to make a plan and fast.

One trick to staying warm in the open is to make yourself small. So I kneel and sit down on my calves. I unzip my parka and tuck my gloved hands in my armpits and press my forearms against my chest, feeling the hard ballistic vest beneath the sweater. The order of business is to keep my core warm. My limbs will take care of themselves.

Where am I?

I have a rough sense, of course. A dim red light high in the air across the river has to be the cell tower at the summit of Pill Hill. I spent most of my afternoon at the trailer park there. It was because I stayed too long—"leave the hill before it gets dark," people had warned me—that I am in this predicament.

Again I check my watch. My sense of time is distorted. It can't have been more than fifteen minutes since I left the cluster of mobile homes. Driving out of that bad place, I kept my eyes on the rearview mirror. It never occurred to me that the real danger lay ahead.

49

If I'd come ashore on the western bank, I would've known what to do. Scramble up to the road and begin jogging to the glowing farmhouse at the bottom of the hill. Mariëtte Chamberlain might still be there, or her daughter at least. Hadn't Bibi Chamberlain said she was the sole occupant of the professor's old manse?

But there is no way across the Androscoggin, not here at least. The nearest bridge is at least two miles north through heavy cover, too far to run in my deteriorating condition. I might try crossing the ice downstream. It will likely be thicker in the calmer waters above Gulf Island Pond. But there are no guarantees I can find safe passage before hypothermia consumes me.

I have to find shelter here, wherever here might be.

Somewhere within the town boundary of Leeds, I think. The municipal line follows the main channel of the Androscoggin. I wish I knew the area better, but I've never had cause to work this district as a warden. I try to recall the map in my gazetteer. One thing I remember is seeing islands in the stream. Acres and half-acres of forest too insignificant to have names.

A fresh fear grips me. What if, instead of being on the Androscoggin's eastern bank, I am on one of those islets, cut off from the mainland by ice all around?

With no shelter in sight and no means of making a fire, my only choice is to move.

I gather up my things, careful to put everything of potential use in the zipped pockets of my parka, even my dead phone.

Thank you, God, for eiderdown.

Thank you for Gore-Tex, W. L. Gore.

Thank you for the lambswool sweater, Leon Leonwood Bean.

As I turn to face the pitch-black woods, I wonder if Shadow is nearby. If I were him, I would have run as far from his cage-keeper as possible. At least he is alive, though. And his chances of staying that way—creature of the north that he is—are better than mine.

There is a small copse of balsams before me, perfect Christmas trees for anyone still in the market. Emma Cronk would have found one of them ideal to decorate my lonesome house. The boughs of these are clumped with fresh snow like cake frosting. I'd rather not try to bull my way through the bristling branches.

I turn back to the river, and that is when I see the vehicle atop the low cliff. Headlights shimmer into space, illuminating the dancing snowflakes. It has to be parked where I went off the road. I wasn't carried as far downstream as I thought. Maybe the driver has seen my tracks going off the edge.

My first impulse is to hope the puny beam of

my SureFire is strong enough to be spotted from a distance of a hundred yards.

But then the memory of the spiked objects in the road returns. I quickly turn off the light.

I remain still.

I can't hear much above the sound of the river. The creaking of ice floes and murmuring current. A breath of wind.

My chattering teeth.

Seconds pass and a handheld spotlight snaps on. A figure stands at the edge of the cliff and shines the beam down at the river. Whoever he is, he doesn't call out. He just uses the searchlight to scan the ice, starting with the place where my Jeep crashed through and continuing methodically downstream.

The light touches the eastern bank fifty feet north of me. Slowly it moves my way. If I step forward and wave for help, he will surely see me.

Instead I step backward into the firs.

The head-high trees aren't as densely packed as I'd thought. As the spotlight touches them, the needles turn from black to dark green to emerald. I clench every muscle in my body to stop from shivering. It takes a terrific effort to force my jaws shut to keep my teeth from chattering.

Step into the light, you idiot. Paranoia is a sign of hypothermia. Do you want to freeze to death out here?

No, Mike. Don't do it, Mike.

The light continues down the bank, and my entire body begins convulsing again.

A minute later the spotlight winks off, but the high beams from the vehicle continue to shine off the cliff into a space alive with snowflakes. I think I glimpse the driver's silhouette. Then he disappears into the shadows of the road, leaving his engine idling.

What is he doing?

The realization hits me like a punch. He's collecting the metal spikes he'd scattered across the asphalt. He's removing the evidence.

I shiver harder, but this time it isn't just from the cold.

6

D r. Elizabeth Holman, I noticed, had gotten a new tattoo. As she leaned over the sedated wolf, his massive body slung along the steel table, his red tongue lolling from his mouth, I spotted an indefinite mark at the base of her neck. I peered closer and saw that it was a tasteful dove with a tasteful olive branch in its tasteful beak.

It was the first truly Christian tattoo I could remember seeing. I had come across many crosses, of course, often flaming or aglow with what looked like radiation, and biblical quotes, sometimes just chapter and verse numbers, other times full quotations, but none of those tats had impressed me as genuine expressions of faith. One reason: most of the religious tattoos I'd seen belonged to people I had arrested for violent crimes.

Lizzie Holman had always given me the impression that she was a true believer. She radiated a serenity that calmed even the most neurotic animals under her care. As someone who had always struggled with the Catholic religion in which I was raised, I envied her faith. I might have resented it a little, too.

I had no tattoos, nor did I have need of artificial mementos; my body was adorned with scars.

There was the permanent starburst of capillaries on my torso where a .45 ACP round had flattened itself against my bulletproof vest. There was the red line on my arm from when I'd fended off a crazed woman with a butcher knife. There was the white stitching along my hairline where a biker had broken a beer bottle over my head. These half-healed wounds told the story of my life more than a tapestry of inked images ever could.

"His heartbeat is fantastic, Mike," Lizzie said, moving her stethoscope around Shadow's furred chest. She was a competitive runner, with those narrow shoulders and twiggy limbs that some marathoners get. "His breathing, too. I'd never know he'd suffered a pierced lung."

The wolf, during his brief sojourn in the wild, had been shot by a crossbow. The bolt had nearly killed him. Lizzie Holman had saved his life. And he had been with me ever since.

"That's good to hear."

"What about the damage to his ligaments? Do you ever see him limping or having trouble jumping up?"

"Sometimes his foreleg gives him problems. That's never going to get better, will it?"

"Not until someone invents a program of physical therapy for wolves."

Lizzie's eyes were sunken, but bright and clear with good health and the serenity I mentioned.

"I understand you brought a stool sample. We also need to draw blood and extract some urine. The usual tests. And I assume you want the full complement of shots. Unfortunately, most of them require a second dose be given in a couple weeks. How did he handle the trip today?"

"Those meds you gave me helped. He complained a lot in wolf-speak. I'm pretty sure he used foul language. I'm trying to get him reacquainted with the kennel."

"You mentioned that you've been entering his pen more?"

"I have this idea he'll be able to come inside my house eventually. I'm probably kidding myself. I doubt he'll ever trust me enough. And I can't say I wouldn't have misgivings. I've watched him tear apart a road-killed deer in five minutes."

She ran a bony hand through the fur along his rising and falling chest. "He's got a divided soul, this one. Neither wild nor tame."

Women had described me in similar terms.

"Don't take this the wrong way, but it's not easy being here. I keep flashing back to seeing him after you removed the arrow. I was sure he was going to die. Thank you for saving him."

"It wasn't me who did it."

I had a feeling she was referring to God.

"I wish I could give him a better life."

"I've seen how he watches you. I think he knows you love him. You two are family."

"I'm his only family. And he's mine, if I'm being honest with myself."

Immediately, I felt embarrassed by the intimacy of this admission.

The examination room was achingly bright and nauseatingly sterile, but the smell of the wolf—like forest loam after a rain—overwhelmed the chemicals they'd used to clean the surfaces.

Out of nowhere Lizzie said, "I'm sorry to hear about you and Dani."

"What did you hear?"

A flush crept up her throat into her cheeks. "Her mom told me about you two breaking up. It didn't sound like it was a secret."

Nicole Tate lived less than a mile away from the Pennacook Hospital for Animals and brought her pets here all the time. Dani's mother had liked me once. She even used to get a little flirty. Nicole had had a habit of stroking my biceps after she'd had a couple of glasses of Chardonnay.

But her attitude had undergone a metamorphosis over the summer when Dani had been hospitalized with a near-fatal fever. I had been working a case in northern Maine and unable to rush to her bedside. Afterward, Nicole had decided that I wasn't the boyfriend her daughter deserved.

Maybe she was right.

Poor Lizzie Holman, though, kept getting redder and redder. She fingered the gold cross around her neck. "You didn't break up?"

"It's OK," I said noncommittally.

"I shouldn't have said anything."

I placed a hand on Shadow's warm, furry ribcage. His heartbeat felt strong and reassuring. "Don't worry about it."

She pretended to clear her throat. "I guess we should get started with his tests. It will take a while if you want to grab some lunch. The Boom Chain makes a great burger."

"I brought a sandwich."

I ate in my Jeep all too often. Like most wardens, I pretty much lived in my vehicle. I took the opportunity to fetch my lunch bag and thermos and found a chair in the vacant "Kitty Korner" where cat owners could sit with their felines, away from bounding dogs.

I have always found hospital waiting rooms, even those of the veterinary variety, fascinating places to people watch. While I ate, a married couple brought in an Australian shepherd with a cone around her neck and a shaved patch on her haunch from recent surgery (a dogfight?). The animal ignored the wife but kept up a whimpering communication with the husband. The couple argued under their breaths the whole time—he wanted to remove the cone, she insisted they wait for the vet.

"Do we have to fight like this?" hissed the woman. "It's Christmas."

"What does Christmas have to do with it?"

It was obvious to me that the dog was playing them off each other and that their relationship was on shaky ground.

The shepherd smelled my Italian sandwich and batted her eyes at me, but I was wise to her con.

My mind was on Dani's mom. Nicole Tate was a gossip and a mischief-maker. She'd known I was headed to Pennacook for Shadow's appointment. Had she spoken to Lizzie hoping that her words would get back to me? To what end?

I considered calling Dani to ask what her mother was scheming, until I remembered about her interview in Portland. Instead, I sent a message to call me when she had a minute.

Eventually, the unhappy couple with the manipulative shepherd was called into an examination room.

I could empathize with their plight. With Shadow, there were days I knew he was manipulating me. He'd ignore the bucket of pig's ears I brought him until I returned with a venison haunch I was saving for myself. Then he'd make eye contact while he gobbled up the ears he'd recently disdained. He seemed to delight in taunting me.

Other days, though, I would catch sight of the wolf through the window, when he couldn't see me, and I would watch him doing something like following an eagle soaring overhead, and his mind would seem unknowable to me. In those moments I missed having a standard-issue dog who would follow me from room to room and lick the crumbs from my floors.

Maybe I just missed having a family.

Eventually, Lizzie Holman emerged through the inner door, smiling but still looking sheepish.

She said she'd given Shadow a large bolus of fluids subcutaneously to keep him hydrated on the drive. After she'd brought him safely out of the anesthesia, she'd also administered a mild sedative—I didn't catch the name—to keep him "mellow" for a few hours. She said not to worry about feeding him until we were home. She told me she'd call with his results, but based on his complete blood count, stool and urine tests, she didn't anticipate issues.

The only problem areas were his teeth. Her assistant had cleaned his yellow fangs while he was under the influence of the propofol. Lizzie asked if I might try brushing them at home.

"That depends," I said. "Do you have any ten-foot-long toothbrushes?"

"We have dental chew toys."

"He swallowed the last one."

"What about beef bones? Deer antlers?"

"I'll increase his allotment."

As a warden, I had access to a near-endless supply of deer and moose sheds. And the local slaughterhouse that provided me with the meat I fed Shadow had plenty of spare bones.

I was permitted to bring the Jeep around to the loading dock. One of her techs offered to help me lift his crate into the vehicle, but I said I could handle it. That was a mistake. A muscle in my lower back spasmed, and it was all I could do to keep a smile on my face.

Lizzie came down to see me off because she'd been obsessing about her faux pas. "Mike, I hope I didn't cause a problem with Dani."

"There's nothing to apologize for."

"Serves me right for gossiping. You're sure it's all right?"

"One hundred percent."

But I kept my eyes open for Nicole's SUV and made a point of avoiding her street on my way out of town. I could never understand why the Tates continued to reside in Pennacook after the mill closed and half of Main Street went dark. The family seemed incapable of imagining life elsewhere.

Dani was the exception. She had always been competitive and ambitious. I wondered how her interview with Chief Jemison had gone since she hadn't messaged me yet.

Better not to dwell on the unknown.

My dashboard thermometer told me the temperature had climbed to a balmy twenty-eight degrees. The GPS told me the drive to Stratford would take less than an hour. From the interior of the Jeep came the heavy breathing of the sleepy wolf.

I engaged the hands-free speaker, instructing my phone's virtual assistant to call former Warden Lieutenant Marc Rivard. I half hoped the number I had for him was out-of-date.

No such luck. "If it isn't the investigator!"

"Hello, Marc."

"When I saw it was you, I almost let it go to voicemail. But you would've kept calling. I know how you are."

My former superior had always seen my persistence as a character defect.

During that brief period when he was the golden boy of the Maine Warden Service, Marc Rivard had overseen the search and rescue team. In that capacity, he'd headed up the efforts to locate Eben Chamberlain, taking over as primary on the case because he wanted the credit. And in fairness, he had a mind for searches.

He had also studied the Androscoggin: its seasonal hydraulics, its changeable river bottom. In theory, he should have predicted the half-dozen places where a drifting corpse could get hung up. But the search had somehow taken longer than expected, nearly a week, by which time the body was decomposing.

"You must want something," Rivard said now.

He had the faintest hint of a French accent that he'd worked unsuccessfully to rid himself of. It was an unusual personal tic in a man of my generation.

"I'm reviewing a search and recovery you ran four years ago. Eben Chamberlain. And I wondered if you have time to talk?"

"You're shitting me."

"The professor's daughter-in-law is still unhappy with your findings. She's making trouble for the department. I'm trying to smooth it over for the colonel."

This, of course, was a lie. I figured blaming the new head of the Warden Service would give me cover.

It had been Colonel Jock DeFord—formerly Captain Jock DeFord—who had artfully maneuvered Rivard out of law enforcement.

"Screw him."

"It'll take ten minutes, tops."

"I'm at work, Mike. It's the week before Christmas. Do you know how busy we are?"

I'd heard that Rivard had taken a job at his uncle's John Deere dealership in Sabattus. He had gone from being a warden lieutenant, on the fast track to become colonel himself someday, to a junior tractor salesman.

"I'm on my way to meet Mariëtte Chamberlain at the professor's old place in Stratford. I thought I owed it to you to get your side of the story first."

"You're going to meet the glamazon in person? Where are you now?"

The nickname didn't jibe with the ornate letter in my briefcase. I'd pictured my correspondent as a pinched old biddy.

"At the moment, I'm in Canton," I said. "I'm driving south along the river from Pennacook."

"Why don't you swing by the dealership. We can chat in person. Just like old times."

The sudden friendliness in his tone set off a warning bell. "It'll mean my back-tracking to get to Stratford later."

"Not far though." He paused as if to take a sip of coffee. "How long has it been, Mike? Since we chatted?"

We had never chatted. Even when we'd patrolled together in the same truck for hours on end. He had lectured me about warden tips and tricks. Occasionally he had engaged in lengthy monologues about his shrewish exes or the stupidity of our superiors. But we had never chatted.

The prospect of being in his presence again depressed me. "You just said you were too busy to have this conversation."

"I can make time for an old friend."

Whatever Marc Rivard had been to me over the years, he had never been a friend. Maybe because of my education—I'd graduated from Colby College while he held an associate's degree from a vocational school—he had resented me. His disdain seemed to run deeper than that, though. It nettled him that I selectively obeyed rules and regulations, and yet still succeeded while his career tanked. Of all my colleagues, former and current, I couldn't think of anyone who nursed such a deep hatred for me. And given the number of game wardens I'd embarrassed, irritated, and pissed off, that distinction put him in a class by himself.

"I'll see you at thirteen hundred hours," I said.

"I'll be waiting."

As I changed course for Sabattus, and my GPS went into rerouting mode, I had the suspicion that Rivard was luring me into one of his signature traps. I'd hoped to get the information I needed from him over the phone. Nothing good would come from meeting in person with the master manipulator.

7

Hypothermia is tightening its grip on me. The snow hitting my face streams down my forehead and into my eyes. It trickles down the front of my shirt.

My shivering has become uncontrollable and violent. My joints are locking up. I am the Tin Man deprived of an oil can. More and more, I lurch after the shaky light on the ground—as if chasing the beam instead of directing it.

The worst thing I can do is work up a sweat since it will depress my body temperature even further.

Even if I find shelter soon, how will I make a fire? Forget about a lighter or matches. I don't even have a ferro stick I can use to strike a spark. Or rather, the ferro stick I always kept at hand is in the console of my submerged Jeep.

After a quick 360-degree survey of my location, I decide to follow the shore south rather than cut cross-country and risk getting turned around. Normally I have an unerring sense of direction. When I am in the woods, I feel as connected to the earth's magnetic poles as a migrating goose. But I know disorientation is another symptom of hypothermia.

Almost instantly, I regret my decision to follow

the river. I find myself clawing through thorny bittersweet and brakes of phragmites. The reed-like plants grow eight feet tall and have swaying tops like ostrich plumes.

Even when I emerge from the stalks, my path gets no easier.

Before me lies an obstacle course of fallen and half-fallen trees. Snagging roots protrude from the snow. I step gingerly over spiked deadfalls where a single slip means impalement. I duck under half-balanced widowmakers, some creaking in the wind, and hope that they won't choose this moment to come crashing down.

I pause to rewarm my hands in my armpits. I stomp my feet like an old-time Chicago beat cop.

A noise behind me triggers my nervous system's early warning system. I listen without turning. Gurgling river, whispering phragmites.

Slowly, I pivot and point the light at my erratic boot prints. The beam shudders and shakes. Beyond thirty feet it fails altogether.

"Shadow?"

Raggedy oak leaves spin and flutter on their branches. They are one of the few deciduous trees in Maine that don't lose their foliage in the autumn. The dead leaves make a dry, papery rustle.

"Come out, big guy." The cold has given me lockjaw. "It's OK."

And suddenly there he is: eyes glowing yellow

at the outer edge of my light. The wolf's heavy coat is chunked white with ice from his dip in the river. He appears to be his own ghost.

Maybe he really did drown?

If I were not hypothermic, if my mind were functioning properly, I would understand the idea is ludicrous. The steam rising from his open mouth is evidence enough of his corporeality.

"It's good to see you," I manage to say.

He doesn't so much as twitch. And a crazy thought enters my mind. *Is he stalking me for food?*

Whatever else Shadow is, he is no man-eater. Wolves are almost never dangerous except in fairy tales. And yet isn't this where I am now—in a German folktale?

I peel up my sleeve to check my watch again. Six minutes and counting. When I raise my eyes, the wolf has receded into the night.

I start forward, quickening my pace. Not caring about the cold sweat rolling down from my armpits. The sensation of being chased becomes overwhelming. If not by the wolf, then by what the wolf represents.

In my carelessness, I miss the drop-off ahead. The Andro, in one of its rages, has chomped a bite out of the land. The result is a deep, sandy undercut. I stumble and fall four feet onto a sheet of ice as hard as a concrete slab.

Once again I have the breath knocked from

my lungs. My SureFire slips from my grasp and drops between two floes the river has pushed against the shore. In a panic I reach my whole arm after it. My numb fingers brush the aluminum barrel and succeed in pushing it deeper down the hole. The bulb shines into my eyes, mocking me. I can't reach it, can't move these heavy, interlocked sheets. I have no choice but to leave it behind.

I crawl up the bank, blind, frustrated, but not yet defeated.

When I pause for breath at the top, I realize I am no longer shivering. That's a bad sign.

I have to wait for my eyes to adjust. Ice crystals reflect light even in the darkest of places—and this is one of them. Hard as it is to believe, I am lucky it is snowing. The paleness of the snow contrasts against the shadows of the trees.

I grab a sapling and pull myself onto my knees, then onto my feet. Something catches my eye on the cutbank above the water's edge, near where I lost the light. It seems to be rectangular in shape, and I assume it is another figment of my deteriorating mind.

Or is it?

As I pick a route up the bank through the scratchy puckerbrush, I am afraid to blink, lest the structure disappear on me like a mirage.

It's real, all right. Too small to be a house or even a cabin.

Recognition comes slowly: It is an ice-fishing shack. And the reason I didn't recognize it is because it is lying on its side. It probably washed down the river and came to rest below. Then someone went to the trouble of hauling it into the trees.

I drop to my knees. I crawl toward the structure like an infant.

Shelter. Salvation.

8

Sabattus Tractors had gone all out for Christmas. The banner above the door advertised: "BLACK FRIDAY SAVINGS ALL MONTH LONG." Inside the entryway was a semi-circle of bright green landscaping machines, outfitted with snowplows, arranged around an artificial tree that was bedazzled with tinsel. Each of the shiny machines bore a big red bow.

Marc Rivard had to be the mastermind behind this over-the-top display. The man had never known where to stop with the pizzazz. The one constant in his life had been a relentless commitment to self-advertisement.

He was the second sergeant I'd had in my career. My first, Kathy Frost, was a teacher, a mentor, and a lifelong friend. Rivard, by contrast, was a taskmaster, a bully, and a politician. He was so naturally deceitful, he seemed unable to differentiate between objective truth and the lies he told to make himself look good.

Since we'd worked together, I'd read that sociopaths were more common than scientists had once believed. Something like one in a hundred people met the standard for antisocial behavior and utter absence of conscience. If Marc

Rivard didn't fulfill the textbook definition, he came close enough for discomfort.

Contrary to his claims of being busy, I saw only a single customer inside the showroom. A white-haired man in a plaid coat stood staring up at the ceiling where a riding mower hung on cables from the exposed beams. The old guy didn't strike me as a buyer, but Rivard practically had his arm around him.

"December's the best month to buy a mower," I heard him say. "For snow-moving machines, people are willing to pay full retail. But anything lawn related—we've got it discounted so much we take a loss on every sale."

Rivard had put on weight since he'd left the service: twenty pounds at least. His hair was still thick and dark, and he hadn't shaved the skeezy mustache that had been his signature as a warden. He was dressed in a holiday-themed sweater— red with a jagged row of evergreens across the chest—chinos, and wheat-colored Timberlands.

He'd seen me come in; his intelligent dark eyes never missed much. But he didn't interrupt his sales pitch to greet me.

"Best of all, we have a zero-interest payment plan."

"How much that thing weigh?" the old man asked.

Rivard's megawatt smile flickered. "Six hundred pounds, more or less."

"How'd you get it up there? Use some kind of pulley system, did you?"

"We hooked a team of oxen to a block and tackle. Is there anything else I can show you today, bud?"

"Don't get pissy with me, mister. Your uncle and I are both members of Le Club Calumet."

I could see it took an act of will on the part of the junior tractor salesman to keep from pile-driving the old man into the concrete floor. "Help yourself to more free coffee and another cookie while you're here."

Then, with a tight smile on his face, he made his way down the aisle of snowmobiles toward me.

"I'll get Gil to watch the floor," he said. "We'll talk in my office."

Rivard's office was the corner of the loading dock. But at least he had a desk, which he made a point of putting between us. He must have read somewhere that sitting behind a desk gives a person authority. The chair he offered me was a stool.

On the wall behind him were framed photos of his several families. Two ex-wives, one current wife. Three daughters, three sons, and judging from the photo of a pregnant blond I didn't recognize, he had another baby on the way. Rivard was an expert at convincing women that he was marriage material, past proof to the contrary.

"You look older," he said, a little enthusi-
astically.

"I am older."

"Middle-aged, I mean. Don't get in a huff. It
happens to all of us, right? I could stand to lose
five pounds. So you haven't met the glamazon
yet?"

He sipped from a coffee mug but whatever was
in it was cold, and he made a face.

"I take it you're referring to Mrs. Chamberlain?"

"Wait till you see her. I guarantee she could
kick your ass. She was probably hot when she
was young. She's from South Africa originally."

That explained the accent I couldn't place.

"You don't meet many of them in Maine."

"That woman is the biggest ballbuster I've
met—with the exception of that bitch Betty
Morse."

I knew Marc well enough not to respond to
his slurs. If I defended the woman he blamed
for his downfall, he would accuse me of being
oversensitive and politically correct.

He leaned his elbows on the desk, probably to
show off the gold Tag Heuer on his wrist. "Why
are you meeting her? Mariëtte Chamberlain?"

"Because she sent me a letter."

"A letter! You've always been a soft touch,
Bowditch. It's a good thing you had the sense to
call me beforehand. You were walking into an
ambush. I assume you've read the case file."

"Skimmed it."

He narrowed his eyes, suspicious I knew more about the Eben Chamberlain affair than I was letting on.

"I'll give you the short version then. The professor was seventy-seven, overweight, diabetic. He had no business being out on the river alone in December. He fell out of his boat—probably retrieving his decoys—and drowned. He wasn't wearing personal flotation, not that it would have mattered. The shock of the water would have likely killed him in minutes. His corpse got lodged downstream, snagged in the stuff piled up underwater at the base of the Gulf Island Dam. When we found him, Professor Chamberlain was in the process of becoming fish food."

The stool on which I was balanced was tilt-y. "You sound certain it was an accident."

"I know you're prone to seeing mysteries and conspiracies everywhere, Mike, but sometimes reality is the way it appears."

I reached into the inner pocket of my parka and withdrew a pad and pen. "What evidence did you find to lead you to this conclusion?"

He regarded the notebook with disdain. "Aside from the fact that he was alone in the boat, you mean?"

He didn't let me respond.

"First, we found his boat, washed up against one of those little islands in the river. He'd had a good morning shooting. There were four geese and maybe ten mallards in the bottom."

"OK."

"Second, our divers found his shotgun at the bottom of the river where the last person to see him reported his location."

"Tell me about the witness."

He drummed his fingers on the desk. "What was his name? I remember it was kind of funny." He squeezed his eyelids shut. "Burch. Arlo Burch."

"Really?"

"You doubt my memory? In my head I picture a low-hanging birch tree on which someone has carved the letter R. *R low birch.* Get it?"

Rivard had once regaled me with the mnemonic practices he used to remember details for his reports.

"Who is this Arlo Burch?"

"Bartender down in Auburn—or at least he was at the time. A hipster hangout called the Brass Monkey. As in 'cold enough to freeze the balls off of.' He owns a mobile home up on Pill Hill. That's not the place's real name obviously. I don't know if it has a name. It's just what people started calling the ridge after they built the trailer park."

I underlined the name in my pad. "Pills as in oxycodone?"

"Narcotics in general. Domestic violence.

Your occasional drunken fracas. The sheriff's department gets a call up there every weekend. I remember when it was just woods. Gil had a deer stand along that ridge he let me use when I was eighteen. Shot myself a ten-point buck."

In reality it had probably been a four-point buck. Or a little spike. Or even a doe. Maybe Rivard hadn't shot anything at all. One could never be sure.

"And you said this bartender claimed he saw Chamberlain alone on the river—"

"Yep."

"That seems convenient, wouldn't you say, having an eyewitness in a place so remote? How did you happen to find him?"

His dark eyebrows lowered. Not for the first time, he interpreted a question from me as a challenge.

"He came forward during the search. The glamazon had issued a reward of ten grand for whoever found the body."

I vaguely remembered this. "That sounds like convenient timing on the part of Mr. Burch."

"You'd think so, but he had no connection to the deceased and no criminal record. I warned her offering a reward would bring out the yahoos. By then, she had lost trust in the Warden Service. She wanted to embarrass us in the public eye. Some concerned citizens even took boats out with homemade dragging hooks. It's a wonder we didn't end up having to recover their corpses, too. How did you get out of working the search? I can't recall."

I shrugged off the implication that I had dodged one of my official duties. "I was working that snowmobile crash in Baldwin. The teenage girl who ran into a guy wire and was decapitated."

"Oh, shit. I remember now. It was, like, her first time on a sled."

"Not exactly," I said. "But the snowmobile was an early Christmas present from her father. Two weeks later, he hanged himself in the woods. I was the one who found both bodies."

His eyes began to well up. "If that happened to one of my kids, I probably would have. . . ." He massaged his forehead to keep me from seeing him wipe his tears with the heel of his hand. "Suicides are the worst."

"Yeah, they are."

"I don't miss seeing shit like that, I have to say."

Here was the riddle of Marc Rivard. Every time I became convinced he was a sociopath, he would pry open his hairy chest to reveal a beating human heart.

I rebalanced myself atop the stool. "Getting back to the day of Chamberlain's death, why did you believe this Arlo Burch if he was just another Pill Hill redneck who showed up for the reward?"

"He didn't strike me as a bad guy. I kind of

liked the dude, in fact. His girlfriend, not so much. She was one of those fiery redheads. Anyway, Burch could describe in detail what Eben Chamberlain was wearing that day on the river. It was a distinctive item of clothing, a camouflage sweater his granddaughter had knitted for him."

"But no life jacket."

"Not that Burch saw. The glamazon said that was bullshit. The professor—that's what she called him—never took off his personal flotation device, she said."

"Was the PFD in the boat?"

"No."

"It must have washed up along the river then."

"If it did, someone picked it up and took it home. One of the guys hoping to find the body and collect the reward. That was our working theory."

At that moment, Rivard's uncle Gil appeared. He was bald and bespectacled and wore the same festive red-and-green sweater. "Break's over, Marc."

"We're finishing up here," Rivard said in the commanding tone I remembered from his days as a lieutenant.

But Uncle Gil was unphased. "Fifteen minutes. No exceptions."

"I'll be right out!"

After Gil left, I found Rivard eyeing me with

open contempt. "You must be enjoying this. Seeing how far I've fallen."

"Marc—"

"I'm doing fine, let me tell you. I've got a new wife who's twenty-four. She's pregnant with our baby. Plus, I'm making more money than I ever did as a warden. I've still got my self-storage business. And I make a good commission here. So you can wipe that superior look off your face."

"I don't feel superior to you, Marc. I'm sorry if I gave that impression." I slipped off the stool. "I appreciate your time."

"Don't condescend to me."

"I'm not," I lied.

"You've always been an asshole, Bowditch."

Rivard dogged my heels into the festive showroom. No new customers had come in since the old guy left. Gil was busy trying to deduce which dead bulb on a string of Christmas lights needed to be replaced before the strand would glow again.

Rivard managed to get ahead of me so that he stood in the door, literally blocking my way. The contrast between his hostile expression and his comic sweater couldn't have been more pronounced.

"How much time do you spend looking over your shoulder?"

The question brought me up short. "What do you mean?"

"You've made a lot of enemies over your career."

I shrugged. "Most of them are in prison—or dead."

"But not all of them. And even the dead ones have brothers and sons eager for payback."

I couldn't help but wonder if he grouped himself into this category of enemies.

"Paranoia isn't my style, Marc."

"I always said your cockiness was going to get you killed."

"It hasn't yet."

"Just wait."

9

The shack lies on its side in the hard frozen snow.

Where do people even ice fish on this stretch of the river? Is there a pond upstream?

Even on the verge of freezing to death, I can't stop my mind from posing questions.

Most Maine fishing shacks are the size of porta potties. By that standard, this structure is downright spacious. I eyeball its dimensions as eight feet by twelve feet. It was built of two-by-fours and sheets of particle board. The inner walls are insulated with pink fiberglass, chewed to shreds by hard-working members of the rodent community. The shanty lost its floor during its float trip down the Androscoggin. One of several opaque plastic windows remains intact. At first glance I see nothing I can use to build a fire.

Snow has blown in through the missing floor—now a missing wall, since the structure lies on its side—and has accumulated over the half-detached strips of Owens Corning's finest.

As I crawl inside, my foot kicks something. It is a glass bottle of Michelob Ultra. There are crushed cans and empty bottles everywhere, I soon realize. Beers mostly but plastic nips, too. Allen's Coffee Brandy, Fireball Cinnamon

Whiskey, Popov Vodka. The teenagers who rescued this shack have turned it into a clubhouse for drinking and drugging. Sex, too, probably.

I sweep the floor with my hands, blindly searching for a blanket I hope one of the young lovers left behind.

All I find is a girl's discarded puffer vest. I'm a beggar not a chooser. I stuff the dirty coat inside my parka as an extra layer.

My eyes are adjusting to the half-light. Wasps have built an oblong nest of paper in one corner of the "ceiling." Everywhere lie cigarette butts and roaches. One is still attached to an alligator clip. Crushed packs of Marlboros and Newports. Ripped bags of Red Man chew.

Rivard used to use Red Man moist snuff, I remember.

Focus.

Matches. There have to be matches.

I continue to brush the floor with my gloved hands, scattering snow-dusted trash left and right.

And then there it is: a book of matches.

When I flip open the cover, I see stubs like dual rows of missing cardboard teeth.

For fuck's sake.

What about a disposable lighter? It doesn't even need to have butane in it. The metal wheel of an empty Bic can still throw a spark that can be caught in a nest of lint, sawdust, what have you. But I am out of luck.

I clear a circle of plywood. Then I empty my pockets again, not even bothering with the bandanna this time in my haste.

When I see the bullets, I experience a fleeting euphoria before reality clamps down.

Sure, I have a knife, but with my stiffening fingers, there's no way I can pry open the cartridges for the tiny amount of primer inside. Forget about the gunpowder. The mix of salt-peter, charcoal, and sulfur is a surprisingly poor fire starter.

I don't recognize the black rectangle at first. Another symptom of my worsening mental condition.

My cell phone is utterly useless to me now. I might as well—

The realization nearly knocks me over.

There might just be a way.

Crawling outside, I feel the wind like a slap to the face. My fingers are beyond arthritic with frostbite. Stumbling from tree to tree, I scavenge for fuel. I snap twigs from the bases of balsams; the resinous branches closest to the trunk are the driest. From a hoary old birch I peel strips of bark and stuff the curling paper into my pockets.

I duck inside the shed and begin building separate piles of fuel. I need to be ready for the moment of truth. I only have one shot at this, and I've never attempted it before.

I pull down the wasp nest.

I strip the cellophane from the discarded cigarette packs and pile up the twisting strips.

Birchbark. Twigs. Sticks. Paper.

I hate to lose my new insulation layer, but I have no choice but to remove the girl's vest from inside my coat. I cut through the outer polyester to get to the feathers inside, and thank God, they're real eiderdown, also flammable.

The shack's fiberglass insulation is worthless, except as a base to keep the fire from burning through the "floor."

With trembling hands, I use the point of the knife to pry open the phone to find the battery.

I remove a wet glove. One by one, I put the fingers of my right hand into my mouth, trying to suck blood into the capillaries. I open and close my fist. The pain is excruciating. I try to put the glove back on, but it's no use. I resign myself to the inevitable chemical burns.

I take a position on my knees above the battery. I close both hands around the handle of my knife.

Please, God. Let this work.

I bring the knife down fast and hard, the tip punctures the nickel-coated backing, and suddenly there is smoke and heat. Acrid fumes curl from around the blade.

Lithium ion batteries, once exposed to oxygen, combust. It's why airlines won't risk stowing cell phones in the luggage compartment. The intense cold of the upper atmosphere can cause their casings to crack.

I pull the knife free and begin tossing cellophane and wasp paper onto the ruptured battery. The treated plastic bursts into flame. I add strips of bark. The curling embers tumble onto the duck feathers which, in turn, begin to smoke. Now it's a mad rush to arrange twigs around the fragile flame. I make a teepee of sticks over the crackling, snapping tinder. I watch the edges blacken, then glow, then spit fire. Soon the chemical smell of the battery is overwhelmed by the burning resins of the wood.

Heat warms my face. Light expands outward— yellow and orange—to fill the entire shack. On the wall, blurred graffiti sharpens into focus.

DONT DRINK THE WATER
FISH HAVE SEX IN IT

And I start to laugh. At the lame joke. At this miserable shelter. At myself.

I am the caveman who first struck flint against a chunk of iron pyrite.

I have made fire.

10

Stratford wasn't much of a town; it was more like the memory of a town. Once it might've been a vibrant farming community, a commercial center near the juncture of the Androscoggin and the Nezinscot rivers, but the old homesteads had been abandoned over decades and left to collapse under the weight of winter, and the new places were just big exurban houses set on three-acre lots. Most of the cornfields planted in the rich loam of the floodplain had transitioned to second-growth forest. Even the mill at the mouth of the Nezinscot was gone; the only vestige of the dam was a broken wall along the far bank of the stream: a moss-covered ruin of a time people didn't seem to feel merited honoring.

That was my initial impression of the hamlet, at least.

Then I turned a corner, emerged from a stand of pines towering over the road, and there on the banks of the river rose a majestic farmhouse and barn so perfectly preserved I involuntarily lifted my foot from the gas. In an instant I had seemingly traveled a century back in time. The clapboards gleamed white in the sun, and the red trim shined as if freshly painted. The roof shingles, wet with snowmelt, icicles dripping from the gutters, might have been nailed on mere months earlier. Even the vase-shaped elms out front had somehow escaped the blight that had decimated their kind from Maine to the Mississippi.

Friends accused me of being a young man with an old soul—the "youngest old fart" they'd ever met—and maybe they were right. For much of my youth, I had suffered under the delusion of having been born too late. I was a displaced person from the era of the Voyageurs who had set out across the Great Lakes in bateaux in search of furs; I was a temporal fugitive from the age of the Klondike Gold Rush when men literally bet their lives against nature with more than riches on the line. Sometimes I still succumbed to this mode of thinking. An overfondness for nostalgia was the crack running down the middle of my character.

I saw Chamberlain's farmhouse, in other words, through some heavily clouded lenses.

Only as I neared the circular drive did I feel myself pulled forcibly back to the twenty-first century. Two newish-looking vehicles, both recently washed of salt and sand, reflected the sun like colored mirrors. One was a forest-green Toyota Land Cruiser; the other was a Mini Cooper Clubman with a hard top and a chassis the color of French vanilla ice cream. The Land Cruiser must have belonged to Mrs. Chamberlain;

the luxury SUV suited a wealthy woman who had grown up on the South African veldt.

Who drove the Mini, I couldn't guess.

Shadow had passed from comatose sleep into a more fitful state; he twitched his tail and growled as if dreaming. Lizzie had said he would doze for four or five hours—time enough for me to conduct my courtesy interviews. The wolf was ahead of schedule, and what would I do if he awakened in a bad temper, willing to break his teeth on the steel gate?

I decided to park some distance from the house to minimize possible disturbances to his rest.

As I stepped outside, I saw my breath sparkle in the afternoon sunshine. I loved the cold because it always made me more conscious of my animal self: strong heart pushing warm blood through my arteries, network of nerves sending electric messages from my fingers and toes to my brain, thin skin that was no defense at all against the elements.

I closed the door quietly and surveyed the massive house with genuine appreciation.

The front shrubs had been securely wrapped in burlap against the coming storms or covered with tent-shaped wooden shelters. The drive had been marked with reflective rods to guide the plowman so he wouldn't tear up the lawn when he pushed aside the inevitable snow.

An antique sleigh had been parked beneath the elms. Its bells jingled in the breeze.

The front porch was stacked with a pile of wood that looked entirely decorative. Fir boughs trailed along the rails. Every window on both floors boasted its own green wreath.

The professor was dead. And Mariëtte Chamberlain had implied she lived elsewhere. So whose house was this that it should be so elaborately decorated?

There was no doorbell; just one of those old-fashioned brass knockers that made me think of Jacob Marley's ghostly face.

Eben must be short for Ebenezer, I realized belatedly.

When the door opened, I half expected to see a house servant in a long coat or a maid in a bonnet.

Instead the young woman who greeted me was as far from a Norman Rockwell painting as I could imagine. She was nearly as tall as me with blond hair styled in a brushed-up undercut. Her blue eyes were rimmed with kohl. Her ears were studded with what looked like shrapnel. She wore a Buffalo plaid shirt, black jeans rolled at the ankles, and Doc Marten boots. We were probably the same age, give or take, but her affect was deliberately retro: a throwback to the grunge era.

"Run, while you still can," she said in a throaty undertone.

"Excuse me?"

"Bibi! Is that the game warden?" bellowed a big voice I recognized as belonging to Mariëtte Chamberlain.

The young woman leaned close enough that I could smell the woodsmoke in her hair. She'd lately been tending a fire. She made a pistol shape with her hand, thumb cocked, index finger extended. "I'm serious, friend, if you value your life and your soul, get out while you still can. Quick! I'll cover you while you make your escape."

"Bibi!"

"Don't say I didn't warn you." She pulled the door wide so I could enter. "It's your game warden, Mother!"

Warm air spilled out, smelling of balsam and baking spices—cloves, cinnamon, nutmeg. An actual nutcracker, straight out of the ballet, stood on a small table beside the door. A gilded bowl of walnuts at his feet.

The ceiling creaked overhead, the boards complaining.

My view of Mariëtte Chamberlain began with her feet as she descended the narrow staircase. Ragg wool stockings and gum-soled shoes. Her legs kept on coming, impossibly long and clad in chocolate-brown corduroy.

She was so tall she was forced to duck her head as she descended. Rivard had derisively called her a "glamazon," but there was little about her that struck me as glamorous. She had naturally blond hair cut in a short, severe style. She wore no makeup, nor any jewelry except for a gold wedding band. Her cable-knit sweater sported holes in the sleeves and along the hem. Based on her wrinkles and sunspots, I guessed her to be in her late sixties, but she might have been half a decade younger.

For all the damage to her skin, she remained undeniably striking. Her eyes, blue as beryls, were spaced wide apart. Her perfect nose showed no sign of the plastic surgeon's scalpel. Cameras must have loved the exquisite symmetry of her face.

"Please forgive my daughter," she said in that accent I hadn't been able to place. "She has an idiosyncratic sense of humor that strikes many people as rude. Her father and I did our best to tame it, but whatever authority I had as a parent is long gone."

"And please forgive my mother," said Bibi, "for believing wealth excuses condescension."

Mariëtte's shoulders were broad in the manner of someone who had swum competitively and still did hundreds of laps in the pool. She projected more vitality than people half her age, her daughter included.

"I am hardly condescending to the warden."

"You've dialed up the eccentricity pretty high,

Mother. We both know that's one of your stratagems when dealing with strangers. Mainers in particular. Befuddling them with your foreignness."

"And we both know that your defiance is just as calculated."

Bibi failed to suppress a smile. I suspected I wasn't the first stranger to watch one of their performative squabbles.

The mother nodded at me. "Warden Investigator Bowditch, I am Mariëtte Chamberlain, née Van Rooyen. I'd like to thank you for making the drive here. I am sure you thought me rude, but I have learned that a woman needs to risk being thought a bitch if she hopes to get anywhere in this world. This is my daughter Bibi."

"We've met," said the young woman. With her Goth makeup and her crude piercings, she'd gone to elaborate lengths to camouflage her own natural beauty.

"Take the man's coat, *bokkie*," Mariëtte said.

As I removed my parka, Bibi Chamberlain appraised the gun on my belt. "Is that a SIG Sauer perchance?"

Few civilians, in my experience, could identify the make of a handgun at a glance.

"Yes, it's a P239."

"I thought I recognized the slide and beavertail. Weren't the P239s discontinued? I have a secret fetish for firearms. Grandfather taught me to shoot with a Pistolet automatique modèle 1935A. It was a trophy his grandfather brought home from the War That Failed to End All Wars. If you have time, I can show you Eben's gun cabinet later."

"I'd like that." An interest in antique firearms was another of my weaknesses.

"Enough gun talk, I think." Mariëtte took my arm and turned me toward the hall with even greater strength than I'd anticipated. "We're having coffee and biscuits in the back parlor. I assume you're not allergic to dogs. I doubt a game warden would be."

The back parlor was, in fact, a winterized porch, with a view of white fields rolling a hundred yards to the river. The low-ceilinged space was warmed by a potbellied stove on which a dented pail was boiling fiercely. The water seemed to contain the spices I had smelled upon my entrance. There was, in other words, no actual baking in progress: just the false odors of home.

A water spaniel, all wavy brown coat and droopy ears, occupied a flannel bed beside the stove. It raised rheumy eyes at me and sniffed. I wondered what would happen if it caught the smell of the wolf on me—some dogs seriously freaked—but it sighed and lowered it hoary chin onto its paws.

"This is Plum," said Mariëtte. "She was the

professor's boon companion. Plum survived the incident in the boat. Someone found her roaming the shore, barking at the water, presumably where my father-in-law had gone in. She hasn't been the same since the tragedy. I believe her spirit was broken that day."

"Oh, please," said the daughter, whose own accent was generically American. "That dog has always been a sad sack."

"Bibi!"

Mariëtte had chosen a seat for me, facing the room instead of the scenery. A Christmas tree dominated one corner: a nonnative Scotch pine with bristling branches. The decoration was minimal: red ribbons, silver globes. A manger scene with pewter figurines—shepherds, angels, magi—was artfully arranged on a blanket at the base.

"Your house is very beautiful, Mrs. Chamberlain. And very festive."

"Christmas was the professor's favorite holiday. Bibi and I have sought to keep his memory alive by continuing his traditions. But it only makes his absence more pronounced, I think."

The mother sat down across from me, so she could watch the radiant fields over my shoulders. Her daughter settled into a love seat to her right. The natural light brought out the vivid blueness of both their eyes.

"You're joining us, Bibi?" said Mariëtte.

The daughter removed an electric cigarette from her shirt pocket. It looked like a USB drive the length of a pencil. As she inhaled from one end, a blue light glowed.

"Oh, I wouldn't miss this for the world."

Mariëtte Chamberlain served the coffee from a polished pot. The cup was bone china, as was the plate on which she had spread an assortment of cookies. They were certainly not home-baked.

It seemed necessary to begin with a pleasantry. "Do I understand that you're South African by birth, Mrs. Chamberlain?"

Out of the corner of my eye I caught Bibi grimace.

Her mother's lips tightened; she had difficulty spitting out a response. "No, I am *Rhodesian.*"

Seeing my distress, Bibi said, "You might know the country today under the name of Zimbabwe."

It was possible Rivard had set me up, knowing the ire I would elicit referring to South Africa, but it was just as likely that Marc didn't know about the bloody histories of the former British colonies. He'd never been interested in the past, anyone else's past at least. His own grievances and grudges, on the other hand, were sources of endless preoccupation.

Mariëtte gripped her knees with her hands and gave me a blue glare. "We were driven out—my family. Forced into exile after the United Kingdom sold us out to Mugabe. I hold dual passports, British and American, but Rhodesia will always be my home."

"I apologize for the presumption."

She glowered at me a while longer, then reached down and began to stroke the water spaniel with such force that the dog cried out. "You need to brush her coat, Bibi. Look how tangled it is!"

"Mother, you're hurting her."

I cleared my throat. "I should tell you in advance I only have an hour."

Mariëtte glanced up from the dog, eyes still fierce. "What do you know about my late father-in-law?"

"That he died while duck hunting—"

"I am not asking what you know of his death. What do you know about Eben Chamberlain, the man? From your blank expression, I can see you know nothing."

I sipped my coffee and let her instruct me.

"Eben Chamberlain held a bachelor's degree in classical history from Cornell and a Ph.D. from Cambridge. But before he entered the academy, he served his country as a member of the foreign service."

"He was a spook," said Bibi.

"He was not a spook. After leaving the government, he began his teaching career at Bryn Mawr, moved to Princeton, and ended as dean of Bollingbrook. He wrote five books, the last of which, about Xenophon and the Ten Thousand, is considered the definitive text. He was a man of catholic interests. An expert in the cause to preserve heirloom apple varieties, he served on the board of the World Seed Vault on Baffin Island."

"You left out his passion for ducks," said Bibi, exhaling a vapor cloud.

Mariëtte indicated several lifelike waterfowl sculptures displayed around the parlor. "He achieved some acclaim as a wood artist late in life. His bird carvings are in the collections of the Ward Museum of Wildfowl Art and the Wendell Gilley Museum."

"They're magnificent."

I was particularly taken with his gadwall hen. The professor had captured the duck's orange underbill. It was a subtle detail many carvers— especially those who didn't hunt—overlooked.

Mariëtte continued as if I hadn't spoken. "He was married to the same woman for fifty years— Glenna predeceased him—and they had two sons, also deceased. I was married to the elder of the two, Artemus. Eben left behind three grandchildren, all girls, of which Bibi is the youngest."

I put down my empty cup beside my crumb-strewn plate.

"It sounds like he lived a remarkably full life."

"Indeed, he did."

"Show him the picture, Mother," said Bibi.

Mariëtte handed me a framed portrait of the man. She'd kept it facedown on the table beside her and presented it now with great reverence. I tried not to get fingerprints on the professor's distinguished mug.

"Here he is on his seventy-seventh birthday," she said.

Professor Chamberlain had been a barrel-chested man with a narrow waist. His smooth cheeks had the ruddiness of an outdoorsman who enjoys a nightly nip. His nose was a ski jump. His steel-rimmed glasses were small and round. His hair, enviably thick for a man of his advanced age, was slick with pomade. He wore moleskin trousers, a houndstooth shirt, a Shetland sweater, and a tweed hacking jacket with a suede shooting patch on the shoulder and patches on the elbows.

He looked to me like a pompous ass.

I handed the icon to Mariëtte Chamberlain who returned it to the table, no longer facedown but propped up, so I could continue my appreciation of his manly form.

"Now that you know something about the professor," she said, "you should know some-thing about me."

I made a show of peeking at my watch, to remind her that I was on a tight schedule. She ignored the gesture.

"I grew up in Salisbury, Rhodesia. My ancestors

were Voortrekkers. My grandfather was a leader of what is today called the Second Boer War. He resettled in Rhodesia, carved a settlement from the bush, and our family farmed the same land for more than a century until the British stabbed us in the back. In the 1970s my branch of the Van Rooyens joined the diaspora during the *Gukurahundi* campaign."

"Objection—relevance," said Bibi. "The warden doesn't want to hear your life story, Mother."

"It is important he knows the woman with whom he is dealing. That I come from a family of fighters and survivors, the women as well as the men. It would be a mistake to trifle with me. I will not tolerate being taken lightly."

I leaned forward. "I don't think I've given you cause to distrust me, Mrs. Chamberlain."

"Not yet perhaps. I made the mistake of trusting your fellow wardens four years ago, when I had misgivings about the thoroughness of their investigation. I will not be patronized by a man in uniform again."

"It's a good thing I'm not wearing a uniform."

My joke fell flat, even with Bibi. I doubted Plum appreciated it either.

Mariëtte continued: "I was modeling in London when I met Bibi's father. Artie worked for the U.S. State Department. We lived overseas until his death—toxoplasmosis—after which I felt it necessary that Bibi and I should move to Maine.

I wanted her to have as much time as possible with her grandfather."

"My dad was a spook, too," said Bibi.

"He was not a spook," said Mariëtte.

"He was totally CIA. Career U.S. State Department official, final posting in Istanbul. I bet the Russians bugged the flats where we lived. I have this theory that my dad was actually poisoned—"

"It shouldn't surprise you that my daughter writes cartoons," said Mariëtte.

"They're graphic novels, Mother," said Bibi. "And I also illustrate them."

"Glorified comic books."

"What she hates is that they're autobiographically based, and she's the visual inspiration for the main antagonist. Women make the best villains, don't you think? Men are so clumsy and obvious."

I hadn't yet found a reason to bring out my pen and notebook. "Do you live here together?"

"Bibi does. I have a house on Paris Hill."

The daughter gestured with her vape when she spoke. "You're looking at the sole resident of the Professor Eben Chamberlain House Museum."

"Are those macabre remarks necessary, Bibi?"

"Grow a sense of humor, Mother."

I leaned forward in my chair as if preparing to rise. "With all due respect, Mrs. Chamberlain, I am here as a courtesy to discuss the letter you sent me. And while your family history is interesting—"

"He's feisty!" said Bibi Chamberlain with delight.

"He's on a tight schedule," said Mariëtte. "The warden lieutenant who oversaw the search for my father-in-law always seemed pressed for time, too. I wondered what could be more important than locating Eben Chamberlain's body."

I settled against the leather headrest. "You're referring to Warden Lieutenant Rivard."

"I understand he was subsequently cashiered," she said.

I kept my tone neutral. "Lieutenant Rivard is no longer with the Maine Warden Service."

"Good! I'd like to think my official complaints contributed to his dismissal." Mariëtte Chamberlain gripped her knees again. "I wrote to you, Warden Investigator Bowditch, because I read about your involvement in the arrests in Aroostook County last summer. You created quite a headache for your department! Your colonel resigned because of the scandals you brought to light."

"I wouldn't characterize it that way."

Others did, however; many of my fellow wardens included.

"My impression of you, Warden Investigator, is of a man who refuses to toe the official line," said Mariëtte. "My subsequent research confirmed

106

as much. You are not afraid of making enemies. You must sleep with that sidearm under your pillow."

"Do you?" asked Bibi, showing writerly curiosity.

"Mrs. Chamberlain, with all due respect—"

Mariëtte lifted an over-stuffed folder from the floor beside her. "Here is the complete file relating to my father-in-law's death. You will see it has been augmented with my own research and assorted news clippings. Please review it, and then we will continue this conversation tomorrow."

"Ma'am, I can't do that."

She brought the heavy folder to her lap. "Why ever not?"

"Because the Maine Warden Service conducted a thorough investigation. With the assistance of the attorney general's office, it produced a report concluding no suspicious circumstances were indicated in the death of your father-in-law—as unfortunate as it was."

"You've read the file then?"

"I have."

"And what did it say—in your own words?"

The question was a test to determine if my visit was the hollow gesture she suspected.

"While returning from a morning of duck hunting," I said, "Professor Eben Chamberlain removed his personal flotation device. He

107

then either suffered a health event that affected his balance or fell out of his boat by accident, perhaps while retrieving decoys. He succumbed to hypothermia in the forty-nine-degree water and drowned in the current, measured that day at 1,200 cubic feet per second at the water-flow meter in Auburn. His corpse sank, floated downriver, and became trapped underwater above the Gulf Island Pond Dam. His remains were recovered six days later. The chief medical examiner determined that the bruises on his body occurred postmortem, and the presence of water in his lungs indicated death by drowning."

Most of the water in the bucket atop the wood stove had evaporated, and now the spices began to steam.

"Mother has an alternate theory," said Bibi.

"I understand your reluctance to accept these conclusions," I said.

"Eben Chamberlain was murdered," declared Mariëtte Chamberlain. "He never would have removed his flotation vest. He nearly drowned as a boy and always wore one when he was in a boat. Someone forced him to do it. He didn't drown. He *was* drowned. Poor Plum here was also forced into the river. The person who killed the professor then returned to shore, relaunched the boat, and tossed the life preserver after it. A near-perfect crime."

A burnt odor arose from the sizzling bucket.

I wondered if either of them was going to add water.

"Do you have any proof of this?" I asked.

"Circumstantial proof—but the state's theory is also built on circumstances and speculation."

"I wish I could help you, Mrs. Chamberlain."

The tall woman shot to her feet. "You're not going to ask what the motive was?"

"I told you this was a bad idea, Mother," said Bibi, punctuating the sentence with a stab of her e-cig.

"I know who the murderer is," said Mariëtte. "And don't tell me you're not interested in hearing his name."

"All right."

"Bruce Jewett."

I remembered the name from the report. Rivard had briefly investigated the man. "He was Professor Chamberlain's regular hunting companion."

"Among other things."

"I don't follow you," I said.

"Bruce Jewett was my father-in-law's lover."

11

I feed the flames with boards pulled from inside the shack. With the missing wall, it is more like a lean-to than a proper shelter. But it provides cover against the wind which would likely extinguish my fire before I can get it burning. Sooner or later I will need to move the smoldering, flickering pile of wood, before it burns through the nominally inflammable insulation on which it sits.

A voice in my head tells me to let the blaze grow until it becomes a massive conflagration and consumes the structure: a beacon visible for miles around.

I have to remind myself to distrust my thoughts. Confusion is a well-observed symptom of hypothermia.

Burning down my only shelter is one of those ideas I should probably refrain from acting upon.

I remember another of my friend Charley's maxims. The old geezer has one for every situation.

"When faced with a crisis, focus on one thing at time."

For me the one thing is warming my core. I pull off my sweater and rip open the Velcro fasteners that hold my concealable body armor in place. Then I undress down to my merino long johns. When I remove my socks, I am shocked by the shriveled pastiness of my flash-frozen toes. I remove the anti-ballistic panels from my vest and hang the wet layers of clothing from nails and other makeshift hooks above the fire. Even damp, the wool items will retain their warming properties. My jeans are a lost cause unless I get them dry. I deserve to be pantless for wearing cotton this time of year.

I roll up my Levi's like I would a sleeping bag to squeeze out as much water as possible. I swing my socks over my head to dry them using centrifugal force. I hang everything so close to the licking flames I smell burning fabric. I'd rather have singed clothes than wet clothes.

The boots are the hardest. I strip out the insoles and prop them beside the orange embers. But the leather uppers are soaked through. I can warm up the exteriors, but the insides will stay damp even if I bake the boots all night long.

The flames spit. The fir sticks blacken and burn, faster than the hardwood pieces.

I feel like I was run over by a snowplow. The struggle to escape the Jeep stretched a few ligaments and twisted a few muscles past their natural limits. My core is so cold it feels as if my heart and lungs are a solid block of ice. And yet my frostbitten fingers sting as if I'd burnt them on a stove. Even my mandible hurts from my teeth chattering.

I examine my injured hand in the brightening light.

Shadow's claws have torn furrows between my wrist and knuckles. When I emerged from the river, the wound was frozen into icy clots, but blood is leaking from the scratches again.

Charley speaks to me again, this time more insistently: *"When faced with a crisis, focus on one thing at time!"*

My sole priority needs to be reheating my core.

I rummage through the litter until I find an empty can of Foster's Lager. I try shaking it out but the dregs at the bottom are frozen. I bring it down to the river and fill my makeshift cup. Cigarette butts boil out of the top. I keep dunking until the water runs clean.

Back in the shack, I stick the bottom of the can in the embers of my campfire. The aluminum blackens. The paint scorches.

I watch my wristwatch for five slow minutes while snow drifts in through the missing wall. My first drink is lukewarm and tastes of tobacco. I wedge the can in the coals to boil. The water will heat me from the inside out. When you are hypothermic in the wilderness, you can't warm up externally. You need to feed your internal engine with hot water and food if you have it. Then wrap yourself in something to trap your body heat between your skin and the outer insulation. What I wouldn't give for a two-dollar space blanket.

My chief worry is a condition called after-drop. As my frozen arms and legs warm, they will inevitably send chilled blood to my already-stressed heart. The shock can be fatal. People have died of after-drop.

I make a point of taking a piss because I remember that the body has to work extra-hard to heat a full bladder. Then I make another barefoot trip to the river to refill the can. I hunch over the fire while the water heats.

For the first time since I went into the river, I have a chance to reflect.

The people I need to focus on are the ones I interviewed earlier, starting with Mariëtte's prime suspect. Who else could have laid that trap for me but Bruce Jewett? The man had been a welder, for Christ's sake.

In my mind's eye I see the spiked objects laid across the road. Leave it to a student of military history, like Jewett, to use caltrops. The Navy vet knew there was only one way down from Pill Hill. I was bound to run over those spikes. Either I'd die in a fiery crash or drown in the freezing river.

Does he think I'm dead? Or will he come looking for me?

There are bridges, up and downstream, where

114

he can cross. He doesn't even need a truck. A snowmobile, with the throttle open, could skip across a frozen stretch of the Androscoggin without having to detour more than a thousand yards.

I don't dare stay here any longer, I decide. I will cut inland to the road that runs parallel to the east side of the river. It won't be easy in the dark, but I prefer my chances in the woods to sitting motionless in the firelight, waiting for a sniper's bullet to find me.

I begin gathering up my steaming clothes. It is then that I see the wolf. I glance out into the trees, and there he is, looming at the edge of the shadows. The reflective lining behind his retinas glows with a yellowy phosphorescence.

My first reaction is to reach for the knife. But I stop my hand before I do.

I love and care for this animal, I feel a spiritual bond with him. I am ashamed of my fear of the wolf.

"Hey, big guy it's good to see you." There's a quaver in my voice. "I was worried about you, Shadow. Why don't you come inside, get warm? You can lie down by the fire."

Having a predator stare at you is one of the most unnerving experiences you can have. Being singled out from the herd. Realizing you are now his prime target. His next meal.

The fear that skitters up my spine is primal.

As he takes a tentative step toward me, I fight the urge to grab the knife. Like any wet dog, his body seems strangely shaped with his fur matted. His ice-clumped coat looks burdensome.

I have to remind myself there was a time when this ferocious creature lived among people.

The man from Montana who'd weaned him had fed him Puppy Chow from a bowl. Even the Maine drug addicts, who obtained him illegally and were his last "owners," had kept him indoors, locked in their foul basement.

I had never planned on keeping Shadow. I told people that the wolf had escaped, but it was just as accurate to say I'd let him go. The distinction didn't matter. What mattered was that he'd begun a new life in the high timber of western Maine. He'd hunted and scavenged in the wild, and he'd thrived. Occasionally, someone would spot him, often in the company of another large canine, thought to be one of the occasional wild wolves that make their way down from Canada. State wildlife biologists denied the existence of Shadow and his female companion. "There are no wild wolves in Maine," was the official line.

Then an idiot shot him with a crossbow. And through a twist of fate, I'd become his protector once more.

God seemed to want the wolf in my life. For what purpose, I still cannot imagine.

What am I to him though?

I sure as hell am not his owner. Or his "pet parent," to use a term I disdain.

Am I the jailer who foiled his many escape attempts? Or the tormentor who put him in a box to be drugged and half-drowned?

His unblinking stare reveals nothing of his mind.

"Why don't you come get warm?" I find myself saying again.

He hangs there at the ragged edge of the firelight. The patience of wolves.

And then, without warning, he trots toward me, leaps the threshold, and plops down at my feet.

With the campfire flickering and the wolf dog beside me, I feel like I've found myself in the most fucked-up Jack London story of all time.

Shadow begins to chew the painful chunks of ice from between his toes. One of his paw pads is bleeding. I move my hand in the direction of his injured foot. His lip curls and there is no missing the message.

"If you touch me, I'll bite your fucking arm off."

12

Mariëtte Chamberlain settled against the upholstered seat and gazed at me through her eyelashes. She knew she had my attention.

"His lover?" I said.

"I don't think Professor Chamberlain understood his own predilections until late middle age. It wasn't until after the birth of his sons that he came to his 'great awakening,' as Artie used to call it. Afterward, he began an exciting new phase of his life. The professor was a loving husband and father, and he had his dalliances, which Glenna accepted as his private business since he harmed no one by them. One of the virtues of the Chamberlains is their refusal to make petty personal judgments. I suppose I should use the past tense since Bibi is the last of the name and likely to remain so."

"Thanks, Mother," said Bibi. "But I haven't ruled out marriage."

"I'm speaking of procreation, dear."

"Have you never heard the words *in vitro*?"

My chair creaked as I leaned forward. "Did you tell Lieutenant Rivard about this aspect of Professor Chamberlain's life?"

"At the time it seemed immaterial."

"But not now?"

"I'm getting to that," she said. "When the professor retired here, to focus on his art and his horticultural research, he was still a vital man. He had a lifelong commitment to physical fitness. It was one of the things we shared. I assumed his robust physicality extended to his sexual life, but he and I never talked about those things."

"Grandfather spoke with *me* about it," said Bibi. "He was very open."

Mariëtte shrugged. "Yes, well."

"As fellow queers and all."

"Bibi, the warden doesn't know you well enough to appreciate your sense of humor."

"I think he's coming to appreciate it," said the daughter, ripping another Juul.

The spaniel arose, did a 360-degree turn that only succeeded in raising a cloud of hair and a musty dog smell, before settling into her bed.

I thought of Shadow outside in the cramped quarters of his cold kennel. I prayed to God he hadn't fully awakened.

Mariëtte ran a hand through her cropped hair. "In any event, the professor had a full life. He had his agricultural research and his wood carving. He was a lifelong Freemason because his role model, Benjamin Franklin, had been one. He volunteered at the polls each election. He took an interest in his community. And that is how he came to be associated with the man, Jewett."

I had resisted the urge to reach for my notepad,

120

not wanting to signal my growing interest. I hadn't wanted to give Mariëtte that little victory. But the time had finally come. I clicked the button on my pen.

"You're referring to the lover you mentioned—the person you're accusing of murder."

"Bruce Jewett," she said, stressing the name's internal rhyme.

I remembered him from Rivard's report. "He's the man who accompanied Professor Chamberlain for the first part of the hunting trip the day he died? But I understand that your father-in-law dropped him ashore hours before he disappeared. Lieutenant Rivard interviewed Mr. Jewett on several occasions, and his alibi for the afternoon was airtight. Now you're telling me that he and your father-in-law were lovers?"

"No one knew about it at the time," said Mrs. Chamberlain. "The idea was so unlikely, given their differences."

"That's not entirely true," said Bibi.

Her mother grew red. "You knew and never told me?"

"I had suspicions, but it was no one else's business. It still isn't, if you ask me."

"Bibi—"

I was concerned that if I didn't interject now I would miss my chance. "What can you tell me about Mr. Jewett that isn't in the file?"

Mariëtte smoothed her pants atop her thighs.

The corduroy was worn there; she did this a lot. "He's a retired Navy veteran who lives about a mile south of here. He's one of those—what's the word? Help me here, Bibi. Preppers? Survivalists?"

"Kooks," said the daughter. "He believes the collapse of civilization is imminent and that the black and brown hordes will flee the inner cities to rape and pillage the good people of Stratford, Maine."

Her Rhodesian mother cleared her throat. Bruce Jewett's views on race relations were not what the self-proclaimed fugitive wanted to stress.

"I never understood what the professor saw in him, honestly, even as a hunting companion," she said.

"Grandfather called Bruce 'an acquired taste,'" said Bibi. "He told me, 'If you can wait out his filibusters, Bruce can be quite insightful. He hides his intelligence behind a barbed-wire fence of SHTF nonsense.'"

"SHTF?" said Mariëtte.

"It stands for Shit Hits the Fan. The Second Civil War. The coming genocide of the white race."

A dark expression passed over Mariëtte's perfect face. She seemed to withdraw inside herself before slowly returning to the room. "Those things are not relevant. They are not part of the motive."

"I wouldn't be so certain," I said.

"It is Jewett's self-disgust that you must focus on," she said. "That is the reason he killed the professor."

"Oh, please," said Bibi with a flourish of her nicotine delivery device. "The man who can't accept his sexual identity—it's a total cliché."

Mariëtte cocked her chin. "Some stereotypes are true."

"For the love of God, Mother." Bibi put her head in her hands.

"I want to return to your accusation, Mrs. Chamberlain," I said. "Based on what you've told me, I believe you'd be better off speaking with someone from the state police's Unsolved Homicide Unit. I can give you the name and number of a victim witness advocate."

Mariëtte slapped the arm of the sofa so hard she awakened Plum again. "You don't think I called them already? It was a waste of time."

"As a warden, I am not authorized to pursue a murder investigation, ma'am."

"What about the search then? You can review the failures of Lieutenant Rivard."

"Marc Rivard is no longer with the Warden Service, as we discussed."

"But your agency could still be held liable in court."

I tucked away my notebook and pen. "In that case, I would recommend your next conversation be with an attorney. I've heard you out, as I agreed to do. There's nothing more I can do for you."

The strapping woman shot to her feet. "There's something else! An important detail not in the report. Tell him, Bibi."

The daughter steeled herself with another draw from her vape. "I was supposed to have tagged along on the duck hunt that morning. I never told Rivard or any of the other game wardens about it."

There had been no mention of this in the file. Of that, I was positive.

"Why didn't you go?" I said.

"Because I was hungover. You have to remember it was four in the morning and still dark and freezing. I'd been out with friends the night before. But I got dressed because I'd promised Grandfather and even went down to the boat. Bruce made a comment about how green I looked. He took out a pint of Peach Schnapps and asked if I wanted some 'hair of the dog.' A minute later, I threw up. Grandfather suggested I return to the house and go to sleep, which I did."

I quickly scribbled down this information into my notebook.

"Why didn't you tell Lieutenant Rivard about this?"

"Because I didn't go, did I? And it wasn't like I had any idea where they planned on hunting or anything that happened between them after I went to bed. And to be honest, I felt guilty because maybe if I'd gone, I would've stayed with Grandfather all day, and he wouldn't have died."

"You can be certain that if I had known any of this," the mother said, "I would've spoken out at the time."

I directed myself to the daughter. "Do you have any idea why Jewett never mentioned it?"

"I assumed it was because I was obviously grieving, and he didn't want the authorities raking me over the coals. I don't like the man—God knows I find his beliefs abhorrent—but in my eyes he did me a kindness."

"The idea that Jewett might've had something to do with your grandfather's death never occurred to you?" I said.

"Bruce had an alibi—and there was a witness."

"You had no suspicions whatsoever."

The young woman looked at the carpet.

"Tell him, Bibi. Tell him what you told me."

"Two weeks ago, my mother and I were discussing my inheritance. The house and property belong to me. I have been thinking of selling the place and moving to Los Angeles. An ex of mine lives in Venice. And there are career opportunities for me in Hollywood. Mother was horrified. She asked what Grandfather would think. I told her I knew Eben Chamberlain a hell of a lot better than she did. I said, 'You don't even know what he told me before he died.' "

Mariëtte had been biding her time, waiting for this moment. "If I had, you can be sure everything would have been different!"

The daughter put her elbows on her knees and hung her head.

"What did Professor Chamberlain tell you before he died?" I asked.

Without looking up, she answered in a choking voice, "He said it would be good having me along on the hunt. He said he needed my opinion of Bruce."

"There!" said Mariëtte Chamberlain. "There it is. She's been sitting on this information for four years as if it doesn't matter when it proves the professor had misgivings about the man."

"It could mean any number of things," said the daughter, raising wet eyes. "You're assuming without evidence that he viewed Mr. Jewett as a threat to his life."

"He might have!"

"Did Jewett expect you to come along that morning?" I said. "Did he know you were joining them in the boat?"

"I have no idea."

"Do you suspect that he offered you schnapps when you were sick to dissuade you from going?"

"I don't know."

I paused to take in the scene. The weak sunlight

streaming in past the statuesque silhouette of Mariëtte Chamberlain. Her daughter, collapsed in her chair. The wood stove crackling. The dog snoring. The air thickening with the burnt vapors of Christmas spices.

"Can you give me his street address, Mrs. Chamberlain?"

"Halfway up Pill Hill," said Mariëtte with a triumphant smile. "More than halfway. It's the last house before all those wretched trailers at the top."

Bibi rearranged herself in the love seat. "You mean you're going to talk with him?"

"Yes."

"He probably won't even speak with you," said the mother. "I tried last week but didn't get past the gate—he has a camera and speakers. He told me to leave before I regretted it. I said I wasn't scared of him. And he laughed. It was comical, really. He thought he was frightening me."

At last I rose to my feet. "Where can I find my coat?"

"I'll get it for you," said Bibi.

"You need to report back to us after you see him," said Mariëtte, forcefully guiding me to the door by the elbow, just as she'd forcefully guided me into the parlor. "I want to hear everything he tells you. Perhaps you can record your conversation so we can—"

"No, ma'am, I'm not going to do that."

"I expect a full accounting, Warden Investigator Bowditch."

I thanked her for the coffee and cookies.

Outside the air had grown colder. The sun, already low in the southern sky, had moved behind the house and the icicles along the gutters had ceased to drip.

I was surprised to find Bibi following me. She hadn't bothered to grab a coat.

"Please don't harass that poor man," she said. "It'll only provoke him."

"If he's so easily provoked, why don't you believe your mom's theory that he had something to do with your grandfather's death?"

"Because I pity him. Bruce Jewett doesn't know who he is. Or he doesn't want to know."

"That describes a lot of people who aren't racist gun nuts."

"Really?" She seemed genuinely surprised by this claim. "Maybe I take it for granted because I've always known who I am—and what I am. I suppose that was my grandfather's greatest gift to me. Acceptance."

"You're lucky then."

She seemed to take the remark as patronizing. "You don't exactly strike me as someone who struggles with self-knowledge."

Little did she know. Most mornings, the sight of my reflection still ambushed me in the mirror.

13

Sparks shoot upward from the fire and are caught in the moving air and carried outside with the smoke. The pink fiberglass near the entrance grows black with creosote. The plywood floor has begun to darken beyond the pink circle of insulation. I break branches and toss them onto the embers to feed the flames.

My instinct tells me I am pushing my luck, staying here when I should be running. But Shadow seems so exhausted. And my parka could use twenty more minutes to dry.

I know I am rationalizing.

Softwood hisses as steam escapes from the burning gas. The flames change color depending on what has ignited. Orange for pine and birchbark, yellow for maple branches, blue for cellophane, monofilament fishing line, and assorted trash gathered from the floor.

With swollen fingers, I reach up to feel the polyester fabric of my undergarment armor, hanging from a nail, and find it damp. There is nothing to do but slide the plates into place and shrug on the vest again. When I pull the sweater over my head next, I smell woodsmoke baked into the wool fibers.

My jeans have dried a little, but not enough.

"Cotton kills" is another of my mentor Charley's backwoods sayings.

My insoles seem warm when I slide them into my boots. But within minutes of tying up the laces, the cold clamminess returns.

The wind has changed direction, swung around from the northwest, causing smoke to back up inside the shack. I want to give the wolf a chance to get warm, but the urgency to flee while I can begins to build again.

How visible the blaze is from across the river continues to worry me.

But a wall of young conifers stands between the shack and the water's edge. And the snow is coming down heavier. Maybe I am all right here.

Shadow seems to know how close he can sprawl to the licking flames without having sparks rain down on his fur.

I wish I had food for him.

I wish I had food for myself.

I decide to take a gamble and lie down several yards from his massive head. He appraises me with those inscrutable eyes but doesn't growl or flinch. We bask together in the heat the wood is throwing off.

No one is a greater defender of wolves than I am. But there are moments when I am in the presence of this fearsome creature, when the Brothers Grimm take authorship of my internal monologue, and I feel as terrified of him as a medieval peasant hearing howls in the night.

Then this monster out of folklore will whimper in his sleep or let loose with a stinking fart, and I will remember he is just another mammal, like me; and that the evils we see in wolves are merely projections of our own moral failings. Since the dawn of history, his kind has paid the price for our ignorant self-regard, our eagerness to blame others, our persistent lack of courage. Wolves satisfy humanity's pitiful need for villains.

The fire grows too hot for me.

Now that I am out of danger for after-drop, I grab my parka and wander down to the river to rinse my scraped hand. My night vision needs time to adjust. The falling snow looks faintly gray in the darkness, like wood ash blown from some distant fireplace. I stand motionless behind my wall of firs, not wanting to risk a wrong step.

Slowly the Androscoggin reveals itself. The river is mostly a blur, made worse by the spitting flurries. Below my feet, I can make out slags of fractured ice piled at the edge. Then a pale sheet stretching away, as smooth as a carpet: a dangerous invitation to cross.

I imagine Bruce Jewett hidden on the heights of the far shore, methodically sweeping the eastern bank with a night-vision scope. Given the extent of his armory, he must possess every modern military device. To set his ambush for me, however, he had foregone contemporary weapons and reached back to the Bronze Age.

The simplest weapons are often the best. Out of reflex, I touch the knife in my pocket.

Jewett is a clever man, I have to hand it to him. He fooled Bibi Chamberlain. And he absolutely fooled me.

Why did I even stop at his house? I could say I'd done it for Mariëtte Chamberlain. But really, I was indulging my twin vices: curiosity and arrogance. Bruce Jewett, meanwhile, had leveraged my intellectual conceit against me. He sent me on a fool's errand up Pill Hill while he laid his steel traps below.

If I am going to survive the night, I will need to dig into my small store of humility.

I have to assume, for instance, that despite my self-assurances, my fire is visible. I have to acknowledge that in staying put I am making myself an easy target. I have to admit that I am facing a human predator who may be smarter, stronger, and more ruthless than I am.

I push through the firs into the circle of light. When forced to travel, the hunter-gatherers of the Pleistocene used to carry hot coals in the horns of aurochs. It's far easier to bring a fire with you than to make a new one in the dark and wet. I scrounge around until I find a rust-bitten can that once contained Maxwell House Coffee. It will serve me as a bull's horn.

Suddenly Shadow lifts his chin from his paws.

His ears go up. He stares past me toward the firs along the river.

Then he bolts.

A split second later comes the gunshot.

I throw myself onto the snow.

The shack starts splintering as bullets rip apart the plywood boards. Again my body reacts without any conscious direction from my brain. Leaving behind the dropped can of embers, I begin to crawl into the trees.

Bullets rip into the flaming logs, raising sparks. The shots are coming so quickly I don't know if it's a single shooter with an automatic weapon or multiple shooters with semi-automatic weapons. I have to fight the urge to stand and run. I keep squirming forward on elbows and knees: making myself a low target.

Somehow I find myself among the roots of an ancient oak. Bullets bury themselves in its massive trunk. Ahead of me is the unexplored forest, infinitely dark. I keep crawling.

14

The river road took me through the dead man's orchard. Between the rows of twisted trees were frozen white paths, wide enough for a tractor to pass, and there were tracks in the snow where a heavy machine had been at work. A picker must have come through since the last storm and plucked the branches clean of every last Winesap (or whatever varietals Chamberlain had cultivated).

I shouldn't have been surprised that the professor's horticultural experiments continued postmortem. Mariëtte Chamberlain would never abandon her father-in-law's studies any more than she would abandon her crusade to prove he'd been murdered.

Past the orchard was a frozen cornfield where I saw dozens of Canada geese foraging amid the broken stalks, some with their elegant necks held high, others with their white asses tilted in the air. Then the forest crept close to the road, and I had a brief view of the river, mostly ice-covered with open water cutting a slash down the channel.

A green truck crept toward me in a low gear. It was a pumper, and the driver was being careful on the grade although the asphalt was dry and free of ice. I waved, as was the neighborly custom in Maine, but he pretended not to see me. It was a septic truck, and I watched it descend in my side mirror, reading in reverse a sign on the bank of the tank.

YESTERDAY'S MEALS ON WHEELS

The driver might have been pumping out a portable toilet up the hill. Although it was highly unusual for a porta potty to remain in operation when the temperature plunged below freezing. Maybe he lived on the summit.

The road drew close to the river, and I saw that the guardrail was missing. The drop wasn't steep: no more than twenty feet. But if a vehicle hit black ice there, coming around that tight turn, the prospects of anyone surviving were grim.

The hill was steeper than it had appeared from the orchard, and near the top was Jewett's place.

Coming upon it from below, I thought it looked like just another New England farmhouse, sitting too close to the road as the old places always seemed to, with a stone wall in front and a small yard and then the parlor door no one used unless the visitors were special guests. Flagpoles were mounted on either side of the entrance with dual banners flapping in the wind. One was the sun-faded Stars and Stripes; the other was the blue standard of the United States Navy. The house was handsome enough, but an air of neglect hung about it. The red shingles had begun to peel in the sun, showing gray wood where the paint had flaked, and the mortar was crumbling in one of the chimneys. Some of the bricks had come loose and tumbled off the roof, but it was too late in the year for a mason to get up there safely. A plume of woodsmoke rose from the functional chimney and was pushed sideways in the wind.

When I came level with the yard, I saw that the stone wall had bottle shards cemented to the top as a deterrent against strollers having a sit-down. I'd seen this unfriendly ornamentation in the snootier neighborhoods of Ogunquit and Kennebunkport but never in a backwater like Stratford. People walking up and down this hill must've been rarer than molars on a hen.

As Mariëtte had said, Jewett's driveway was guarded by an iron gate.

I stopped short of it. Shadow was snoring again.

When I stepped from the Jeep, I felt a cold blast that sent a shiver through me. I made my way to the squawk box mounted beside the gate and pressed the red button under the keypad.

"Yeah?" The voice came through the speaker so suddenly I almost jumped.

A camera was surely watching me from a place of concealment. "Mr. Jewett?"

"Yeah?"

"My name is Mike Bowditch. I'm an investigator with the Maine Warden Service. I wondered if you might have a few minutes to talk with me about your late neighbor, Eben Chamberlain."

"You're pulling my chain, right?"

"No, sir."

"Eben drowned four years ago. The investigation was closed. How can there be any more questions?"

"It's standard procedure to review old cases."

"Like hell it is." He paused long enough for me to hear a crow caw as it rode the wind overhead. "Now you've got me curious, though. Yeah, I'll answer your damned questions. Give me a minute. I'm downcellar in my workshop, and I'd better clean up the C4 I'm making."

Jewett had an odd sense of humor: joking about plastic explosives to a law-enforcement officer.

While I waited, I dug my hands in my pockets and surveyed the river. The ice reflected the weak sunlight like an antique mirror. Beautiful in all its imperfections.

After a while, I heard a buzz and the gate swung inward. I made my way up the plowed drive to the house. Jewett stood at the side door, waiting for me.

He was small enough to have been a jockey. Unblinking eyes glared up at me through black-framed glasses. His complexion was as gray as his hair.

"Would you like to see my badge?" I asked.

"Anyone with half an ounce of brains can recognize you as a LEO."

By which he meant law-enforcement officer. Bruce Jewett was wise to the jargon we used.

"Would you mind if I came inside?"

"Why do you think I'm holding the door open?"

I stepped into a mudroom devoid of boots and coats. Just a bare bench and a row of naked hooks above it.

The door beeped when Jewett closed it behind me. Locks were engaged. Alarms were armed.

Mariëtte had described him as paranoid survivalist. Bibi had said he was preparing himself against the coming race wars.

To me, he appeared unremarkable. Like some former military men, he was fit for his age. I suspected the skinny old bird could do twenty pull-ups without taking a breather. He was dressed in a blue chambray shirt buttoned at the wrists and tucked into dark-wash dungarees; his black boots were polished, as was his belt, as was the holster holding a Glock 17 handgun. I had no doubt that the barrel of the weapon was polished, too.

"I was headed out to my range to do some shooting. Care to join me?"

"I'd rather we talk somewhere we could sit down. I promise it won't take long."

An odor came off him of some grooming

product from a bygone era; an aftershave or deodorant I'd only ever smelled in barbershops that cut the thinning hair of old men.

"I'm going to the range with or without you. So if you want to have a conversation, that's your choice." He worked hard to mimic a human smile. "I'll happily let you out again."

"All right."

He led me through a kitchen that was as clean as a frigate's galley, down a dust-free hall, and into what would have been the entryway if he ever received visitors through the front door. Then he stopped.

"It was the African Queen who sent you here."

His black-framed glasses held my attention. There was a smudge, a thumbprint, on the left lens.

"I'm sorry?"

"The protector of the late professor's memory. Mariëtte Chamberlain. Don't bother lying. I know she did. What's she saying about me now? That I'm a crazed crackpot?"

There seemed no point in being cagey when he could see through my lies. "She didn't use that particular word."

He grinned like he'd won five dollars on a scratch card. "You'd think, given her personal history, what happened to her family in Rhodesia, she'd want to prepare herself. She lived through her own Boogaloo when she was younger. But

140

some people don't have brains to pound sand into a rathole."

The house had the drafty feel of a place that had sat on the market so long the Realtor had stopped showing it.

Jewett caught me surveying the room with my peripheral vision and showed his teeth again. "I suppose you want to talk about the day Eben died. There's no other reason for another LEO to show up on my doorstep."

"I realize you've been over it many times."

"And each time, I've told the truth. My story hasn't changed. But I accept I'm an easy target."

"For what?"

"Suspicion. Harassment. Censure by TPTB."

"TPTB?"

" 'The Powers That Be.' What happened to Lieutenant LePeau?" he asked, resting his hands on his thin hips.

"Lieutenant Rivard is no longer with the Warden Service."

"I didn't think it was possible to fire a state employee. You people are dug into the body politic tighter than ticks."

"Are you sure you wouldn't rather sit down for this conversation?"

"We're going to the range. But first, I've got to water my horse."

He correctly interpreted my vacant expression as not understanding.

"I need to take a piss. Don't go anywhere. I've got mines hidden in the floor. Step on the wrong flagstone and *ka-boom*."

After he'd left, I took my chances and explored the entryway. My footsteps echoed. The walls were blank. Paintings or portraits had been removed. There was subtle shading in the paint where the frames had been, and a few hooks remained in the drywall. Maybe I'd gotten it right the first time, and Jewett was preparing to vacate.

As I turned from the wall, I was startled to find myself face-to-face with an ancient woman. She wore a flannel bathrobe with dried food down the front, and underneath, she was as thin as a bundle of sticks. She had limp hair, a bent spine, and the same gray complexion as Jewett. Her brown eyes were wide with fear.

"Tom?"

"No, ma'am. My name is Mike." I made a guess. "Are you Mrs. Jewett? Bruce's mother?"

There was not the faintest flicker of under- standing.

"Tom, you need to help me. I'm being held prisoner by a strange man." She pressed her veined hands against my chest and clutched the fabric as if she feared it being torn loose. "Quick, before he finds us. We have to escape."

Very carefully, I folded her frail, trembling hands in mine. I wanted my touch to be reassuring. She was so scared.

"No one is going to hurt you, Mrs. Jewett."

A tear ran down her wrinkled cheek. "But he *is* hurting me."

I had seen enough cases of elder abuse not to shrug this off. "Are you talking about your son? How is Bruce is hurting you?"

"He's poisoning me."

"Poisoning?"

"It doesn't taste right. Shhh! He's coming."

Jewett appeared in the hall with an expression that mixed exasperation with embarrassment. "Mama! I told you not to leave your room."

She clutched my sweater again. "Please, Tom."

"She thinks you're poisoning her." I wanted to see how her son reacted.

"It's medicine for fuck's sake! Cholinesterase inhibitors. Mama, you know I'm not poisoning you. Let's get you back to your room."

He took her upper arm, but with more gentleness than I might have expected from his raised voice.

Could there be anything more sorrowful, I wondered, than a mother not recognizing her own son?

Yes, there was. Seeing him as her mortal enemy.

Just when I was feeling sorry for Jewett, thinking I'd been too hard in my judgment, he turned to me and hissed, "If you leave this room while I'm putting her away, I swear to Christ I'll shoot you in the face."

15

Not until I've crawled under a fallen log and taken shelter behind the stump of what must have been a massive pine do I notice the trail in the snow. It looks black in the half-light. But it's just a trick of the shadows. Everyone knows blood is red.

I'm hit.

It can't be true. I never felt a thing.

Panicked, I slap my torso, but find nothing, move my hands down to my pelvis and groin until I find a spreading wet stain on my left leg. I feel the ripped fabric and find a deep gouge along the outer thigh. The instant my fingers touch the exposed tissue, I feel an electrical charge that causes me to bite my hand to keep from screaming.

The light coming from my dying, distant fire is too faint. I have no choice but to probe with my fingertips. If the bullet—it had to have been a hollow-point—nicked the femoral artery, I'd be spraying blood like a dam without a Dutch boy. The slug has carved a burrow along my upper leg half an inch deep and four inches long. Blood pumps through my fingers when I clamp my whole hand over the wound, trying to use pressure to slow the hemorrhage.

I left home that morning with a fully stocked first aid kit. It contained antibiotic gel, a packet of hemophilic clotting agents, and an adhesive combat bandage invented by the Israeli army, not to mention a surgical stapler that can stopgap a wound long enough to find a doctor. That first aid bag is probably halfway down the river to Lewiston now.

In the dark I can't even tell how badly I'm bleeding. Shock worries me. Blood loss worries me.

The wound has to be dirty. Bullet fragments, cloth from my jeans, maybe dirt and bits of wood. But I have nothing to irrigate the exposed tissue. Add sepsis to my list of worries, although an infection won't kill me in the next hour.

Snow maybe? Pack snow into the wound? Let the cold constrict the blood vessels and slow the outflow of blood.

No, that's a stupid idea.

Ideally, I'd have a clean absorbent cloth to use as an improvised bandage.

Ideally, I'd be a hundred miles from here with no perforations in my person, enjoying a bourbon neat beside a crackling stove.

I fondly recall the magical time, two minutes earlier, when hypothermia was my major concern in life.

I keep pressing my hand against my thigh. I

clench my teeth so hard, it's amazing the molars don't crack.

I need to get gravity working for me. Sitting up, I try to elevate my injured leg by resting it on a fallen log.

Meanwhile Jewett is out there with his rifle, waiting for me to poke my head up. The kind of scope he is using matters a great deal. Does it rely on image intensification, active illumination, or infrared thermal imaging? It's one thing if he has to pick out my fuzzy shadow from amid the monochrome trees. It's another if he can see my heat signature glowing red and yellow against a magenta backdrop.

Does he know he hit me? How long will he wait before he crosses the river to finish the job?

The blood, pumping through my fingers, shows no signs of slowing.

There is something truly awe-inspiring about how fucked I am.

My campfire continues to blaze away happily beyond the brush. I did a good job building it. That ice shack might become a bonfire yet.

If I were John Rambo, I'd crawl out there, thrust my knife into the coals and cauterize my wounds with red-hot steel. And then I'd pass out from shock or be dead from blood poisoning in a matter of hours. Because Rambo is a bullshit macho fantasy.

But the image of an over-muscled Sylvester

Stallone with his signature headband slaps me awake.

Where's my bandanna?

Did I leave it drying over the fire?

I pat my pockets, unzip every zipper, dig everywhere, it seems. But the bandanna is nowhere to be found.

I sure as shit am not using my belt or bootlaces for a tourniquet. Not just because I'd rather not lose my leg, but because the only way out of my predicament is to go mobile. I know that the medical thinking on tourniquets has done a 180-degree turn because of lessons learned during the wars in Iraq and Afghanistan where lives were saved from their quick application. Many limbs were also lost though. I'm not going to attempt a tourniquet until I begin feeling woozy from blood loss, by which time it will probably be too late.

As I bring my free hand to my face to stroke my chin, I brush cloth at the hollow of my throat. It's the bandanna. I tied the damned thing around my neck because I was afraid of losing it.

I undo the knot, shake out the cloth, fold it into a triangle, roll it tight. I slide the bandanna under my leg and grab both ends. I pull hard and tie off the ends with a square knot.

I recline against the stump and look at my leg but, of course, I can't see anything. I reach down and find the cloth already warm and wet with blood. But there seems to be less of it.

And, if the situation turns dire—can it get any more dire?—I can slide a stick under the bandanna and begin to twist and make a last-resort tourniquet.

Suddenly, I hear a gunshot. I throw myself to the frozen ground.

Another shot.

I sit up again against the stump.

What the hell?

There were no bullet impacts anywhere near me. No bursts of bark. No snow kicked up from the laden pine boughs. Jewett wasn't blasting away around the shack, hoping to get lucky.

What was he firing at, if not me?

It must have been Shadow, I realize.

Jewett caught sight of the wolf in his scope. The second shot sounded fast, unaimed. Both misses, I hope and pray.

As racked with pain as I am, as hard as it is to think straight, I need to put myself in my enemy's head. Jewett is a careful man. He will wait patiently for me to crawl into view, hoping for a clean shot. But he won't wait long. He can't chance me slithering away into the woods.

Sooner or later, the son of a bitch is going to have to cross the river and come looking for me. What other choice does he have? He needs to be sure I'm dead. He needs time to hide my body where it can't be found. Because, as far as Bruce Jewett knows, game wardens will be swarming all over this river come dawn, and when they find my bloodless corpse, they will be lining up outside his door with tac gear and Windham Weaponry AR-15 rifles, fighting one another to be the first through the breech to exact revenge.

If I am going to see the sunrise, I have no choice but to go.

I need to run until I can run no more.

And then I have to find the strength in myself to keep running.

16

When Jewett reappeared, he was wearing a U.S. Navy command cap and a nylon windbreaker over his button-down shirt. The front of the hat bore the name of a ship, the USS *Thresher*, above an insignia of two fish, facing each other, above the hull classification: SSN-593.

His boxer's face had the pugnaciousness of a fighter climbing into the ring. "I bet you enjoyed that pathetic, pitiable tableau."

"Your mother has Alzheimer's?"

"No, I'm actually imprisoning her downstairs. Of course she has Alzheimer's. She's ninety-four."

"Who's Tom, if you don't mind my asking."

"I do mind. I mind everything about your being here. Did you have enough time to snoop around my house while I locked my mother in the dungeon? Did you find the bags of nitrogen fertilizer I'm using to build my truck bomb?"

"Mr. Jewett—"

"Are we going shooting or not?"

From the start, I had misgivings about being in the same room with this high-strung man while he engaged in active-fire target practice. His heightened agitation now had me on the verge of bowing out altogether. But he barged out of the room so fast that I found myself pulled along, like a needle after a magnet.

The general sense of emptiness was pervasive throughout the house. Every footstep echoed. There was not a single Christmas decoration to be seen. It was worse than my home in its utter lack of cheer.

As we passed through the kitchen again, we came upon a tomcat.

He was big, the size of a lynx, with scratches across his gray face and a milky eye that may or may not have been functional. He hissed at me from the chair on which he'd been resting.

"What's his name?"

"Nemo. Why don't you pet him? He likes being scratched behind the ears."

We passed again through the mudroom, but instead of stepping outside, continued along an ell that had been added after the farmhouse was built. It provided a sheltered walkway to a barn behind the main building.

"I love these old Maine farmhouses," I said.

"Sorry, but I'm not selling." He kept walking.

"How long have you had it?"

"A hundred-and-fifty years, if you mean how long has it been in my family. The Jewetts were the original settlers in Stratford, Turner, and Keen's Mills. Would you like to see the family plot when you're done grilling me? It's over there in the trees."

I ignored the provocation. Better to remain friendly. "You must have a nice view of the river from upstairs."

"I'm not inviting you into my bedroom."

He had to pause at the next door to tap a code into a keypad, and then we entered his personal shooting range, inside the barn. The floor was solid concrete with drains against floods and leaks. The lights were dim, as they often are in indoor pistol ranges, with a spotlight focused on a berm at the far side of the barn. Jewett had dumped a couple of tons of sand there to serve as a backstop to the bullets and bullet fragments.

There wasn't a shooting stall, per se; the whole interior functioned as a firing lane. But there were three separate target retrievers mounted to the ceiling. Jewett could attach a paper target on any or all of them, push a button, and watch them be carried along on chains to the back of the room, twenty-five yards away. There was also an upright reactive target—a man-shaped sheet of upright steel—if he wanted to take out his anger on a hunk of metal. Granted it was early in our acquaintance, but it was my impression that Bruce Jewett might have a bad or two day occasionally.

This personal range couldn't have been cheap to install. I had shot at commercial facilities that felt more makeshift. Maybe he had hocked the rest of his household possessions to pay for it.

The barn was unheated, and I could see my breath. "This is quite the setup."

"Coming from you, Warden, that means the world to me."

He busied himself at a locked locker. When he turned to me, he had swapped his black-framed glasses for a pair with yellow lenses. He held two sets of cupped earphones that would cushion the sounds of the gunshots. He put one around his neck and tossed the other to me.

"We're not going to be able to have a conversation wearing ear protection," I said.

"That's the plan, Stan."

"Come on, Jewett. I just want to ask some questions, and then I'll leave you alone to take out your anger at humanity at your paper people. This can all be over in ten minutes."

"Paper people?" The turn of phrase provoked an actual smile from him. "I'll give you your interview—but only after we each take a turn. I want to see how poorly you wardens are trained."

He removed a military surplus ammo can from the locker and dropped it at my feet. The metal rattle of loose rounds rose from the container. "You guys still use .357 SIG cartridges, right?"

"Yes."

"Figures the state would pay extra for the most expensive, least necessary caliber out there."

Inside the can I found loose frangible rounds, designed to reduce ricochets. This kind of ammo was standard issue at shooting ranges.

I couldn't recall what the regulations were for the use of a service weapon in this situation. We were certainly permitted to practice with our guns as needed. And if it was necessary to get Jewett to speak with me, I doubted Colonel DeFord would mind my taking a turn with the targets. In truth, I'd always enjoyed shooting and wanted to disprove Jewett's low opinion of me.

While Jewett attached a paper target to one of the retrievers and sent it whirring to the back of the barn, I unloaded one of the mags in my pocket and reloaded with his cartridges. The target was printed with a vaguely human silhouette. You scored extra points for head shots and bull's-eyeing the center mass.

I barely had a chance to get my noise-canceling headset on before Jewett drew his pistol from the holster. The Glock 17 comes with a magazine that holds seventeen 9 x 19 mm Parabellum rounds (hence the name). Jewett's shooting technique was the old-school power isosceles stance; he stood with his legs apart, his arms extended, making himself a human triangle.

Hot cartridges bounced down and rolled around the floor. Blue smoke wafted at me. As it cleared, I saw that he had shredded the heart out of the target. And he'd put one in the forehead in case

I hadn't gotten the message. Bruce Jewett was a deadeye marksman.

But I was too pissed to compliment his shooting. "You were supposed to tell me the range was hot," I said, meaning that he had a pistol ready to fire.

"Oops."

He hit a button and the paper target trolled back to us. Up close, his clustering was even more impressive. He'd brought me here to show that his skills were superior to mine. Insecure men were always quick to engage you in a topic or pursuit where they held an advantage. They needed these dominance displays to bolster their fragile egos.

"Now you." He pulled off the ear protectors and hung them around his neck.

"No."

"How's that?"

His protective eyeglasses had slid down the bridge of his nose. He pushed them up with his middle finger. The yellow lenses lent a sinister quality to his unblinking gaze.

"If you want proof you're a better shot than me, you'll need to talk first."

I knew I held the trump card because it would irritate him to death not knowing for sure that he was the superior marksman.

"What are you—afraid to be shown up?"

"As I understand it, you went duck hunting with

Professor Chamberlain the morning he died."

"Yeah, you're chicken." He ejected the empty magazine, lifted a loaded one from a pocket on his belt, and used the heel of his palm to slam it home at the base of the grip.

"You met him at his house at what time that morning?"

"At 0430 hours. We motored from his dock down to Gulf Island Pond and set a couple of strings of decoys, then drew the net over the boat. Birds came in, geese and mallards. We shot fourteen in all. Most were mine. Eben had acquired a tremor that gave him trouble leading his targets. I had a late morning appointment: dentist. He dropped me off at 0930. That was the last I saw of him. End of story."

"What guns did you both use?"

"What does that matter?"

"Just curious." I wanted to see if he remembered what he'd told Rivard.

"Remington Versa Max for me. Eben used that old punt gun of his. I call it a punt gun because the barrel of the Marlin 55 is so long. Your divers recovered it from the bottom of the river. I'm surprised the African Queen doesn't have it displayed in the shrine she's built to St. Eben of Stratford. Did I pass your test, Warden?"

"You did."

"I've thought about that gun and the rest of Eben's collection. He owned some beautiful shooting irons. I'm guessing the *lesbienne* sold the best of them to pay for drugs."

"You're referring to Bibi Chamberlain?"

"She goes by the house a couple times a week in that English go-cart of hers. Heads up the hill to score. You'd think she could find a dealer somewhere classier than a fucking trailer park. If Eben knew what a scheming bitch she is, he would have written her out of his will. The way that dyke played him. . . ."

"Played him how?"

"It doesn't matter. He's dead. She's rich. End of story."

"I'd like to hear more."

"I'm sure you would! But I am going with a 'no comment.' What else do you want to know about the day Eben drowned? I wasn't there when he died; I was in Lewiston getting a crown replaced. I don't know how he went overboard but I can guess. The man was seventy-seven going on twenty-seven. I used to tell him he couldn't do everything he did when he was young but he laughed and said, 'Maybe *you* can't.' "

"That sounds a little harsh."

"No worse than the shit I gave him."

"Could he have committed suicide?"

"The man loved himself too much to end it. He must have lost his balance and fallen, hooking the string of decoys. There's no other explanation."

"What did you two talk about that morning?" I asked.

"Our favorite Taylor Swift songs."

"Be serious."

"We talked about what we always talked about. Politics. How this country had a last chance to save itself and blew it, and now we're all fucked. Eben was a moon bat, but he was a good debater who kept me on my toes, and at least he could admit when his arguments had holes in them, which was always."

"So you argued that morning?"

He tilted his narrow hips and rested his hand on the grip of the Glock, as he had a habit of doing. "We debated. There's a difference."

"Did he ever remove his personal flotation device in your presence?"

"No, he did not."

"In your experience did he ever remove his life vest when he was on the water?"

He cast a glance at the berm at the end of the barn. "Are we going to shoot or not? Because I'm running out of patience."

I made a mental note that he hadn't answered. "Have you ever met the witness who saw him alone in the boat and said he wasn't wearing his PFD?"

"I don't recall."

"You don't recall?"

"I've seen him in his new Rubicon often

enough—this is the only road to the top. I've been behind him in line at the variety with those girls he supposedly lives with. It doesn't mean we're acquainted."

His prior evasions had been more artful. "It sounds like you've forgotten his name?"

"Why should I remember it? All I know about the guy is he's a meeks who lives with a couple of red-headed sluts on the hill."

"What's a meeks?"

"Pretty boy piece of shit. Forgive me for not giving a fuck about him."

"I don't believe you, Mr. Jewett."

He removed his glasses and cleaned the gunpowder residue from the lenses with a crisp white handkerchief. It gave him a moment to focus on something other than my statement. "And why is that?"

"Because you're too smart to have forgotten the name of the last man who saw your friend alive."

"Is that supposed to be a compliment? You don't know the first thing about me, Warden."

"I know you're a Navy veteran. Submarines?"

"What gave it away? Oh, right. The hat. I bet you don't even know what happened to the USS *Thresher.*"

"It sank with all hands somewhere off Cape Cod." I had finally remembered the name and the incident. During the hottest days of the Cold War, a horrible malfunction led the Maine-built submarine to go down. Hundreds of sailors died in one of the worst ways imaginable.

"Am I supposed to be impressed?" said Jewett. "I could tell within two minutes of looking at you that you never served. Bone spurs?"

"I decided to serve my country by becoming a law-enforcement officer."

"A fish cop! Good for you. But you went to college, first. I can tell from your diction. Where?"

There was no right answer to his question—a contempt for higher education rose off Jewett's person like a foul odor—so I told the truth. "Colby."

The mocking smile returned. "You're the first game warden I've met with a fancy-pants degree. I bet that helps a ton when you're ticketing some fisherman for exceeding his daily bag limit. Colby is one of the Little Ivies, right?"

"No one uses that term anymore."

Jewett snorted and turned again to the ammunition locker. "I'm done answering questions. You're going to shoot now."

Whatever sympathy I'd had for him as a beleaguered son caring for a senile mother was gone.

He returned with a paper target which he clipped to the retriever. It wasn't the same design as the one he'd used himself. This target depicted a cartoonish African-American mugger.

"Seriously?" I said.

"Shoot."

"No."

"Then I guess it's time for you to leave."

I ejected his shells from the magazine into the ammo can.

"You don't even want to know what Mrs. Chamberlain told me—the reason why I'm here today?"

"She thinks I orchestrated Eben's death for some inexplicable reason, despite that being impossible."

Carefully I pushed my own bullets into the empty magazine. "She said you and Eben were more than friends."

His face emptied of emotion. His eyes seemed to recede behind the protective lenses. Slowly they reemerged, but now the pupils had grown wide with anger. And his nostrils flared.

"That's a disgusting lie."

"Then tell me the truth. How would you characterize the nature of your relationship?"

His hand tightened around the grip of his Glock. "You come into my house and you accuse me of being a degenerate."

I made no threatening movements but casually let my own hand wander into the vicinity of my reloaded SIG. "I am not accusing you of anything."

"Butt buddies," he said. "Fucking butt buddies?"

"Calm down, Mr. Jewett."

"Get out of here. Get out of here now, or so help me—" With his left hand he pointed at a door. It was not the one through which we'd entered. I presumed it led outside.

"I'm sorry if what I said upset you."

"Like hell you are. I can see through you, Bowditch. You put up a good front. But I know you're a fraud."

I felt for the doorknob behind me, gave it a twist, and felt it open outward. Cold air rushed in around my shoulders, making the hood of my parka flap. Keeping my gaze on the armed and angry man, I stepped backward.

"Ivy League fraud!" he said.

I closed the door.

Years earlier, I had watched Charley Stevens goad a dangerous man to anger. He claimed it was a strategy he used to trick information out of stonewalling suspects. I'd never seen anything more reckless.

"Do you deliberately provoke everyone you meet?" I'd asked him.

To which he'd answered, "Everyone? No, not everyone. Just 90 percent or so."

It had taken years, but I'd finally come to appreciate the method behind Charley's madness.

I had seen the truth in Jewett's face, heard it in his voice. He and Eben Chamberlain had been lovers, as Mariëtte suspected.

17

I stagger through the trees, holding my left hand tight against my weeping leg. The makeshift bandage is already soaked through. In subzero temperatures blood flow can go from a flood to a trickle—it's why you should ice a cut—but the process is insufficient to form a protective clot over a gunshot wound.

I'm making no effort to cover my tracks because I don't have the energy or the time. No doubt I'm leaving drops of blood, too. A blind man could follow my trail.

The way through the woods is an obstacle course. Ice jams are annual occurrences along the Androscoggin. As the snow melts, freshets course down from the White Mountains and the river begins to rise against its banks, five feet, ten feet, sometimes higher. On occasion it overflows the entire floodplain, clearing out shrubs and saplings but leaving behind a tangle of deadwood through which I must now pass.

The concealable ballistic vest I wear under my clothes these days weighs only a fraction of the heavy-duty body armor I used to use as a patrol warden. But it feels as heavy now as a coat of chainmail.

After a few minutes, I take cover behind a

boulder the size of a Volkswagen van. A glacier left the giant stone behind on its retreat north when the last Ice Age ended.

The silence worries me. I haven't heard a gunshot since the two I believe were aimed at Shadow. *What if he was hit?*

Jewett will be crossing the river soon. Whether by foot or using one of the bridges. My bet is he'll take his vehicle. Why risk venturing onto the ice when he knows I'm on foot with no place to run? My guess is he'll use the road to loop around and come at me from the east.

My only advantage is he doesn't know I lost my gun. He has to assume I am still armed, and that means he must approach me with caution. And while Jewett might be a better marksman than I am, I know in my heart that I am the superior hunter.

The exertion has made me sweat. But whatever heat I feel from the exercise dissipates quickly as the perspiration cools. I start shivering again. There will be no more campfires tonight.

I lean my head against the cold, lichen-crusted rock and close my eyes, trying to formulate a plan. The pain in my leg—all those exposed nerves—is too intense.

Something cold touches my nose. I raise my face and open my eyes.

From my perspective, looking up through the tree branches, the sky seems woven of gauze.

The snow, which has been as light as powdered sugar, is falling now in fat flakes.

Emma's spell is working. She's conjured up a White Christmas for everyone. The thought of the precious little girl makes me smile. Seeing her and her family again provides extra motivation to keep fighting. I will need it.

My night vision has improved since I left the firelight. But the snow in the air also reflects light, making it easier for me to make out my surroundings. An ancient oak tree looms over my boulder, creating a natural chokepoint. And sure enough, as I peer closer, I begin to make out deer tracks at my feet.

Maine deer almost never raise their eyes in the woods because they're rarely attacked from above. I lean my head against the rock again. The branches above me are long, gnarled, and thick. Fifteen feet in the air, a man-made platform takes shape. I recognize the squared-off outline immediately—it's a hunter's deer stand.

Now my eyes search the trunk, and yes, I see it now: the ladder of rusty spikes the hunter has driven into the tree to ascend to his place of ambush. They resemble the iron steps a linemen hammers into a utility pole to climb up to the crossarms.

Some deer stands are big: platforms on which a kid could build a treehouse. This one seems more like a chair strapped to the trunk with nylon bands that have probably rotted in the sun and rain. I'm surprised a strong wind hasn't dislodged it yet. Surely my weight would cause the seat to come crashing down.

I don't have the energy to climb up there, anyway.

And while deer may not look up into the tree-tops, men do.

I've got to keep moving.

Following the deer path as best I can, I continue over a ridge that runs along an esker, parallel to the main channel of the river. Pushing through a clump of cedars, I trip and fall chest-first onto the frozen ground. The impact doesn't do anything to alleviate the pain radiating from the gunshot wound in my leg.

But as I recover the energy to raise myself on hands and knees, I notice more deer prints, a dozen of them, all leading in the same direction.

Most hunters don't realize that deer use different paths at different times for different reasons. Some nimrod, having discovered what looks like a well-traveled deer trail, will set up a stand overhead and wait. Eight hours later, he'll walk out of the woods without having seen a mammal bigger than a squirrel. These disappointed hunters don't understand that the deer are only using this road at night, when their only concern is avoiding coyotes and bobcats. They'll switch to an entirely different trail when humans are out and about. And make no mistake: deer know exactly when legal hunting hours begin and end.

When you are a prey animal, you must devote your entire being to outwitting your pursuers.

It's a lesson I am slowly relearning.

During my rookie years, Charley Stevens and I used to roam around different habitats—from leatherleaf bogs to heath alpine ridges—and he would give me a private Ph.D. seminar in the natural history of Maine. The old woodsman would point out a line through some cinnamon ferns, more like a crease than a path, and he'd say, "You'd never know it, but that there is a historic byway. The local deer have been using that skinny trail to cross coyote country for generations. It's not just we humans who have heritage. Critters do, too."

Charley taught me so much. I owe the man more than my life.

Will I ever see him again?

Or Ora?

Or—?

I stop myself before I can speak the name. Even so, a hot tear runs down my numb cheek.

You're crying now, Bowditch?

So what if I am?

I am in pain and I am afraid. Mostly though, I am mad as hell for getting myself into this predicament.

Dangerous people have tried and failed to murder me, and always I have found a way to outwit them. I have walked away intact from traps and ambushes, gun battles and truck chases. I'll be damned if I let myself die at the hands of a nobody like Bruce Jewett. In that moment I vow I will do whatever it takes to return alive to the people I love.

Rage can be a poison, but it can also be fuel.

Following the deer path in the snowy half-light, I slide over the ridgeback and find myself descending again. The subtle change in terrain worries me. By all I rights I should be continuing uphill, toward the paved road that runs along the eastern bank of the Androscoggin through Leeds and Greene.

Instead the ground levels out. I push through a copse of sumacs and find myself overlooking a flat white field. There is a pause in the snow, and I am surprised how well I can see.

Bent and broken vegetation juts up through the surface. Weeds?

No, bulrushes.

This isn't a field. It's a frozen wetland.

The absurdity of my latest problem almost makes me laugh out loud. I'm not on the eastern shore of the Androscoggin after all. I am on an island in the river, cut off from escape by many yards of uncertain ice.

18

I found the cat, Nemo, waiting on the hood of my Jeep. He'd left prints all over it. God knows how he'd gotten out of the house. Jewett, with all his high security, didn't strike me as the cat flap type. Maybe he preferred the risk of a pet door to the certainties of a dirty litter box.

Nemo greeted me with a fluffed tail and an extra-long hiss. He was one of those enormous Maine coon cats, a twenty-pounder. In a fight between him and an actual lynx I wasn't sure which feline would prevail.

"Yeah, yeah, yeah," I said as I put on my sunglasses. "I'm going."

He whipped his frazzled tail.

I'd never been a cat person. Dani had a stray she'd adopted named Puddin'. She'd tried to give the little thing a more dignified name, but the cat, being a cat, refused to respond.

Nemo jumped clear when I got within grabbing distance and, even then, he acted as if the idea had been his.

Cats, I have often said, are strange visitors from an alternate reality where they are the overlords.

I raised the lift gate to check on Shadow and found him sleeping again. It worried me that he was still sacked out this way. Had Lizzie Holman given him too heavy a dose of Midazolam after the anesthesia?

I hadn't assumed I had time to visit the bartender, Burch. But with the wolf conked out, maybe I could stretch my visit an hour longer.

I drove slowly at first, taking in the view. Behind Jewett's barn were shimmering white fields that stretched two hundred yards before running into a wall of oaks, birches, and pines. The distant trees were tall and picturesque; they looked like the woods in a Robert Frost poem.

Snowmobile tracks crisscrossed the field and converged behind the barn. I hadn't caught a glimpse of Jewett's sled, but I decided it must be a dependable, touring model with a scabbard on the side for an AR-15. He struck me as someone who patrolled his land regularly, looking eagerly for signs of intruders he could scare off at gunpoint.

I felt the automatic transmission downshift as the grade grew steep and the road entered a tunnel of trees. NO TRESPASSING signs were posted at state-mandated intervals: clearly visible, with less than a hundred feet between them. Bruce Jewett wasn't allowing interlopers the slightest excuse to "accidentally" wander onto his land.

He struck me as a type I often encountered in rural Maine: a person who held strong yet contradictory views of the law. These men zealously guarded their own property rights yet thought nothing of taking multiple deer a season, in violation of state rules. They built buildings without permits and wantonly cut trees in protected wetlands.

I'd come to the conclusion that these hypocrites never suffered cognitive dissonance because they genuinely believed the law existed to protect their own selfish interests. Except when it became an unconstitutional encroachment on their God-given liberties.

But Jewett struck me as intelligent enough to recognize when he was actively violating statutes. He must have known his shooting range, for instance, wasn't up to code.

Was he a murderer, though?

One of the perils of detective work is that, if you investigate enough crimes, every death begins to look suspicious. I had to check my own biases. Sometimes old professors fall out of boats without being pushed.

I was still seeing NO TRESSPASSING signs stapled to roadside trees when I rounded a turn and the pastoral forest transformed, all at once, into a wasteland. Someone had come into these postcard woods with chainsaws and a skidder and taken every tree thicker than a baseball bat. The bulldozer had even knocked a hole in a century-old stone wall to gain entry onto the property.

In the distance, beyond the handful of crooked

trees still standing, I saw the dirty machines at work.

I braked, grabbed my 10 x 42 Leica binoculars from the dash, and scoped the brutalized hillside.

I counted three men: one driving the skidder, a second wielding a chainsaw, and a third supervising the job from atop an all-terrain vehicle. None of the loggers wore helmets, ear protection, goggles, chaps, or other safety gear.

Real geniuses, these three.

While I watched, the skidder drove into a sugar maple and began to push against the trunk with the bulldozer bucket until smoke belched from its exhaust. (With a skidder you don't need a saw or an axe to take down a tree. You simply rip it from the ground with the stick and grapple, or you use brute force to knock it down.) The maple snapped. The subsequent crash was loud enough that I could hear it above my hot air blower. The moment the tree fell, the young guy with the saw went to work severing its silvery branches. The loggers would then haul the de-limbed trunk to their improvised woodpile for later removal.

The signs along the road suggested this was still Jewett's property, but he hadn't mentioned logging it. Even if this was his operation, he didn't strike me as the sort of landowner who would approve denuding the family estate. The savagery of the clear-cutting went beyond the limits allowed by Maine law. There was slash strewn everywhere, even near the road where discarded branches were not permitted.

Logging didn't bother me; raping the land did.

One of the men—the driver of the faded yellow skidder—must have noticed my Jeep. He cut the engine and signaled to the others. I saw the man on the ATV lift his own pair of binos from around his neck and train them on my Jeep.

Then he shouted something up at the driver who dutifully moved onto the next maple.

The kid with the chainsaw, meanwhile, continued de-limbing the fallen tree. That idiot would be deaf before his thirtieth birthday. Maybe before his twenty-fifth.

While I watched, the man on the ATV had swung his machine around. He gunned the engine, zigzagging through stumps, toward the road. The four-wheeler looked like a recent model, but even the new shocks couldn't cushion the ride across the deeply rutted ground.

I didn't wait for him to arrive but stepped from the vehicle and unzipped my parka. I wanted the badge and gun on my belt to be plainly visible. I circled around to the passenger side, folded my arms across my chest, and waited.

The man on the ATV was dressed in winter-weight coveralls that made most people look tubby. Not this guy, though; he had to be a beanpole under that padding. He wore dark sunglasses and a black balaclava that he had pulled up around his head so only the oval of his face was visible.

He must have caught sight of my badge and gun because he braked hard before he reached the stone wall. The machine slid across the icy, torn-up earth. The rider didn't dismount but sat with his hands on the vibrating handlebars.

"What do you want?" he shouted above the idling engine.

I made a motion with my hand, signaling for him to turn the key. He didn't catch my drift.

I cupped my hands around my mouth. "Turn it off."

"What?"

"Turn it off!"

Like Nemo the cat, he obliged but in a way that suggested the choice had been his all along.

He was still far enough away that I had to shout. "Is this your land?"

"Who are you?"

"Game warden."

Tired of shouting, I stepped through the gap the skidder had knocked through the wall.

The rider looked naturally pale, but the cold and exertion had brought blood to his cheeks and the tip of his nose. He seemed to be trying to grow out a reddish-blond mustache and goatee, but the beard refused to flourish. His eyes were hidden behind a pair of dark Ray-Bans.

I scratched my scalp behind my ear. "Did this forest do something to insult your manhood?"

"What?"

"It must have seriously disrespected you for you to beat the shit out of it like this."

His cheeks grew redder. "You think you're funny?"

"Sometimes. But usually I'm the only one who does."

It bothered me that he hadn't removed his sunglasses. Not that I expected to recognize him. It was a simple courtesy.

"If you ain't a forest ranger, what we're doing ain't none of your business, man."

"I may not be a ranger, but I know enough about state forestry laws to count a dozen violations here. Has Bruce Jewett been up to oversee your work?"

He reached into the chest pocket of his Carhartt's to find a tin of chewing tobacco. He stuffed three fingers worth of Skoal into his cheek. The bit of business with the dip was intended to provide the young logger with time to think.

"Yeah, he's seen it."

"And Mr. Jewett doesn't mind the mess you're making?"

He spit a brown stream onto a patch of snow. "This is how cutting looks, man. You want to call a ranger, go ahead and call a ranger. I ain't got nothing else to do but wait. I'm still getting paid, sitting here. How about you?"

He was probably nineteen or twenty, I decided. He had the appearance of dozens of kids I'd met on patrol: wannabe outlaws looking for any way to demonstrate they were real men. And yet, for all his generic posturing, there was something naggingly specific about him. He looked familiar.

"You mind taking off your sunglasses?"

"Hell, yes, I mind. It's bright out here."

It was not bright.

"What's your name?"

"I don't got to tell you shit. I'm on private property minding my own business."

"You're on private property, true, but it's not yours. How do I know you and your buddies aren't stealing Mr. Jewett's wood?"

Wood theft was, in fact, a widespread crime in the most forested state in the nation. I had heard of summer people who closed their camps in the fall, went south to Massachusetts, Connecticut, and New Jersey for the winter, and then returned to find their sheltering pines missing. That said, it was not a common occurrence for thieves to steal wood in plain view, in the light of day, half a mile from the landowner's house.

"Call the man and find out," the young rebel suggested.

"I don't have his number."

"I do."

He shouted seven digits at me.

I keyed the number into my phone.

The voice that answered was, unmistakably, Jewett's. "For Christ's sake, what do you want now?"

"Mr. Jewett, this is Mike Bowditch."

He fell silent. Clearly, he'd assumed I was someone else or he might not have answered. "Where did you get this number?"

"A young man on an ATV gave it to me. I came upon him and two associates scalping the hillside above your house. He says he's cutting here with your permission. Is it true you hired these amateur lumberjacks to cut your woodlot?"

The ATV rider expelled another stream of tobacco juice.

Jewett made a noise that I took to be an affirmative.

"Have you been up here to see it?" I asked.

"Yeah."

"And you're fine with their forestry practices? You don't mind your woods looking like no-man's-land?"

"What I mind and don't mind is none of your business. Now are you going to leave me alone or am I going to have to file harassment charges against you with your superiors? I Googled your name and it won't be the first time."

"Bruce," I said, "you and I both know you're

not going to do anything that results in more officers paying you a visit."

"Don't call this number again!"

The kid grinned at me as I put away the phone. "What did I tell you? We got permission. Now me and my cousins got work to do. Money ain't gonna make itself, man."

With a smug grin, he started the engine and revved it so loudly he must have damaged his ear drums. I watched the kid ride off, wondering where I'd seen his cocky face before.

19

Snow blows in waves across the frozen channel. The far side is hidden in darkness. The vegetation at the near edge suggests the water beneath might be shallow, perhaps even frozen down to the mud. Ice needs to be only two inches thick to support the weight of a man. I might be able to walk safely across.

But if I am wrong in my calculations, if I go through the ice again—even if it's only up to my knees—I am doomed. I won't be lighting another fire, not tonight.

What choice do I have, though?

I start making my way upstream along the marshy shore. What I want to find, as paradoxical as it might sound, is the deepest stretch of the stream. Shallow water is often turbulent and doesn't freeze easily. The irregular river bottom causes the current to roil, and the ice above never thickens.

I hope for deer prints. I weigh as much as a big buck, and where he can cross, I can cross.

But the snow has accumulated more in the open than it did under the trees. Half an hour ago, I could still have spotted tracks. But any prints that might've been here were smoothed over by the wind.

I take a breather to lean against a snag and check my bandanna. The cloth is soaked, and blood continues to ooze down my pants leg. It puddles inside my already wet boot, making every step squishy. I don't feel lightheaded yet, but if the hemorrhage continues, it's only a matter of time before I enter the danger zone.

At 10 percent blood loss, I will feel dizzy, then nauseous. My blood vessels will constrict, as my circulatory system tries to protect itself, and the cold I am feeling now will become even worse. At 20 percent, I will experience disorientation and rapid breathing. My body will go into the state of shock I have so far avoided. At 30 percent, I will lose consciousness, and I will die without Jewett needing to fire another shot.

Ahead of me, a shadow detaches itself from the near trees and floats out onto the ice. Then it stops.

I can't see the creature clearly, but I don't need to.

The wolf is waiting for me. That much is obvious. Don't ask me how, but Shadow knows it is safe to cross here. He wants me to follow him.

Carefully, I take a step onto the ice, then shuffle out my other foot. My balance is poor, and I totter for a moment like it's my first time on skates.

After I have steadied myself, I call to Shadow. My voice is hoarse from sucking cold air into my voice box. "Hey! It's good to see you."

He merely waits.

When I am twenty feet from him, he trots forward and disappears into the dark. He over-estimates how well I can see him in the storm.

But I can follow his tracks at least. They are huge, clawed, and the size of my open hand.

Soon I see that he is leading me toward a domed shape that I mistake for a boulder before realizing it is a beaver lodge. The top is crusted with snow from a prior storm. The logs and sticks jutting up from the mound appear gray and weathered.

The sight gives me confidence. Because beavers remain active all winter, they need the surrounding water to be deep. They spend the cold-weather months under the ice, hauling up the leafy branches they've dragged into the mud all summer. With their orange teeth, they carry these lengths of wood into their lodges to eat.

When I reach the den, I cast a glance behind me, and my heart drops. It seems like I've barely made progress. I reach out a hand to steady myself against the mound of sticks, and as I do memory returns. Despite my prior despair and general misery, I can't help but laugh aloud.

I am thinking of Charley Stevens and a story he once told me about his stay in a "beaver house."

He'd once found himself fleeing through the woods. A trio of poachers had unleashed their bear-hunting dogs on him, and the hounds were hard on his heels. He thought he knew a shortcut to safety, across a stream, but he found his escape route blocked by a newly created beaver pond.

"If I'd tried swimming across, those poachers would have pot-shotted me sure," he said.

There seemed to be nowhere to hide. Then he'd gotten an idea. Fully dressed, he plunged into the pond and swam out to the lodge. With the dogs baying behind him, he took a deep breath, and dove down into the murk until he found the underwater entrance into the den with his blind hands. He'd wormed his way inside, up onto the raised platform where a mother beaver was nursing her three kits.

"A beaver has a nasty set of choppers so you can be sure I minded my manners," he said. "When she saw I meant no harm to her family, she calmed down. I spent the night there, listening to those frustrated hounds. The dogs could smell me among the rodents, but fortunately their owners weren't sharp enough to put two and two together. It must've seemed to them that I'd drowned. I caught up with those gents later, when I had a few armed wardens behind me, and they looked at me like I was Lazarus."

It had to be a tall tale, I concluded. Game wardens are storytellers of the highest order, and Charley ranked among their elite. Then I'd met a warden who could vouch for his account.

"Stevens came into the office stinking of mud and beaver shit," said Warden Mack McQuarrie.

"We thought for sure he'd die of beaver fever."

Meaning giardiasis. It's a parasitic infection of the gut, usually contracted from swallowing water in which animals have defecated.

"I did have a wicked case of the scoots afterward!" Charley admitted.

Thinking of my grinning friend is almost as good as having him beside me. I feel the strength of his resolve as he fled the bear poachers, and it gives me new energy to follow Shadow. Humor brings me hope.

I drag my feet to keep from slipping. Then a mischievous gust yanks down my hood.

Before I can cinch it in place again, the wind drops and everything becomes still. The snow settles. I find I can hear the ice rumbling behind me in the Androscoggin.

I hear something else, too. Very faint. An engine.

It's not a car or truck. The sound is higher pitched, like the whine of a giant, mechanized insect.

A snowmobile.

I cup my hands around my ears trying to echolocate the machine. It seems to be coming straight down the channel. Under the circumstances, that can mean only one thing. The rider is actively searching for me. And the odds are against him being a Good Samaritan.

Like Charley Stevens, I am being hunted. But

for me, there is no hiding inside this frozen lodge.

Nor can I reach the far shore before my pursuer catches me in his headlights.

Having no other choice, I stagger back, slipping and sliding, to the unnamed island I thought I'd left behind.

20

The hills across the Androscoggin were low and mouse-brown, except for the white of the snow fields. Here and there, were also stands of pines, dark against the hillsides like the shadows made by heavy clouds. Swirls of smoke rose from houses hidden among the trees. I could see a crease in the woods where a road cut through, parallel to the river.

Shadow was snoring again. The odor coming from his cage wasn't entirely doggish. There was also a hint of earthiness that often put me in mind of his native North Woods. It was as if I could smell his essential wildness.

The road entered a mixed thicket of pines and maples, and I saw a wide spot ahead where school buses and snowplows turned around. A single vehicle was parked in the pull-out, beneath the swaying branches. It was an ivory-colored Mini, the all-wheel drive model.

Bibi Chamberlain was waiting for me.

By reflex, I pulled in behind her the way police are taught to do when we conduct traffic stops. Positioning the front of your patrol truck—or cruiser—so that it juts into the road gives you cover as you approach the driver's window. You're not as likely to be struck by a careless passerby who refuses to pull into the opposite lane.

Bibi had put on a man's tweed topcoat that she might have picked up in a thrift shop. Her hat was a gray wool newsboy with the brim pulled low. Everything the woman wore seemed intended as an ironic statement. As usual, she had her e-cigarette pinched between the first two fingers of her left hand.

I stepped from the Jeep, hitching up my belt. It always sagged under the weight of my service weapon.

"So you talked to Bruce then?" she said.

"I told you I was going to."

She took a hit off her Juul. "I don't see any bullet holes in you, so that's something."

"Why are you following me, Bibi?"

"My mother is desperate to blame somebody for Grandfather's death. I thought it would help if you understood why. They met in London, you see, and he was the one who introduced her to my dad. Eben was the father she never had, by which I mean he wasn't a violent, displaced farmer from a country that no longer exists and never should have existed in the first place. So this wild-goose chase she's sent you on—it's not just about closure. My mother needs someone to be punished. The universe has been thrown out of balance by my grandfather's dumb death. Mariëtte Chamberlain sees herself as an agent of cosmic justice."

I thought of the slanders Jewett had hurled at Bibi: that she had deceived her grandfather about her affections, that she was addicted to drugs, that she had come out of Chamberlain's death with riches and a sweet living situation.

"And what about you?" I asked. "What do you need?"

"To have my mom back, the way she was before. I know it won't happen. Life doesn't move in reverse."

Just because Jewett was a crank and a bigot didn't mean he was wrong about everything. Bibi might well be a liar who didn't welcome anyone taking a fresh look at her grandfather's death. I decided to test her.

"I think there's something else you haven't told anyone," I said, "and maybe it's weighing you down."

In an unconscious imitation of her mother, she lifted her chin so that she seemed to be looking down her nose at me. "Where'd you get your degree in psychology, Warden?"

"The usual place: a box of Crackerjacks. What's on your mind, Bibi?"

"Grandfather loaned Bruce money. I don't know how much or why. Enough that it became a bone of contention."

"Is that why he asked for your opinion of Jewett, do you think?"

"No, he never mentioned anything about a

loan." She sucked some nicotine from her little plastic stick. "I overheard a phone conversation when I was visiting the farm one day. Grandfather had a booming voice. He spoke loudly because he refused to wear his hearing aids."

"You're sure it was Jewett on the other end?"

"Grandfather called Bruce 'Cap'n,' even though he was never an officer. So, yes, I'm sure."

"Do you remember the specific words your grandfather used?"

" 'I'm not your banker, Cap'n. I agreed to give you six months and I want my money.' "

"Any idea what Jewett needed the funds for?"

"His pistol range, maybe. Did Bruce take you down there? He likes to show off how well he can shoot. It makes him feel better about being a failure as a man. His marksmanship is something he doesn't need to lie about."

"What does he lie about?"

"Bruce Jewett never went to sea *ever*. He was a hull technician at the Portsmouth Naval Shipyard. His area of expertise was marine sanitation. Boat toilets."

Maybe he'd built the heads on the *Thresher*, I thought. No, he was too young for that.

"You mean he wasn't second in command to Hyman Rickover?"

"Who's that? Some legendary submariner?"

"Father of the nuclear navy."

I watched Bibi watching me through narrowed eyes. I hadn't been studied this closely since the last time I'd played poker.

"I've never been interested in history," she said at last. "I mean, I get that those who forget the past are yadda, yadda, yadda. It just doesn't seem to have anything to do with my life. How old are you anyway?"

"Thirty-one."

"You seem older. Your affect."

"So I've been told."

Rivard had made a crack about middle age that morning. And Dani had recently ribbed me about preferring to read a book rather than play Fortnite with her. Maybe the hard life I'd lived was aging me prematurely.

The breeze came up and rustled the pine boughs. I heard a blue jay chortle in the distance. This late in December, most of his kind had left for warmer climes. Mainers didn't realize that our local jays migrate and are replaced by jays from the north. To most modern people a bird is a bird is a bird.

Spoken like an old man, I thought.

"I want to get back to the conversation you overheard between your grandfather and Jewett," I said. "Did it sound like there was some animosity there? Like maybe the professor had run out of patience?"

"That was my impression."

"You don't know how much money it was, I take it."

"Enough that Grandfather minded. He was a generous man by nature. But he didn't appreciate being jerked around."

"Why didn't you tell Lieutenant Rivard or the state police detective assigned to the case about the rift over the money Jewett owed?"

"Because it had nothing to do with Grandfather's death!"

"That wasn't for you to determine, Bibi."

She hadn't minded my using her first name before, but it seemed to get under her skin now. "I didn't say anything about the money for the same reason I didn't mention Grandfather and Bruce hooking up. It was no one else's business."

"The police might have disagreed."

"I don't know anything about cops, but I'm a writer, and I know a shitload about the power of narratives."

"I'm not following you."

"My grandfather drowned because he was careless. He wasn't murdered by a closeted lover who owed him money. Of those two stories, which one do you think people would be most interested in?"

"So you lied to protect Bruce Jewett?"

"I omitted information I considered unimportant. And it wasn't like I was under oath. Besides, that Lieutenant Rivard barely gave me five minutes. Not a fan of the non-conforming community, that man."

She was right there.

"Why tell me this now?" I said. "If you believe Jewett had nothing to do with your grand-father's death, why did you come chasing after me?"

"I looked you up on the InterWebs after you left the house. Your life would make a great graphic novel if you're ever in need of a ghostwriter." She winked at me to be cute. "One of the things that came through in the articles was how relentless you are. I knew you'd catch Bruce in a lie or something."

I wondered if she knew that the man she was defending considered her the human equivalent of something you found stuck to the bottom of your shoe.

She actually put away her hookah pen to make her final appeal. "The best thing for everyone—Mother most of all—is for you to let this drop and go home. That'll be the end of it, and we can all get on with our lives."

The wind, rushing down the river valley, pushed snow from the boughs. It fell around our heads like glitter.

"What can you tell me about Arlo Burch?" I said.

"Oh, for fuck's sake! Really?"

"I can't put this case aside until I have a

conversation with the last man to see your grandfather alive."

The sound of an engine straining to climb the hill made us both pause and wait for the vehicle to appear. It turned out to be a growling Pontiac Grand Prix, one of the last of the V8s. The once-white body was pockmarked with rust like the worst case of acne you've ever seen. There were at least two people inside, both women, maybe a kid in the backseat.

The driver slowed to have a look at us as they passed. The female passenger scowled and made a comment that I didn't need to be a lip reader to decipher.

"Do you know who that was?" I asked, after the Grand Prix had roared out of sight.

"Not by name. Half the people living up there moved in over the past year. They're all related, my friend Felice says. And they're no fans of cops. The worst of them—the one to watch out for—is the old lady they call 'Grambo.' "

"Grambo!"

"I don't know what her real name is. She's an old hillbilly who sits on her porch with a shotgun. Sometimes she aims it at passing cars if she doesn't like your looks."

"Is this another story you heard or something you've actually experienced?"

"It was a rumor going around town, and I figured it had to be bullshit because it's such a

194

caricature, right? Then I went up there to visit Felice—I don't know how she stands it—and I saw Grambo on her porch. I never believed in the evil eye until that old crone looked at me."

She illustrated the baleful gesture by pulling down her lower eyelid with her index finger.

"Grambo sounds like someone else I should meet."

Bibi threw her hands in the air. "It's like everything I say to persuade you to leave has the opposite effect."

"You never answered my question about how well you know Burch."

"My friend Felice lives up there, like I said. I don't know why she stays in that shithole, but I guess it's because she's worried about her dad. He has a gambling problem. Anyway, she introduced me to Arlo at the bar where he works. So he's not a stranger exactly, but we're barely acquaintances. I couldn't even tell you which trailer is his."

"But Felice would know?"

"You're *seriously* going up there alone to confront those people." She added an eye roll for effect. "I know you've got a gun and all, but the deputies who get called to the hill won't even go without a backup. It's always two cop cars, at least. Every weekend, I see them race by the house with their lights flashing."

"Lucky for me it's not nighttime."

"Yeah, but it's December, and it's going to get dark faster than you think. I wouldn't get caught up there after nightfall if I were you."

"It wouldn't be the first time someone slashed my tires."

"There are worse fates." She took a step toward her Mini, then turned. "How long have you been a game warden?"

"Eight years since I entered the academy."

"You must have made lots of enemies in that time."

It was the exact same thing Rivard had said to me. The coincidence was uncanny, but that's the nature of coincidences. We never notice the millions of times they don't occur.

"I've encountered some dangerous people. The worst of them are off the board."

"But the ones who aren't—don't you worry that they'll come looking for you?"

"If you're asking do I spend my life looking over my shoulder, the answer is no."

She reached for the door handle. "Maybe you should."

When I opened the Jeep door, an odor rushed out: nose-burning, industrial-strength ammonia. The wolf had pissed himself. Lizzie Holman had lined the kennel with absorbent pads against this eventuality, but they had made no difference.

The phone rang as I turned the key in the

ignition. Charley's face appeared on the screen. The old man was one of the only people in my life with whom I engaged in video chats. It gave him such obvious pleasure to see me that I indulged his whim. I enjoyed seeing him, too, I had to admit. He had a weathered face and a chin like the toe of a boot. His head of white hair had grown back after he'd shaved himself bald for an unsanctioned investigation, in June.

"Did I catch you at a bad time, young feller?"

"Never."

"You wouldn't tell me if I had. I'll cut right to the chase then and ask if you've given any more thought to Christmas supper? If you're free, Ora and I would like you and Dani to join us. Stacey will be here, of course. The Boss says that might be a dealbreaker for you."

It was his affectionate nickname for his wife, Ora. No man of my generation could get away with using it for his spouse.

"Things are still up in the air," I said.

Charley was my mentor and my closest confidant in the world. But now was not the time to tell him that according to Nicole Tate, Dani and I were no longer a couple.

"We understand if you have to decline," Charley said. "But we'd dearly like you to join us, son. The holiday won't be the same without you."

For half a dozen years, I hadn't missed

Christmas supper at the Stevens house. But that was before Dani and I had gotten serious.

"I hope to have an answer for you tonight."

"Good enough," said the old pilot. "So what are you up to on this fine December day?"

"I had to bring Shadow to the vet in Pennacook."

"You got the werewolf into a kennel? How'd you manage that feat?"

"I started putting an electric blanket inside the crate to get him used to sleeping there."

"That's a nifty trick!"

"Honestly, I think he chose to go of his own free will. He's smarter than any dog I've ever known."

"How is the old boy?"

"Dozing at the moment. Dr. Holman shot him full of drugs. But he's healthier than he has any right to be."

"Good to hear! So you're about to head home then?"

The man's curiosity was as bad as my own. "I had to make a few stops in Stratford."

"Stratford! I won't ask what mischief brings you to that Podunk."

"Thank you."

"You should keep your eyes open for a crow roost while you're there. Used to be a big one nearby. At dusk, the sky would turn black with thousands and thousands of birds. Crows roost up in winter for warmth and safety. Otherwise they're easy picking for owls, you know."

"I'll keep an eye out."

"What mischief brings you to Stratford?"

I knew the old busybody couldn't stop himself from prying.

"It's a long story. I'll tell you over Christmas supper."

It was only after I'd gotten off the call that I realized the promise I'd made to him.

21

I crouch behind a crooked cedar, listening. Sounds travel strangely in the woods at night—especially when the wind is up—and I can't be sure if the snowmobile is following the main channel or coming around the island.

I don't have long to wait. The engine grows louder. The rider must have the throttle wide open. Then I see headlights, shining down the ice. The blowing snow is thick in the beams.

With luck, my pursuer is traveling too fast. He will miss the impressions left by my boots as I staggered back to the island.

But the beaver lodge is too obvious a point of interest. The twin cones of light turn toward the heap of weathered wood. The sled slows and stops before the abandoned den.

Game wardens learn to identify snow machines and all-terrain vehicles with the same expertise that state troopers memorize the makes and models of street cars and trucks. This one is a chartreuse Arctic Cat ZR 6000: a fast and furious ride. But not super-maneuverable in dense cover. It's a flashy sled that doesn't suit Jewett, but I wouldn't be in this mess if I hadn't misjudged him once. He will, in any case, have trouble navigating the twists and turns of my private island if he attempts to follow me here on his ZR.

He's wearing a black jacket over gray snow pants: a unisex outfit. The helmet concealing his face has a visor, a spoiler, and an opaque shield. A shotgun is slung over his shoulder.

That voice in my head, the one that sounds like Charley, speaks again.

What if it's not Jewett?

The height and build seem close, but I can't be certain. But who else can it be?

Jewett climbs off his idling machine, and I duck my head.

When I dare take another peek, I see him circling the beaver lodge. There is a tactical flashlight mounted to the black barrel of the twelve-gauge. The gun is likely a Remington 870 or a Mossberg 590: a combat weapon. To search for tracks he points the muzzle at the ice as if preparing to blast it into smithereens.

The circle of illumination lingers on a patch of snow on my side of the beaver lodge. Suddenly Jewett straightens. The light follows my wind-blown path back to the island. Once more, I retreat behind the cedar.

Now I hear the squelch of a hand-held radio. Not words. Just a series of button pushes: a wordless, indecipherable signal traveling over the airwaves to report what? That the target has been located?

Who's he communicating with?

I have no time to watch and wait. I am injured and, except for the knife, unarmed. My enemy is on high alert and equipped with a long gun designed for house-to-house raids. I begin crawling into the trees.

Only when I reach the enormous root clump of a toppled pine, do I dare stand. It doesn't occur to me that the tangled roots offer imperfect concealment—there are holes between the inter-laced tendrils—and so when a blast of buckshot obliterates the deadwood ten inches from my head, I just about leap out of my skin.

Now I'm off at a full gallop, snapping branches and whipping evergreen boughs as I make instinctively for the one cover I remember: the narrow gap between the glacial erratic and the tree stand.

At least Jewett doesn't seem have brought along his night-vision goggles or an infrared gunsight. (Why didn't he bring them along?) He'd have no need of a tactical flashlight if he could pick out my heat signature.

I pull my injured leg over the ridgeback, only vaguely sure of my direction. To my side I see a beam of gauzy light from my pursuer's gun. He's hurrying, too. He should be tracking me slowly like the wounded animal I am, but he must be caught up in the thrill of the chase.

I nearly smash myself against the boulder, I'm going so hard.

Is this even the right rock?

I don't see my boot prints, but as I circle the monolith, I come to the crevice where I rested. The impression of my body, like the bed of a stag, shows as a gray-blue shadow. I recognize the sentinel oak and the tree stand above.

I remind myself that Jewett must assume I'm armed. He can't know that I lost my pistol in the river. Just because I haven't returned fire doesn't mean he can approach in safety.

Behind me, I see the brightening glow of the flashlight beam. I hear branches snap. Jewett has discovered my trail, and now he's moving cautiously. He is hunting me like the dangerous prey I wish I were.

Looking up, I follow the ladder of spikes to that barely balanced chair fifteen feet above the ground.

I don't have the strength to climb up there.

I need to find the strength.

What choice do I have?

I pause beneath the lowest rung to take a centering breath. I lower my shoulders, bend my knees as much as I can, and push against the hard ground. As I explode upward, I extend my arms over my head. My palms hit the first foot-long spike hard. My left hand closes tightly around the ridged steel, but my right loses its grip. I swing like a monkey by one arm, gritting my teeth to keep from letting out a groan.

Even when you're healthy and well rested, one arm chin-ups are arm-busters and back breakers. But in the gym you don't have adrenaline powering you to save your own life.

Engaging my arms, my core, and muscles I can't name, I raise myself until I find a firm grip with my right hand. Then, legs swinging, I pull my chest up to the level of the spike and throw my right elbow over the rung.

I pull hard, reaching for the next rung, until my kneecaps are balanced on the rebar. The posture is pure agony. I pull again until I am standing on the lowest spike, seven feet off the ground. I see the flashlight poking at the lower entrance to the gap. I don't dare move, for fear of alerting Jewett to my position. All that needs to happen is for him to raise his eyes.

But he has grown careful. Maybe the question about whether I am armed or not has begun to worry him. I see the beam of light probe the chokepoint between the tree and the boulder. It stops when it finds my blood trail. Then it rises, scanning the boulder from the base to the top.

The radio squelches again. Jewett fumbles to kill the volume, but it takes seconds for him to find the knob in the dark.

The distraction gives me a chance to ascend to the next rung. Now I am standing ten feet above the frozen earth, holding onto the ladder for dear life. I am afraid that if I draw my knife, I will lose my grip.

It's apparent that Jewett suspects an ambush. He thinks I'm crouched atop the glacial erratic. He can't see the tree stand from the bottom of the snow-filled alley. He has given no thought to the seemingly unclimbable oak tree to his left.

My heart is beating like a war drum.

He begins creeping forward, probing the rock face with the light, illuminating the mosaic of orange and sage-green lichen. The pattern is intricate, beautiful. In the dark I never saw it.

If Jewett's finds the place in the snow where I leapt up, I am dead.

But he is preoccupied with the boulder. He searches for footholds with the beam, continues its slow ascension of the rock.

Come on.

It takes everything in me to keep from shivering, to avoid knocking snow loose, or making the faintest noise.

Then Jewett is beneath me. I am looking down on his black-helmeted head and snow-dusted shoulders. The barrel of the shotgun drops suddenly. The flashlight finds my deep footprints, the spot where I leapt into the sky. I can sense his thought process as he lifts his head.

I let go of the ladder and fall as hard as I can upon him.

22

The crown of Pill Hill had once been forested. Now it was an exposed, windswept place. Whoever had developed the hilltop had sawed and knocked down every tree for twenty acres around the cell tower that loomed above the mobile homes. Between the huddled trailers, not a single sapling had been planted. The sheet-metal houses must have shuddered every time a storm blew through. One good nor'easter would send them all packing to the Land of Oz.

As far as I could tell, the road consisted of a loop—one way in, one way out. At the entrance stood a mail kiosk with maybe twenty boxes. A foot of aged snow covered what must have been a lawn around it. Sunny days and subzero nights had caused the snow to melt and refreeze, and dirty boots had punched holes through the crust to the softer stuff beneath.

Adjacent to the parking lot were two dumpsters. One was closed; the other had been left open and was overflowing with waste. Crows were hopping around inside, tearing apart trash bags and scattering pizza boxes and Styrofoam food containers in their pirate's quest for booty. These birds must have belonged to the massive roost Charley had mentioned.

The crows took to the air when I parked the Jeep. Three of them landed on the power lines to wait me out.

I powered down the window and scanned the mailboxes, but only a few had names on them. Arlo Burch's was not among them.

Across the plowed and sanded road was a sad playground with monkey bars and a swing set. The plank seats hung from chains. They swung in the wind as if from ghost children at play.

I hadn't even noticed the living kids. There were two of them, and they had been lying flat on the hard frozen ground. Their hats and coats were white when they rose to their feet. They'd been trying and failing to make snow angels in the packed crust.

I had always been bad at judging the ages of children. All I could say about these two was that they were closing in on puberty but hadn't hit it yet.

"Hey, kids. Do any of you know where Mr. Burch lives?"

The boy had a moon face, dusky skin, auburn curls. The girl was so pale and blond she looked as if she'd once fallen into a vat of bleach.

"You a cop, right?" said the boy.

"Close," I said. "I'm a game warden. My name is Mike Bowditch. What's yours?"

His broad nose was running. He sniffed hard to

reverse the flow of gravity. "I ain't telling you."

"His name is Levi," said the girl.

"Shut up, Treasure!" He returned his attention to me. "What do you want Arlo for?"

"Can you tell me which house is his?"

"These ain't houses," said the boy, Levi. "These're tornado magnets. No one's gonna lead you to Arlo's crib, cop."

The wind spirited shopping flyers from the open dumpster and tumbled them across the open space.

"You give me a dollar, I will," said the girl, Treasure.

"All right."

"Show it first." Her voice was more little-girlish than she was.

I removed a bill from my wallet. She marched to my window and held out a mittened palm.

"Make it two dollars, you want to know so bad."

I pressed the crinkled bill into her hand, afraid the wind would catch it unless I held on tight. "A deal's a deal."

Her eyelashes were so pale it looked like someone had plucked them out as a punishment. "Arlo lives at number four."

"Thank you."

"He's gonna be mad, you telling," shouted Levi. "He's gonna whoop you, girl."

"Is that true?" I said, concerned I had created

a potential problem. "Will Mr. Burch be mad at you?"

"Hell, no," Treasure said. "Arlo lives with my mom's cousins. They'll give me another dollar when I tell them a cop's on the way."

"You're quite an entrepreneur."

"What that?"

"A businesswoman."

"You're full of shit."

She removed her mittens and pulled a cheap Tracfone from her coat to text her relatives about the law-enforcement officer who would soon be knocking at their door.

Arlo Burch was the owner of the most tricked-out mobile home I'd ever seen. Underneath all the additions, it was your standard double-wide: low-slung with vinyl siding stamped to resemble wood clapboards. It sat on concrete piers with a skirt of aluminum wrapped around the crawlspace. The furnace probably lay on its side beneath the building.

The crazy add-ons were what got me: the stained-glass door; the bow windows; the exterior porch wide enough to hold a square dance; the hot tub on said porch; and the eye-popping diameter of the satellite dish in the dooryard. Honestly, the antenna was as big around as a wading pool. It looked capable of picking up transmissions from Alpha Centauri.

Just as impressive was the fleet of vehicles overflowing the property. A new-looking Jeep Wrangler Rubicon (the recent model); matching black Chevy Monte Carlos; a sweet Harley-Davidson street rod. I counted three snowmobiles under tarps, two all-terrain vehicles, a Jet Ski that should also have been sheltered from the elements, and a very large object under a protective coating of white shrink-wrap. My guess was that the concealed watercraft was a pontoon boat for summer cruises on Lake Auburn or wherever Arlo liked to party.

Bartending obviously paid better than I'd thought.

It was standard operating procedure, before approaching what looked like a drug den, to alert fellow officers to your location. In my case that fellow officer was going to be Maine State Trooper Dani Tate who, while many miles away, had become my default go-to. I had the phone in hand when the trailer door opened and a skinny young woman stepped onto the porch.

From a distance, I could see that she was gaunt and fair, but her identifying features were mostly hidden. Her hair was bunched beneath a knit cap emblazoned with a pot leaf. Her eyes were concealed behind aviator sunglasses. She was dressed in a man's chamois shirt, bedazzled jeans, and buckskin moccasins.

The girl's text had preceded me.

The pale woman didn't so much as pause but sprang lightly down the stairs and made a line for my Jeep. She had the energy of someone whose metabolism runs twice as fast as a normal human's. I watched her hands, but they were empty.

I disengaged my seat belt (never a bad idea if you might need to reach for your sidearm) and slid down the window.

"Game warden, right?" she said. Even her words came out fast.

"How'd you guess?"

Up close, I could see that her nose and cheeks were covered with connect-the-dots freckles.

"I didn't need Treasure to tell me. You guys aren't as stealthy as you think you are. What do you want with Arlo? It can't be about poaching. The dude doesn't even hunt. You want to show me your badge and identification?"

"I'll show you mine. How about you show me yours?"

"I don't think so."

I brought out the badge and the ID. "Are you Mrs. Burch?"

She made a snorting laugh, then peered at my identification closely. I had never seen someone do a double take in real life until that moment. Her head snapped up, and she removed her oversized sunglasses for a better look at me. Her eyes were the blue of faded denim. False lashes, eyeliner, and eye shadow gave her a catlike appearance. Her gaze was searching, intense, and borderline hostile.

"You're Mike Bowditch? No fucking way."

"Do we know each other?"

Like the teenage logger I'd challenged earlier, she looked familiar in the sense that she resembled other people I had busted. Maybe I'd arrested her brother or uncle. People convicted of crimes never forget the officers who sent them to jail. They throw our names around with disdain. Hard-ass cops, in other words, achieve a modicum of notoriety within certain social circles in Maine.

She returned her sunglasses to the bridge of her freckled nose as if to frustrate my attempt to place her.

"No, but I've heard about you, *Mike*."

Her free and easy use of my first name was intended to get a rise out of me.

"I'm getting that a lot today. Is Arlo home? I'm not here to hassle him or you. I've got a few questions about a cold case."

"Not that professor again."

"It shouldn't take more than fifteen minutes."

"That's what you guys always say," she said, showing bleached teeth. "Arlo's got to leave for work soon, but he might have time to answer your questions. I don't know why you guys keep wasting your time with him. Seems a misuse of our state tax dollars."

As I got out of the Jeep, Shadow moaned in his sleep. In his dreams he returned often to the mountains where he'd roamed loose for several years. Sometimes he seemed to be chasing deer again through the landscape of his mind.

The pale woman heard him. "What the fuck do you got in there?"

"A wolf."

"Be serious."

I winked at her. There was no reason that she should be the only one keeping secrets.

She watched me get out of the vehicle, giving special attention, it seemed, to my right side. Everyone took an interest in my handgun.

There was a bite to the air that I hadn't felt down in the river valley. The sun had grown pale in the windy sky.

I towered over her by almost a foot. "Are you going to tell me your name or are you in witness protection?"

"Tori."

"Tori what?"

Her response was another snort.

I followed her thin hips up the stairs and through the outer stained-glass door. The decorated panel showed a naked woman holding an apple while a snake, wrapped around a tree, whispered enticements in her ear. There was a second door beyond the glass one, but it was made of steel and four inches thick. The barrier would easily have stopped small-caliber bullets and maybe even bigger rounds. Security doors like this one cost thousands and weren't readily available at your local Home Depot.

Inside the trailer, the thermostat had been turned up to Amazon rain forest. Even the light had a greenish tint. The color, I quickly realized, was on account of the terrariums.

There were three coffin-sized glass boxes arrayed around the living room, each with a heat lamp shining down into its steamed-over interior. Every one of the glass chambers, I was fairly certain, held a very large snake.

"Arlo's in the shower," said Tori. "Have a seat, and I'll go get him."

Instead of sitting, I took a tour of the terrariums, making sure not to turn my back to any doorway.

I thought again of texting Dani, but I was too eager to see the snakes.

The first box contained a serpent as big around as my forearm. Its color was pinkish-beige with orange mottling. If I had to guess, I would've said it was a species of boa. The next constrictor species, also unknown to me, was a vivid green and equally muscular. The third snake I recognized on sight. The previous summer, I'd gotten too close for comfort with a Burmese python in Florida's Big Cypress Swamp. It had nearly chewed a man's face off in front of me.

There wasn't a proper chair in the room: just matching sectional couches arranged around a coffee table made from a barn door and littered with tabloid magazines, wine and shot glasses, and ashtrays needing to be emptied. I remained standing with my back to the nearest exit.

I heard Tori shout, "Hey, Arlo, there's another game warden here. He wants to talk with you about old man Chamberlain."

A drop of sweat rolled down the side of my face.

Tori returned, having removed her sunglasses and overshirt. She wore a thin tee that might as well have been transparent. Her small nipples poked through the cotton fabric. She held two cans of Twisted Tea.

"Thanks," I said, "but I'm not allowed to drink on duty."

"Who said one of these was for you?" She kept an alcoholic beverage for herself and set the other on the table. "So you're *the* Mike Bowditch. The warden who killed those prison guards last spring."

"Actually, I didn't kill anyone."

"But you were an accessory."

"Accessories are people who assist in the commission of crimes. I was a law-enforcement officer defending innocent people."

She threw herself onto one of the couches.

"That's why the entire nation hates cops. You're all so fucking racist and corrupt. You get away with shit that would send someone like me to prison for life. How many people have you abused personally? And how many of them were Black?"

There were people I was prepared to have a serious conversation with about the state of policing in America: the problems and possible solutions. This Tori person was not one of them.

I heard a man's voice and another woman's voice at the far end of the house. Their words were muffled by a door closed between us.

I nodded at the second terrarium. "What's that green one there? I recognize the boa and the Burmese python."

"Emerald? She's from Australia. We bought her in New Hampshire. Reptile Warehouse. You ever been there, *Mike?*"

She seemed to take pleasure in saying my name. "No, but I've rescued a few animals that came from that business."

Her face was magnificently freckled. The skin beneath was as thin and pale as rice paper, but the sheer number of freckles on her forehead, nose, and cheeks made her look almost tan.

"Really?"

"One was a pit viper that got loose in its owner's garage. Unfortunately, it killed the guy's dog before we managed to capture it. You know, Tori, it's kind of rude not to tell me your last name. You have me at a disadvantage."

"Do I?"

"You do."

Her blue eyes held mine a moment, drifted away around the room, then came back to me. "It's Dillon."

"Tori Dillon?"

"Don't wear it out."

I heard a door open down the hall, fast footsteps, and then a second woman stood in the threshold between the living room and the kitchen.

She was wearing a terrycloth robe bearing the insignia of a fancy Portland hotel and a purple towel wrapped around her wet hair. She had the same height, build, and general coloring as Tori, but she lacked the freckles, and her nose was distinctively pink. She wore a copper ring in one roseate nostril.

"So you're the famous Mike Bowditch. In our fucking house. What are the odds?"

She, too, spoke as slowly as an auctioneer.

"I'm hardly famous."

"We've seen you on the news," said Tori, cracking her can of Twisted Tea. "Tiffany saw your picture and thought you were hot. Didn't you, Tiff?"

Tori and Tiffany?

Tiff Dillon reached for the unopened can of booze. "You're older-looking in person, though."

"Sorry to disappoint. You two are twins, I'm guessing."

"Gee, what gave us away?" said Tiff. Her rabbit nose twitched when she smiled.

"Mike here is a warden investigator," said Tori. "That's like a detective, right? Only your cases involve dead moose?"

"And occasionally a dead hunter."

"Ain't you funny," said Tiff in a faux Maine accent. Her eyelashes and eyebrows, not yet made up, were rusty red. "He's a *smaht* one, ain't he, sistah?"

"He thinks he is."

From the back of the house came a crashing sound.

Then: "Shit! Ouch! Damn!"

Half a minute later, Arlo Burch blundered into the room, dressed in nothing but a towel and cupping one elbow in the palm of his opposite hand.

"I hit my funny bone!" he said, shaking his arm. "Don't you hate that? The tingling."

He was a tall man, slim, but well-muscled. His skin was tanned from a tanning bed, and one arm was inked from shoulder to wrist in a sleeve of well-drawn tattoos. (More snakes, intertwined.) He hadn't shaved for several days, and his stubble beard was darker than his curls. His eyes were extraordinarily large, friendly, and empty of intelligence.

"When Tori said we had a warden visitor, I expected it was my man, Rivard."

"This is Mike Bowditch," said Tiff.

"Nice to meet you." He advanced on me with a warm smile and an outstretched hand, calloused from a weight bench. "Welcome to my abode. Have a seat."

"I'm fine, thank you."

"Did the girls offer you a beverage?"

"He can't drink, Arlo," said Tori. "He's on duty."

"He can drink a Muscle Milk."

"No thanks. I'm fine. This is quite the place you've got here."

His voice dropped to an intimate level, "Do you think it's over-the-top? I worry that it is. There's a line between luxury and tacky. The girls and me—I trust their taste, but we don't always see eye to eye. I worry it's over-the-top. Hey, did they introduce you to my snakes?"

He now presented the three serpents: Babe (the boa), Emerald (the Emerald python), and Lucifer (the Burmese python).

"You sure you don't want a Muscle Milk? Or a Gatorade?"

When I refused, he sat down in his towel on the couch between the women, extended his arms along the top, and spread his legs. If he shifted position by a matter of centimeters, he was going to give me a show I didn't want to see. I would have thought Burch was showing off—"Dude, look at me, I've got *two* women sharing my bed, and they're twins!"—if he didn't seem like such a good-natured dimwit. My first impression of Arlo Burch was that he was an entity I'd formerly considered mythological: the man without a care in the world.

"First I want to say," he began, growing solemn, "that my second cousin is a cop over in Nashua, New Hampshire. So I've got a lot of respect for you guys. Police, I mean. Wardens included."

"We appreciate your support."

"Tori said you wanted to ask me something about Professor Chamberlain. What can I do for you, man? Ask and you shall receive."

Putting on some clothes would be a start.

"The Warden Service is taking another look at the Eben Chamberlain case. My superiors gave it to me for some fresh perspective. I've reviewed the file and been briefed by Lieutenant Rivard."

"Former lieutenant," said Tori.

I hadn't been surprised that Mariëtte Chamberlain had heard about Marc's fall from grace. But how the hell did Tori Dillon know about it? Maybe I wasn't the only warden whose career she followed. That seemed like a stone worth turning over—but not at present.

I locked eyes with Burch. "I understand you were the last person to see the professor alive the day he disappeared."

"That's what people tell me. But I mean, someone else might've seen him alive after me, and I wouldn't know, right?"

Tori grabbed a handful of his chest hair.

"Ouch!" he said. "What did you do that for?"

"Because you're being a tool. You were the last one to see him. Don't pretend it's some unknowable mystery."

Still scowling, he snatched her can of booze and took a swig. "I'm only trying to be helpful. Have you talked to Bruce, yet? Bruce Jewett, I mean. He was a friend of the professor's. You would've passed his place here. Old farmhouse behind a stonewall."

"Of course, Mike spoke with Bruce first," said Tiff between clenched teeth.

"What did he tell you about us?" said Tori. "I can only guess. That nutcase thinks he's living down the road from the Manson family."

I kept my attention focused on Burch. "Can you tell me about the day Eben Chamberlain died? When and where did you see him?"

"It was about eleven o'clock," he said. "I was headed into work. At the pullout I saw a man alone in a boat."

When I removed a notepad and pen from my pocket, his mouth tightened. People get squirrelly when a law-enforcement officer starts writing their words down.

"How far were you from this man?" I asked.

"Three hundred yards."

"You sound pretty certain."

"I played quarterback in school. I estimate distances in terms of football fields. But I'm just a simple bartender now."

"He's a mixologist," said Tiff, sounding affronted on his behalf.

"I pour drinks," he said with a self-effacing smile. There was something of the golden retriever about his shining hair and eagerness to please. "You know the Brass Monkey on Mechanics Row in Auburn? Come in some night when you're off duty. First round is on me. Maker's Mark, Belvedere, whatever you want."

"Getting back to Professor Chamberlain. . . ."

He nodded and tried to look serious. "Right. He was alone in his duck-hunting boat, like I said. It was too far to see any details, but I knew it was Professor Chamberlain. And he was alone, like I said."

"How did you recognize him?"

"I'd see him working in his orchard, and he would wave at me so I stopped sometimes, and we'd shoot the shit, you know? The prof would always give me a bushel of apples."

"The professor liked Arlo," said Tiff with her usual deadpan. "He liked him a lot."

I bet he did. Burch could have worked as an underwear model.

I clicked my pen a few times. "There's one thing I don't get. If you were three hundred yards from him, how did you notice that he wasn't wearing a life vest?"

"Huh?"

"The professor was duck hunting, and I understand from the file that his personal flotation device was a Mustang MIT. Those vests are thin and light until they get wet, then a sensor goes off, and the automatic gas canister fills the internal bladders with CO_2. I wear mine every time I'm on the water. So did Professor Chamberlain, according to his granddaughter."

"You mean Bibi," said Tori with no affection in her voice.

"You know each other then."

"Not really. I know she comes up here to buy her Addies—not from us, from our neighbor, Felice. I bet that isn't in your file. That the poor little rich girl is an addict."

Addies was slang for the drug Adderall, prescribed to people, often young, with attention deficit hyperactivity disorder. It is bought illegally and abused by adults wishing to sharpen their mental focus or seeking instant stimulation. People were known to crush the pills and snort them like cocaine.

"She inherited all that professor's money,

you know," said Tiff. "Is that in your report?"

"The Warden Service concluded that Chamberlain's death was an accident," I said. "Do you have reason to say it wasn't?"

Tori, who struck me as the quicker of the two, sensed the trap. "My sister's not saying the dyke killed him. Bibi Chamberlain is just a rich bitch who likes kiddy coke and thinks her shit doesn't smell."

I was perspiring pretty furiously under my bulletproof vest. I was the only one in this hothouse fully dressed.

"I want to talk about the professor's PFD." I pretended to look at my notebook as if refreshing my memory. "My Mustang MIT happens to be red, but Professor Chamberlain's was camouflage. The pattern is called Mossy Oak Shadow Grass Blades. This is where I have another problem, Arlo. If he was dressed in camouflage, as he was when we recovered his body, and his life vest was also camo-patterned, how could you have seen or not seen it from a distance of three hundred yards?"

"Don't answer that question," said Tori with the abruptness of a defense lawyer at a deposition. "He's trying to trick you into incriminating yourself."

"Don't trust him," echoed Tiff.

"Why not?" asked Burch.

"Because I know all about him," said Tori

through her teeth. "Arlo, honey, this guy is as bad as they come."

I'd been called worse. But never by someone I'd just met.

23

My ambush is fucked from the start. Maybe my boots squeak, inching along the spike. Maybe a handful of snow dislodges itself from my person.

Whatever the giveaway is, Jewett jerks his head up.

By then, I'm dropping fast. I am 100 percent committed. But the split-second warning is time enough for Jewett to spring forward. Instead of my coming down on top of him, it's more like I come down behind him.

The one thing that saves me is that, lunging, he loses his footing. He lands on his kneecaps with his left arm outstretched to arrest the fall. The shotgun swings up under his right armpit on its bouncy bungee sling.

Somehow I land in a crouch, but I don't have time to plant my weight. Instead of springing on top of my attacker, I collapse on him. My armored chest hits his boots, the side of my face hits his butt, and my arms close like pinchers around his midsection before he can twist around.

Now that I'm on top of him, I can feel how small he is under the padded snow suit. Jewett is a short, wiry guy, but something feels wrong. My arms have closed around a narrower waist than I expected.

Not that my brain has time to process this information. My wrestling partner manages to glance the butt of the shotgun off my forehead. There is nothing like a hunk of synthetic fibers knocking your skull to chase stray thoughts from the mind.

Meanwhile he's trying to worm his way out of the grip I have around his waist. I feel clothing moving, a belt yielding, snow pants coming loose.

The flashlight, mounted to the barrel, causes the beam to shake—a strobe light in the trees.

I let go with my right hand, make a fist, and deliver a punch to where I hope one of the bastard's kidneys is.

The audible expulsion of breath tells me I hit the mark.

He twists before I can drive my fist into his kidney again. Somehow I find myself on my back in a desperate attempt to keep him from slipping free. He presses his bony ass against my sternum while he stamps his boots on my shins.

Under normal circumstances, I would be winning this bout, no contest. I have practiced hours for this scenario, both at the criminal justice academy and with Dani, who holds a black belt in Brazilian jiu-jitsu. I have the advantages of size and strength, and on the ground, brute force matters more than martial artistry. Because if there is one iron rule in hand-to-hand combat, it's never let a bigger opponent pin you.

Jewett, on the other hand, doesn't seem to have been trained in any fighting style. He's just slippery as an eel and determined as hell.

I arch my shoulders and rock from side to side—Dani calls the move "bridging"—trying to roll us both over so I'm on top again. Finally I push up with my hips: the kind of pelvic thrust people do in booty-building classes.

But the little bastard drives an elbow at my face. It doesn't hit, but it causes me to shut my eyes and lose focus. Worse, it allows him to brace the butt of the gun against the ground.

So instead of rolling on top of him, I roll off his body altogether. He might as well have thrown me clear.

I land on my hands and knees while he scrabbles away, kicking snow. In the process he inadvertently jerks the trigger of his shotgun. The barrel flashes as an unaimed shell explodes from the chamber, scattering buckshot into the trees overhead. Broken branches and splintered bark rain down.

The gunshot wakes me up.

I've been treating Jewett the way I would treat some random asshat resisting arrest. Despite his having tried to kill me—twice!—I'm holding back. I'm pretending this is a high school wrestling match instead of a fight to the death. My restraint is going to get me killed.

My hand closes around the knife in my pocket and presses the button that causes the blade to spring out.

He's struggling to get the barrel of the long gun around so he can pull the trigger again. I close one hand around his ankle. The heavy pack boot prevents me from cutting his Achilles tendon. So I go higher and slash his quad through layers of Gore-Tex and wool. I'm not aiming to sever his femoral artery. I only want to hurt him enough to gain possession of the firearm.

He screams, a surprisingly high-pitched scream, and reflexively presses a hand to the cut. I grab hold of the bungee sling and give the elasticized strap a good yank.

The weapon slips over his head. In the process his helmet pops off.

I'm sitting in the snow, but this time holding the shotgun butt, while my unmasked opponent gasps for air. He has a balaclava around his head. In the darkness I can't make out identifying features except to note the paleness of his face.

I reposition my grip on the gun to get my finger in the trigger guard.

With one hand he clutches his bleeding thigh. With the other he massages his throat where he was clotheslined by the strap as I pulled it over the lip of his helmet. Then he straightens his shoulders. I raise the shotgun's sights and with it the flashlight. In the blue-white beam I see a strand of red hair peeking out from beneath the balaclava.

That's not Jewett.

The freckled, contorted face turns to me full of pain and anger, but absolutely no fear.

It is Tori Dillon.

24

Tori curled into her boyfriend's armpit and pressed her left hand flat on his furry pectoral muscle. She was barefoot. Her toenails were painted with glittery polish that sparkled in the green light of the heat lamps.

I have a good memory for names and a better memory for faces. The Dillon twins definitely reminded me of someone else. It ate at me that I couldn't make the connection.

"Are you sure we've never met, Tori?"

"You'd remember if we had, *Mike*."

One of the snakes rubbed its scaled belly against the gravel in the heated box, the sound dry and rasping.

"This seems personal for you," I said. "Usually people get to know me before they decide they hate my guts."

Arlo laughed.

The freckled twin scowled. "I've known you for five minutes—that's long enough."

"Ease up, Tori," said her sister.

I found Tiff's dead eyes hard to read. Cannabis, maybe. Or something stronger.

Tori detached herself from Burch to reach for a pack of cigarettes. "I'm telling you, this asshole specializes in fucking people's lives over."

"Anyone in particular you have in mind?" I said.

The Bic flamed before her face as she lit her Parliament. "Those people out on Maquoit Island, for example."

She was referring to my first case as a warden investigator. I had been called to the scene of a hunting homicide on a remote coastal island. The woman who'd died had been an unwelcome stranger whose murder no one wanted solved. It wasn't my finest hour. By the time I left Maquoit, the entire population hated me. If I'd stayed another day, I'm fairly sure I would have been stoned in the public square.

"You seem to have followed my career closely," I said.

She exhaled at the ceiling. "A friend of mine lived out there."

"Who?"

"Like I'm going to give you their name! But don't worry, Warden Bowditch. I'm not your personal stalker."

Isn't that what every stalker says?

"Tori, you're being kind of rude to our guest," said Arlo in a fatherly tone that didn't suit him. "You should, maybe, apologize."

"Everyone's entitled to their opinions," said Tiff.

"Damn right they are," said Tori.

I tapped my pen against the spine of my

notebook. "The case file is unclear about one last point. I'm hoping you can help me with that one too, Arlo. Did you mention seeing Professor Chamberlain alone in his boat to anyone else?"

"Lieutenant Rivard."

"I mean the day he died."

The question seemed to rattle Burch, based on his stuttering reply. "It wasn't unusual to see him in his boat. He liked to hunt. He was out there a lot."

Tori perked up. "Arlo, honey—"

But I ran right over her. "What about after you heard he was missing? Did you tell your 'roommates' that you'd seen him alone?"

Tiff covered a yawn with her hand. "We didn't live here then."

"Oh?"

Tori cast her sister a look to shut up. I wondered why she did that. What didn't she want me to know?

Burch had recovered some of his natural mellowness. He was a concerned citizen with nothing to hide. He only wanted to help. "My last girlfriend had just moved out. There weren't many homes here. Back then, it was me and old man Bazinet. It was my cousin who developed the hill. He sold me this lot at cost when he was putting in the loop road."

"You've done well managing your money," I said.

Tori sat forward. "Arlo—"

But Burch again missed the warning in her voice. He smiled with pride as if I'd congratulated him on his well-earned success. "I've done OK."

"More than OK. The renovations you did on this place. That new Rubicon parked outside. All the cool toys you've got on the property. Bartending must pay well."

"He thinks you deal drugs," said Tiff.

"What?" He sounded more confused than insulted.

Tori bolted from the couch. "For fuck's sake, Arlo! He thinks you bought all this with drug money."

"No way," he said, glancing from her to me. "I mean, in high school I sold some weed, which is legal now. But I'm no dealer, man. How could you think that?"

Poor Arlo; he had thought we were friends.

"When a place gets nicknamed Pill Hill, it's not because someone is selling vitamins door to door."

"Funny," said Tiff.

"What about you two?" I asked the sisters. "What do you do for work?"

"We're high-class escorts specializing in threesomes with older gentlemen," said Tiff with characteristic flatness. "We draw the line at cops and guys with micropenises. So I guess you're out of luck."

"These two girls," said Arlo, tossing his wooly head. "You never know what's going to come out of their mouths. They're just teasing you. They're not hookers."

"We're home healthcare workers," said Tori. "We look after old and sick people who can't manage for themselves. But because we·ride sleds and live in a trailer, we're just white trash to you, right?"

"I've lived in plenty of trailers myself," I said.

She made a miniature clapping motion with her two index fingers. "Good for you. Congratulations on pulling yourself up by your bootstraps."

"Where do you work, if you don't mind my asking?"

"We do mind," said Tiff, flaring her pink nose.

"He'll find out anyway," said Tori. "We work at Aventa Home Health. Do you want to call our supervisor? I can give you her number."

"That won't be necessary." Again I fastened my attention on Burch. "Getting back to Chamberlain, you said the first person you told about seeing him was Lieutenant Rivard?"

His eyes went blank. "I think so."

"Three days after the professor was reported missing, it says in the report."

"I didn't put it together. That what I'd seen was important. I'd never been an eyewitness before."

Burch could have been acting the idiot, but

it's hard to persuasively portray yourself as less intelligent than you are. Smart people have great difficulty playing dumb.

"What prompted you to come forward?"

Now he did something interesting; he cast a glance at Tori.

She nodded her head.

"I heard about the reward Mrs. Chamberlain was offering," he said. "I didn't care about the money. I wanted to help them find the old dude. No one should be buried in an empty coffin."

It was going to take me a while to untangle that sentence. "But you accepted the reward anyway?"

"Why shouldn't he?" said Tiff. "That's why the woman offered it."

One of the interview tactics I'd picked up over my career was to bob and weave. I never wanted the people I was interrogating to anticipate my next question. I didn't want to give them time to plan their responses.

"What's your opinion of Bruce Jewett?"

"My opinion?"

"Jewett was hunting with Chamberlain the morning he died. Other than you, he was the last to see the professor alive. The police were looking hard at him as a suspect—until you came forward. You saved Mr. Jewett more aggravation than you might realize. I'm curious how you would describe your relationship with him."

Arlo smiled, open-mouthed. "Relationship! I've probably had, like, three conversations with the guy over the years. He was here before my cousin developed the hilltop. Bruce tried to stop it from happening. He hired lawyers to fight the permits, etc. He hates my cousin, but he's always been friendly with me. Generally, I have a good rapport with people."

"What do you know of his background?"

"Don't answer him, Arlo," said Tori.

"I can speak for myself, babe," said Burch. "Jewett's from New Hampshire originally. Served onboard nuclear submarines from what I hear. Top-secret stuff he can't talk about. His mom moved in with him a few years ago. She has Alzheimer's. She got out of the house once and wandered into the woods, and Bruce was racing around on his snowmobile trying to find her before she froze to death. He even came up here asking for my help—which was a first."

"He didn't alert the wardens?"

Burch's reaction was a shrug. "I don't remember seeing any of you guys around that night. We found her, in any case. It was below freezing, but she'd taken off half her clothes. It was one of the weirdest things I'd ever seen."

Experiencing feverish heat is a symptom of moderate hypothermia. A person's core gets so cold, they lose the ability to form rational thoughts. They engage in what is called "paradoxical undressing." Sometimes they burrow into the snow or even hide from the people searching for them. The confusion would be worse in the case of a woman already suffering from dementia.

"I met Mrs. Jewett," I said.

"You were *inside* his house?" asked Tiff with real surprise.

"I wondered if she was still alive," said Burch. "She doesn't make a lot of public appearances. Neither does Bruce, though. He stays holed up in his house, waiting for the end of the world with all his guns and books. He gave me a book once—it's on the shelf behind you."

I half turned, still cautious, and found a paperback under an ashtray. The title was *Enemies Foreign and Domestic.* The cover was yellow with a "don't tread on me" snake, wrapped around an AR-15 rifle.

"Did he want you to join his book club?" I said.

"Ha! No," said Burch. "It was kind of a thank-you for helping him find his mom. I figured he gave it to me because he knew I liked snakes."

Arlo thought the militia manifesto was a book about the care and feeding of reptiles.

I had spoken with Jewett and Burch, and their stories matched. And even though I had nagging questions about Pill Hill and its residents, they were mostly unrelated to the Chamberlain case. I had a wolf in my Jeep that might already be wide awake, mad as hell, and ready to devour a toddler.

"If you have no more questions—" began Tiff.

"Then you can leave," finished Tori, rising to her bare feet. She was just a scrap of thing, as Charley might have said. Barely five feet and a hundred pounds.

"You want to see Lucifer eat a bunny?" Arlo leaned forward. His towel opened. And I got the peepshow I desperately hadn't wanted. "He's due for his weekly meal."

"Thank you, but I think I'll pass on that spectacle."

"You're sure you won't stay?" said Tiff.

I paused with my hand on the doorknob. "I hope you don't consider it rude of me."

One of the cell phones rang from the table. Tori checked the number, her eyes widened, and she hurried from the room.

"Baby, you're going to be late for work," Tiff purred, pulling her man's earlobe.

I checked my watch. It was after three. I'd already been in Stratford longer than I'd planned.

At that moment, Tori came charging into the room. "Gram wants to see you."

"Grambo?" I said.

"I wouldn't call her that to her face," said Tiff, dryly.

"I appreciate the invitation, but I need to get on the road."

"She has information about Chamberlain's death!"

Tori's exclamation caused Tiff to catch her breath.

But the more interesting reaction came from Burch. His eyes widened and his mouth dropped. I could have sworn Tori's words frightened the piss out of him.

I had to remind myself that expressions are notoriously easy to misread. When I was younger, I'd thought I had a rare gift for interpreting people's emotions. Then I had discovered all the scientific studies proving how bad we are sizing each other up at a glance. I still fell into error more often than not—but I was trying to avoid making snap judgments.

Burch sure looked alarmed, though.

"Did your grandmother say what kind of information it is?" I asked.

"That's for her to explain" said Tori. "Don't expect her to rat out anyone, though. And mind your manners if you know what's good for you."

"I always do."

"She lives at the cul de sac. Number nineteen."

"I take it your niece texted her to tell her I was here."

"Didn't need to. Our grandmother can smell a game warden like a skunk, a mile away."

"What's her name? Her real name. If I can't address her as Grambo."

"Lynda," said Tori with a smile. "Lynda Lynch."

Tiff kept her poker face, but Burch turned to Tori with a look of childlike befuddlement.

I pretended not to notice.

25

Tori Dillon takes full advantage of my surprise.

She snatches up the snowmobile helmet and lets it fly at my head. Her accuracy is impressive. Out of reflex I bring up the shotgun to deflect the thrown object. The projectile knocks the barrel aside and before I can retrain the sights on Tori, she's up and running. I have a shot, square between her shoulder blades as she vaults over a deadfall, but my finger doesn't move. Maybe she judged my character and concluded that I was not the type of person who would shoot an unarmed person—even one who's tried to murder me—in the back. She gambles with her life that I am a man of honor. And she wins her bet.

My finger is so stiff from frostbite I probably couldn't have pulled the trigger even if I were feeling homicidal.

I have a harder time regaining my feet than she did, and by then, she's disappeared into the balsams, leaving waving boughs and puffs of powdery snow like confectioner's sugar in the flashlight beam.

"Come out, Tori! I know you're wounded."

My voice is so hoarse, from cold and general lack of use, I sound like I'm a hundred years old.

There is no answer, of course.

If I blasted wildly at the firs, a shotgun pellet might catch up with her. But even now, as mad as I am, I can't bring myself to fire.

Besides, she has left a trail for me to follow: boot prints in the snow, some speckled red. She's losing blood from the cut I made into the meat of her outer thigh.

As am I from the gunshot wound.

But I was shot by a rifle bullet, not a shotgun pellet or slug. It is unlikely to have been Tori. My money is on Tiff, using a scoped rifle.

Why the Dillon sisters want me dead manages to be simultaneously of great importance and not at all urgent.

In a crisis, Charley's voice reminds me, *you must focus on the urgent.*

The heavy firearm in my hands is the urgent matter requiring my immediate attention.

As I expected, the shotgun is a black tactical model. But it's neither of the makes I had expected; not a Remington, nor a Mossberg. It's a Benelli M4 Super 90 which retails for close to two grand and is the standard-issue combat shotgun of the United States Military. It has a semi-automatic action, which means I don't need to rack another shell into the action after I have fired. There is a pistol grip beneath the shoulder stock for me to close my right hand around and improve my aim. The rail mounted atop the receiver is fitted with after-market "green dot" night-sight inserts: glowing radioactive tritium to assist with target acquisition. The flashlight is side-mounted to the magazine tube.

The Benelli M4 wasn't designed to shoot geese from a blind or to use stalking deer in the misty hours of dawn.

This gun is purpose-built to be a man killer.

And as blasphemous as the thought is, I can't help feeling like the weapon is a gift to me from God.

I do a quick check of the action. Tori fired two shots at me. This model holds up to six shells, if I remember correctly: five in the magazine plus one in the chamber. So I should have four left.

But if there is one thing I have learned about firearms, it is never to assume anything.

I eject the shells to get an accurate count, and yes, there are four of them. The ammunition is the same Federal Law Enforcement Tactical 00 Buck I use in my Mossberg. Each plastic casing contains primer, a wad, and nine lead pellets. When fired at close range, a burst is capable of cutting a man—or a woman—in half.

I waste no time reloading.

I do not engage the safety.

I lift the butt to my shoulder, press my index finger against the trigger guard, and raise the barrel so I'm looking through the sights. The beam coming from the side-mounted light is dead-steady as I sweep the now motionless balsams.

"Tori?"

The wind has died, but it is snowing again, harder than before. The flakes fall straight down, sparkling in the cone of light. I hear nothing except the stomach-rumbling of the river.

It occurs to me that Tori might have a second firearm on her. A small pistol, for instance. Again, I can't assume anything.

If I were her, what would I do?

Call for help.

Especially if her sister is nearby.

Tori Dillon is clever. She thinks things through. But she also struck me as being as tightly coiled as a mainspring. Waiting doesn't come naturally to a person with that kind of jacked-up metabolism.

She's going to run.

Where?

The answer arrives like a slap to the head. Back to her snowmobile, of course. She's going to circle around to her sled and take off up the river to rendezvous with Tiff and whoever else she's enlisted in the hunt for me.

And I've just given her a minute head start.

Unfortunately, the struggle has loosened the bandanna around my leg, and I have to take a moment to retie it. The continuous trickle of blood falls into the urgent category.

I turn and begin to lope toward the beaver lodge, using the flashlight to make a path through the darkness. The heaviness of the weapon in my arms is not a burden. Far from it. If anything, the weight is a comfort. No longer do I feel powerless. Armed again, I might just survive the night. Provided I don't bleed out first or freeze myself into a state of confusion.

I have almost reached the channel when I hear the whine of snowmobile engines.

There is more than one machine.

More than two machines.

More than three machines.

And all of them are approaching from upriver and at a high rate of speed.

It's the fucking cavalry.

Tori must have called for reinforcements as soon as she found my tracks. I am about to be surrounded, outnumbered, and outgunned. All of those good feelings I experienced a moment before are extinguished as thoroughly as a campfire doused with water.

26

There was a note on my windshield, torn from a kitchen pad (*"Groceries & Shit Shopping List"*), and pinned beneath the wiper blade.

LEAVE NOW, <u>PLEASE</u>!

You find decent people everywhere, even in the worst of places, but I didn't honestly believe that I had a friend on the hill.

This wasn't a warning then, but a chess move. *Someone wants me to stick around.*

I made a show of turning in a slow circle to scan the street and the nearest mobile homes. No cracked Venetian blinds or parted curtains revealed secret watchers. Even the kids I'd spoken with earlier had vanished from the playground. But that didn't mean someone wasn't staring at me through binoculars or even a telescopic rifle scope.

I folded the note and slid it into a pocket.

Then I opened the Jeep's lift gate to check on Shadow. The wolf was awake but groggy. He growled and curled his black lip to show a fang that Lizzie Holman's tech had brushed while he was KO'd on the steel table.

"I know you hate me," I said. "If I were in your place, I'd hate me, too."

The growl moved deeper into the throat. He gave a half-hearted snap.

Now there's a threat, I thought.

"Look, I've got one more stop, and then we can hit the road. Seriously. We'll be home in two hours, tops. I've got a treat for you, too, when we get there."

It was a top round roast that had reached its expiration date and should have been yanked from the butcher's case the day before. I'd been planning on saving it for his Christmas dinner. But I owed the wolf something for boxing him up all day.

He snapped his fangs again, showing me he would not be won over so easily.

My phone rang as I was standing there. The cell tower beyond the trailer park guaranteed that Pill Hill's residents had excellent coverage at least. I glanced at the screen and cringed.

The wind was loud enough that I had to cover my other ear to hear.

"Well?" Marc Rivard said.

"Well, what?"

"What did Mrs. Chamberlain say about me?"

"You gave me the impression that you considered this water under the bridge."

"It is!"

"So why do you care about Mariëtte Chamberlain?"

The question seemed to stump him. "I don't

like having my name dragged through the mud. I didn't tell you she sent a complaint to the governor after I filed my report. Professor Chamberlain had been a big-money donor to his first campaign. Malcomb defended my investigation, but that was the beginning of the end. They were already looking for a reason to take away my bars. I hope you stood up for me at least. I think I deserve your support given everything I did for you."

Among the things Rivard had done for me, as my sergeant, was to release a live skunk in the trailer in which I was then living. He'd considered it a splendid prank. Even after months of scrubbing and shampooing, I had never been able to get the odor out.

"I told Mrs. Chamberlain that the investigation had been thorough."

"It was fucking bulletproof. We didn't miss a thing. Not one thing."

"Actually, Marc, you did."

"For fuck's sake."

"Your witness, Burch—there's a problem with his account. He told me that he glimpsed the professor from a distance of three hundred yards."

"You spoke with him?"

"I'm standing outside his trailer now. It's quite a lavish place."

"What are you talking about? It's a shithole."

Like many people who had been born into humble circumstances, Rivard had become a snob the moment he received a paycheck bigger than his father's. He viewed every mobile home as a twenty-first-century hovel.

"You told me you were just going to humor the old lady," he said. "Now you're reinterviewing my witnesses? It's a closed case, asshole."

"Burch claims Chamberlain wasn't wearing a personal flotation device. But the professor was dressed head to toe in wetlands camouflage, and his life preserver was also camo-colored. There's no way Burch could've seen definitively from that distance if he was wearing it or not. Why did Burch lie about it then? Why is he still lying about it?"

"Misremembering isn't a lie. Can you recall what you had for lunch last Tuesday?"

"A roast beef sandwich with lettuce, tomato, and mustard. And a pickle."

"Go to hell."

"Mariëtte Chamberlain swore up and down that the professor never *ever* took off his PFD because he'd nearly drowned as a kid."

"Maybe it came off when he fell overboard," said Rivard. "That part doesn't matter. What matters is Burch saw Chamberlain alone in the boat."

"But if he lied about one thing—"

"I knew you were going to undermine me."

"What?"

"It's not enough that you sabotaged my career and helped get me fired, you want to strip me of my accomplishments, too. You're going to go to DeFord and tell him that I fucked up the Chamberlain case. You don't even need to prove anything. It's enough for you to punch holes in my report. You're a sadistic son of a bitch, Bowditch. Has anyone told you that?"

Rivard was the first boss I'd ever had whom I truly hated. The experience had been hellish, but I wouldn't have traded it for anything. Those miserable months had taught me an invaluable life lesson. They'd shown me how power can pervert a person.

All of Rivard's many character defects—his pettiness, his personal vanity, his paranoia— became magnified with his new station. All of the motives he was accusing me of were projections of how he himself would have behaved in my place. I could waste time trying to persuade him that he was wrong about me, but he would hear every word as confirmation of my dishonesty and disloyalty to my fellow officers.

"I don't suppose the name Lynda Lynch rings a bell? I didn't see her mentioned in your report."

"Should it?"

"She's the matriarch up here on Pill Hill."

"That development was under construction when Chamberlain died. Aside from Burch there was only one other person living up there, some old trucker. He and the professor weren't friends, but they knew each other from around. Both were serious duck hunters."

"Do you remember his name, this old trucker?"

"I remember it was French." He paused to use one of his mnemonic devices to retrieve the half-forgotten name. "Bazinet. Vic Bazinet."

"What do you remember about him?" I asked.

"He didn't have much use for the Warden Service. Our guys had pinched him a few times for exceeding his limit of geese. He was out on the river the same morning as Chamberlain and Jewett. But he came in before they did."

"So Bazinet was a witness?"

"Only in the sense that he saw them together from afar. He didn't tell us anything we didn't already know."

If I had been the primary on the case, you can be certain I would have made a notation that Vic Bazinet had been hunting in the vicinity the morning the professor disappeared.

"He seems like someone I should talk with," I said.

"I'm done trying to have a polite conversation with you," Rivard said. "So what are you going to do next? Are you going to petition the colonel to reopen the case on the basis of what Arlo Burch could and couldn't have seen? Are you going to try to persuade the state police it was a possible homicide? I guess as long as it gives you a chance to smear me, it doesn't matter. That's all that you want, isn't it?"

I have always found that when I am angry, sad, or afraid, it helps to recenter myself in the natural world. I took a breath and looked around.

The only signs of life were a dozen crows scouting the park perimeter. More had perched atop the fenced enclosure around the cell tower. Once again I remembered the huge roost nearby that Charley had told me about. In a little more than an hour, as the sky turned from blue to purple, they'd begin assembling from every direction: hundreds, possibly thousands of crows.

I thought Rivard was about to hang up. But he came back with a question: "You said you were outside Burch's trailer. Who are you going to interview next?"

"Is there someone in particular you'd like me to avoid?"

"I don't remember you being a comedian, Bowditch."

"I've been working on my stand-up."

"Don't quit your day job."

"I genuinely wish you and your family a happy holiday, Marc. I know you don't believe that, but it's the truth."

"Yeah? Well, I have two words for you, and they aren't 'Merry Christmas.' "

Number nineteen was another double-wide, but far less palatial than Burch's. Dove-gray siding, black trim. The only addition to this one was a roofed porch that an amateur carpenter had tacked to the front. It was easy for me to imagine Grambo sitting in the shadows with a twelve-gauge across her lap.

But not on a bone-chilling afternoon like this one.

I was surprised, therefore, to see a woman hanging in the doorway, smoking a cigarette. She hadn't bothered to put on a jacket against the cold. She wore a flannel shirt over ripped jeans. She was also a redhead, but unlike the Dillon sisters, she was tall, buxom, and wide-hipped. Her hair was tied in a horse tail, and her face was painfully red as if someone had scrubbed her skin with steel wool.

"You're the warden?" the new woman said in a voice that creaked.

"I am."

She exhaled smoke through her nostrils. "You shouldn't be wandering around up here alone. You might be mistaken for a trespasser and shot on sight."

She made a hitchhiking motion with her thumb toward a POSTED sign nailed to the porch. Her hands were big and raw, too. It looked like she'd been washing dishes in boiling water.

"You have a problem with trespassers up here?"

Even her laugh was rasping. "What do you think?"

"I think you settle your problems without calling the cops. My name is Mike Bowditch. I am a game warden investigator. I'm reviewing a case from four years ago. A man drowned on the river while duck hunting. Professor Eben Chamberlain. Is Mrs. Lynch home?"

"What do you want to talk to her for?"

"She called me. Are you her daughter?"

"Granddaughter."

On cue, a voice bellowed from within, "Let the man in, Tina."

The big woman cast a peeved look into the darkened interior of the trailer.

There were no fancy snowmobiles or Jet Skis in Grambo's drive. The only vehicle was a salt-splashed Subaru Outback with studded snows. It was a modest home. A grandmother's home.

As I came up the stairs, a scrawny dog shot out of the house and past me. It was tawny, sharp-eared, with ribs showing, and a tail that curled toward its spine. It reminded me of the street dogs I'd seen in photos of desert bazaars: half-tame mongrels that no longer possessed the characteristics we associate with domestic breeds.

I could tell the little mutt had caught the scent

of the wolf on me because he screeched to a halt, bared his teeth, and snarled.

"Kick him if he tries to bite you," said the woman named Tina. "It's the only way he'll learn. Treasure told me you were prowling around up here, asking questions."

"You're her mom?"

"Uh huh." The breeze blew the smoke from her cigarette into her eyes. "She said you were looking for Arlo. You must have met my cousins. What did Tori and Tiff have to say for themselves?"

"They were very gracious."

"I bet! Too bad Arlo was home. The twins might have shown you a good time."

Given their hostility toward me, that would have been unlikely, even if I'd been amenable.

The old voice bellowed again from inside the house. "Let the man in, Tina!"

With a groan, the red-haired woman flicked her cigarette down into a patch of snow littered with butts. It sizzled a second, then went out.

We passed from the porch into an improvised mudroom, created by walls of quilts and blankets nailed to the ceiling to prevent drafts from creeping inside. Tina peeled up the edge of a down comforter and slipped beneath it. I heard music through the hanging bedclothes.

The air smelled resinous from fresh fir garlands draped across every table and shelf, strung up along the lintels, and sagging from the ceiling. As if that wasn't enough balsam, a pine-scented candle flickered beside a display of miniature Santa Clauses engaged in comically offbeat activities: Santa riding a moose, Santa in a Hawaiian shirt and sunglasses, Santa seated in an outhouse making his list that unspooled at his feet.

The music was some orchestral Christmas staple I recognized but whose name escaped me.

A muscular woman, somewhere between forty and fifty, with a torso like a keg of beer, occupied the seat of honor. Her features were surprisingly delicate in contrast to her physique. I suspected she had been pretty once. Even now her dark curls didn't appear to have been dyed but had retained their youthful color. She was wearing a University of Maine sweatshirt promoting the 1999 national champion ice hockey team, gray sweatpants, and fleece socks that extended beyond the toes like elf slippers. She wore reading glasses and had her face in one of those oversized cell phones the size of an eBook reader. She was texting—thumbs typing with scary speed—and did not look up as I entered.

"Mrs. Lynch? I'm Mike Bowditch. I'm with the—"

"I know who you are." She had a small, bow-shaped mouth made larger with lipstick. "My granddaughter Tori says you were asking her boyfriend about that fag Chamberlain's death."

"That's right."

"Why can't you people let the dead rest?"

I took the question to be rhetorical and remained silent.

Lynda Lynch possessed not one freckle, nor a single strand of red hair. The odds against this olive-skinned woman being the *biological* grandmother of the Dillon twins, or cousin Tina, seemed astronomically high.

The recliner was a model fitted with its own cup-holder. This one held a pint glass of what looked like white wine and ice cubes. She reached for her drink without removing her gaze from the screen of her phone.

"Turn up the volume, Tina. This is the Russian dance."

My first serious girlfriend had adored *The Nutcracker* and played it all the time around the holidays. She'd tried to drag me to a performance down in Portland, but at twenty-two I had been too insecure to attend a ballet.

"I don't see why you can't get an Alexa," said Tina.

"And have Jeff Bezos eavesdropping on me all day long? You don't think those tech companies are recording everyone's conversations?"

She had a strong Maine accent: the variety I associated with the lobstering islands Down East.

In my experience accents tend to linger within families, being passed down to children and grandchildren. They can be stubborn, only fading over the course of generations.

The Dillons had no such accent, nor even the hint of one. That, too, struck me as odd.

Lynda Lynch fell silent as her cell phone chimed. She squinted to read the illuminated screen. Finally she raised her head to meet my gaze. Her irises were the syrupy color of motor oil.

"You wanted to speak with me," I reminded her.

"I want to know what you're up to!"

"I'm afraid I don't understand what you mean."

"Don't play games with me! You've invaded our privacy here. And you're pestering my family with personal questions without saying what's behind them. What is it you're trying to find out, Warden Bowditch?"

"It's one of my jobs to review closed cases, to ensure that all official protocols were followed."

"As if!"

"Your granddaughter Tori said you had information about the death of Professor Eben Chamberlain."

She became quiet, and I could sense her cold calculations.

"Maybe I do," she said, nodding toward a rocking chair. "Tina, go make the warden a cup of coffee. Use those good Dunkin' Donuts pods, not the cheap stuff from Marden's. And get me another Bartles & Jaymes while you're in the kitchen, dear."

She pronounced the last word *dee-ah*.

Tina bit her chapped lip. "Sure thing, *Gram*."

27

It's a three-legged race. Tori Dillon is lame in one quad from a knife cut, while I am limping from a bullet wound. We have only two functioning legs between us, and we're both staggering as fast as we can toward her snowmobile.

I crash out onto the frozen channel, slip, and land awkwardly on the shotgun. More bruises if I survive the night.

When I raise my snow-dusted face, I see something so uncanny I can hardly believe it.

Tori Dillon has beaten me to the channel. She would have made it to her sled easily if not for the black monster blocking her way. The wolf has reemerged from the far trees.

Was he returning to the island to find me?

He stands there, long legs apart, huge head lowered, hackles raised. Tori meanwhile is paused in mid-step as if she doesn't dare move a muscle. Shadow has to be the largest canine she's ever seen, as big as a young bear.

Run away, you stupid animal.

Rising to my knees, I turn the flashlight on her. She has a red hand clamped to her wounded thigh. She's shed her balaclava, and her pale eyes are huge with fear. It's not every day you meet the big bad wolf.

I have a thousand questions for her, but the sound of the approaching sleds makes my priority clear.

"Throw me the keys!"

"Go to hell!"

"He's going to attack you if you move, provided I don't shoot you first. Either way you're going to be dead unless you give me the keys."

"You won't do it."

I begin limping toward her. "I can't control what he does, Tori. He's a wild animal."

She considers this and reaches into a zipped pocket on her jacket.

"Don't be stupid and try something cute," I say.

She cocks her arm. I don't like the look of her wind-up.

"Underhand!"

Tori's expression changes in the snow-fuzzed light. The fear passes, and the old belligerence returns. She's clever and I know she's trying to think of a way to prolong the stalemate. She needs to stall long enough for Tiff and the rest of their associates to come racing to the rescue. I am sure she considers making a break. But the wolf is an unknown quantity. Maybe fleeing will trigger his predatory impulses.

"Shadow!"

As if the wolf will obey my command.

Tori tosses the keys. She makes sure to miss me. I follow the trajectory with the flashlight because I can't afford to lose them in the snow.

I steady myself with the butt of the gun and drop to one knee and swipe a hand through the snow until I feel the set of keys, beneath the fresh powder.

As I push myself to my feet, I hear the first sled coming around the top of the island. Out of the corner of my eye, I see Shadow bounding again toward the mainland. So much for my guard dog. I wonder if, during his years in the wild, he was pursued by someone on a snowmobile. Somehow he knows to tear ass, in any case.

Tori does, too. She takes off toward the beaver lodge, moving better on her injured leg than I do on mine.

Again I have my chance. My attempted murderer has turned her back to me. Her head, spinal column, and heart and lungs are all easy targets. But I made a decision long ago never to become my father's son.

With the shotgun slung over my shoulder, I step one foot onto the running board of the Arctic Cat. The engine is still radiating heat. I turn the key in the ignition and brace my legs. Then I grip the pull-start with both hands. I don't pause because I know how much this motion is going to hurt. I grunt and yank the cord, and the engine roars to life.

Gasoline fumes rise around me in a choking cloud.

I fall side-saddle onto the seat. I use my hand to pull my left knee up and over the center console to the opposite footboard.

The sound of a gunshot snaps me alert.

I release the brake and squeeze the thumb tab to give it gas. The machine practically takes off out from under me. Hardcore sledders would call this a jack-rabbit start.

There are more shots. One hits the snow flap which hangs over the track and the rear suspension. But it doesn't seem to damage anything important.

I sneak a peek into the side mirror. Tori limps from behind the beaver den, into the approaching headlights, waving frantically. A rider slows to pick her up.

The channel ice may be smoother than the broken surface of the river, but there are still pressure ridges that lift me into the air every time I hit one.

I have to focus because I've reached the tip of the island and see the river ahead again, pale where it is frozen and scarred with jagged dark spaces where the water is open. I turn toward shore but can't make out a path through the trees. There haven't been any more shots since the first ones. It could mean they're conserving their ammo for my firing squad.

The question returns.

Why though?

I understand why Jewett would want me dead. But why are the Dillons after me?

Meanwhile, open water looms ahead. I am almost out of ice.

28

As much as I craved caffeine, I did not drink the black coffee Tina offered me.

The music coming through the speakers was fast with lots of busy strings. Lynda kept time, tapping her fingers on the armrest. I would have wagered she played piano.

"So you're looking into that professor's death," she said. "And that's what brought you up here to our little Shangri-la-dee-da."

"Yes, ma'am."

"Ma'am! Ain't you the charmer." Again she dropped the *r*. "You know we didn't live up here when it happened?"

"We?"

"My family and me. Tina and the twins you met and my brother, diabetes took his leg, and his boy, and *his* family, that girl of his is pregnant again, she's like a cat, and, well, fuck, I don't know how many of us there are anymore. I don't keep count. We started moving in three years ago this past October, the twins first. The girls met Arlo and couldn't decide which should have him. But they've always been good at sharing. Ain't that right, Tina?"

The brawny woman stood by the window, smoking. From time to time she peered through the heavy drapes as if expecting a visitor. "I wouldn't call what those three are doing 'sharing.' "

"Tina's always been the family prude," said Lynda, who then cackled. "Family prude! Rhymes with *Family Feud.*"

In a few short hours I'd gone from the salon of a Rhodesian doyenne to a firing range housed in a nutcase's barn to an overheated serpentarium to the chambers of a hillbilly queen.

Just another day in Mike Bowditch's Maine.

"And yet you seem to know things about Eben Chamberlain despite never having met him. His sexual orientation, for one thing."

Her cell chimed. She glanced at the screen. Her lips didn't move as she read the text, but it seemed to take effort to stop them.

"That's just small-town gossip," she said, flipping the phone over, hiding its light. She took a sip of greenish wine cooler. In addition to the cup-holder, the chair had a storage compartment for the television remote control. For all, I knew, Lynda kept a snub-nosed thirty-eight inside.

When I leaned in the rocker, I brushed some fir needles loose from the garland on the mantle.

"What about Bruce Jewett? What do the local gossips have to say about him?"

The phone chimed, and again, she checked it before replying.

I was detecting a pattern.

"He's one of those end-of-the-worlders," she said. "Not a Jesus freak waiting for the Rapture. He's looking forward to the Boogaloo when it's open season on darkies. Now me, I don't see color, but for Bruce everything is racial. The man stays up all night stroking his gun."

"In fairness, he owns some expensive guns."

"Huh?"

"He's making fun of you, *Gram*," said Tina from the window. But there was a hint of a smile on her face, as if she didn't mind.

The ballet continued to play from concealed speakers about the room. The piece had moved into a section full of harps and horns.

I knocked a few more dead needles onto the rug. "I was under the impression that Jewett's family used to own all this land. He seemed to take pride in the fact that his ancestors were the original settlers. But as I was driving up here, I talked to some guys who were logging his upper woodlot. They wouldn't be relations of yours?"

"They would."

"It seemed puzzling to me that he'd given permission for them to rape that nice forest."

For the first time her smug expression gave way to something else: anger. "Have you ever been raped, Warden?"

The question—and the fierceness with which she asked it—made me blush with embarrassment.

"Because if you had," she said, "you wouldn't use that word to describe cutting down a few fucking trees."

The phone chimed—seemingly with irritation—and again Lynda checked the screen. This time, she felt compelled to answer. Her quick thumbs typed in a long sentence. Within a second of sending it, the phone chimed with an immediate response.

"Your granddaughter told me you had information that might help me," I said.

"Did she?"

"But since you and your family didn't know the professor and weren't living in Stratford at the time—"

"Do you have a family, Warden? A wife?"

"Not yet."

"I saw you weren't wearing a ring, but lots of men don't wear them, especially the tomcats. What about children?"

"None that I know about."

The laughter came out of her so hard she had to pat her chest.

"He's funny! Cute, too! What do you think, Tina? I could see you as a warden's wife."

The woman at the window coughed into her arm.

Lynda regarded me from her reclining throne. "I knew you didn't have a family—I can tell that about a man. There's a certain lostness to a

274

man drifting through life alone. I can read your isolation in your aura. Yours is red, by the way, *dark* red. Just like that Jeep of yours. But it's been damaged, your aura. There are broken sections. You have suffered deep and grievous wounds to your spirit, I can see."

"I don't know about my spirit, but my body's taken a few knocks."

She didn't appreciate my mocking disregard. "Have you ever had your tarot read? I'm not talking about some dumb college girl who burns candles and calls herself a Wiccan. I'm talking about the real thing."

I had once dated a woman with an interest in the tarot. She fit the stereotype Lynda had described in some respects; except this woman had been a teenage mom, a high school dropout, and worked in a McDonald's. Most tragically, her romance with opioids was even more passionate than the fling she'd had with me.

"This doesn't sound like new information about Professor Chamberlain, Mrs. Lynch."

"I'll explain the connection after I finish your reading."

I arose from the rocker, shedding needles from the shoulders of my parka. "Maybe some other time."

"He's afraid, Tina."

"Let him go, *Gram*."

The phone chimed once more. This time, Lynda

opened the storage compartment in the arm of the chair and threw the cell inside without even glancing at the screen. There was no revolver that I could see, but there was a box of tarot cards. The deck was old school: Rider-Waite. The woman I'd dated—if that was the right word for a relationship that had taken place almost entirely in bed—had used the same cards.

"*Gram,*" said Tina leaving her spot by the drapes. "Stop fucking around."

"Don't curse in my house."

"*Your* house?"

Lynda shook the cards from their box and then, with a dexterity that would have shamed the best blackjack dealer in Vegas, she shuffled them. She held the deck out in one of her small hands and said, "Cut them."

I pulled the top third off the deck and handed it to her. With a practiced flourish, she created a perfect fan for me to choose my card.

"Pick one."

"Mrs. Lynch, I don't know much about tarot," I said, "but I'm pretty sure this isn't how you do a reading."

"Don't be a pussy! Pick!"

When she raised her voice, I could smell the cloying wine cooler on her breath.

I selected a card.

She hid the face from me as she studied it. Her eyes grew merry. Then she flipped it around for me to see. The card showed a man lying facedown on the ground, in front of what looked like a blue snowscape. Ten swords protruded from his lifeless back.

"I'm guessing this is bad."

"Only if you take it literally," she said.

I didn't believe for a second that I had "picked" the ten of swords myself. Lynda Lynch had talent; she'd pulled off this sleight of hand perfectly.

"Nice trick. Where did you learn it?"

Tina was the one who answered. "The Taj Mahal in Atlantic City, when she was dealing blackjack there a million years ago."

The outburst surprised me, but it enraged Lynda. The squat woman leaped off the recliner with more energy than I would have expected and tossed the deck into the face of the much taller Tina.

"Show some goddamned respect!"

One of the cards must have hit Tina's eye. She now clamped a hand over it. "You *hurt* me!"

"Boo-hoo."

Tina glared at a closed door, leading to the rest of the house. I wondered who might be on the other side of it, eavesdropping on our conversation. It was the person, no doubt, who had been sending texts to Lynda Lynch.

The real Grambo?

Lynda pointed a finger at the threadbare rug. "Now, pick up my cards!"

Tina flared her nostrils. For a moment, I wondered if she might drive a fist into the older woman's imperious face. Instead she dropped to her knees and began gathering cards.

"You promised me information, Mrs. Lynch," I said.

"So I did," she said. "Someone who I won't name found that missing life jacket. He was helping with the search and found the vest by the river and took it for a souvenir instead of turning it into the wardens. I've seen it. The buckle was snapped, like it was torn off."

"Not Burch."

"You've met Arlo. Does that sound like him?"

"Where can I find this unnamed person?"

"Maybe you already have."

"Are you talking about Jewett?"

"Here's the thing you law-enforcement guys never understand. You come into a place, asking your prying questions, stirring up trouble between neighbors. And then you get to go home to your families. Not in your case. I mean in general. But we've got to continue living with each other. If you want to know the man I'm talking about, figure it out yourself, smarty-pants."

"Why tell me about it then?"

"Because I promised I would. I'll give you one clue. He has a red aura, too."

"In that case it should be a piece of cake."

Despite her feigned outrage at my intrusion on

Pill Hill, she seemed to want me to stick around and continue asking questions.

But why?

Another realization hit me on my way out the door.

Sometime during Lynda Lynch's magic trick, the phone in the recliner had gone quiet. I wondered how worried I should be.

29

I have no choice but to leave the ice. I let up on the gas, looking for an escape route.

Off to my left, I catch the stuttering flashes of headlights through the trees—a vehicle moving parallel to me, only faster. There must be a road up there, running along this branch of the Androscoggin. A road means cars, houses, people. A road means help.

I just need to find a way to get there.

The answer appears so suddenly, it's like wish fulfillment: a boat launch.

It's no municipal lot with a paved parking area and a ridged concrete ramp plunging into the water. It's more of a Jeep trail that sneaks out of the woods and peters out at the river's edge. I can't imagine someone backing a trailer down that narrow cut, but boaters must manage it in the summer.

I wrench the handlebars to the left and hit the gas again. My side mirrors are reflecting so much light from the machines chasing me, it's amazing I'm not blinded. The Dillons have stopped shooting which can only mean they have something worse planned for me.

One of the riders tries to slip past on the left, but I veer toward him—or her—and they ricochet off an upright ice floe to avoid a collision. The crunch of metal resonates in my teeth.

I reach the launch seconds before the rider can regain control of their dented sled.

Branches and boughs crowd together over the uphill trail, and there is less snow here than in the open. There is just as much as ice, however. A stream of meltwater, following the steep path, has frozen hard, forming a natural bobsled chute.

The night roars. The forest flickers and flashes with artificial lights.

I stand up straight and pull hard on the bars. The skegs on the sled don't appreciate the slickness of this path.

I have in my mind the annual Snodeo in Rangeley where the organizers stage contests called hill drags in which two riders race up an incline. I've never competed in one, but I've stood in the crowd along the racecourse. I've seen sleds tip over and crash. I've helped evacuate a racer whose machine landed on top of him. I have no illusions about the odds of my making it to the road—Tori and the others are that much up my ass.

Now I am past the ice patch and on firmer ground.

The rider behind me is less fortunate. I hear a shout, glance into the mirror, and see the nearest sled sliding away as if on a greased sheet. Its picks, if it has them, can't find anything to grasp.

I can't hear above the sound of my own engine the metal-on-metal screech of the runaway snowmobile colliding with the machine behind it, but I can imagine it.

Two down.

For an instant, I congratulate myself on having caught a break.

Then I see vaporous cones of light through the trees beside me. A blue Ski Doo has swerved around the pile-up and is slaloming uphill through the oaks and pines. It's got to be the Backcountry model, built for busting a trail through deep powder. These mountain sleds aren't built to carry two people, but this one is. It helps that Tori weighs so little, but still it's a precarious position, and the engine is laboring under the added stress.

The driver is skilled and experienced, though. Past the slippery stretch, he or she returns to the boat launch trail. The powder being kicked up by my track forces them to hang back or be blinded. It's not like a car chase where they can accelerate and ram me from behind. They can only hang as close as they dare to my tail and wait for me to mess up.

Fortunately for me, Tori literally has her hands full, holding tight to the driver's waist. Otherwise, she could easily shoot me, assuming (as I have to) that she has access to a firearm.

The driver keeps pressing, then falling back the

moment airborne ice pellets begin striking his windshield.

I touch the brakes, hoping that'll back them off, but they're not fooled.

That's when I see the chain ahead. In the snow-blown beams, a sagging silver line stretches across the trail. When the town closed the launch for the winter, someone must have locked off the entrance. As powerful as the engine is of my stolen Arctic Cat, it can't snap chain links made of zinc-plated steel. If I don't stop or turn aside, the impact will send me somersaulting onto the road beyond. I wouldn't survive even if I were wearing a helmet.

I don't think my situation can get any worse. Then I spot the snowmobile waiting for me beyond the chain. Those stuttering lights I'd seen along the hillside—they belonged to a sled shooting along the road to cut me off at the literal pass.

Nearing the chain, my headlights illuminate a dismounted figure dressed in black coveralls and a black helmet. The size and shape of the rider suggest it might be Tori's sister, Tiff. She points a scoped rifle down the trail. A red light flickers atop the rail of the AR-15. A laser sight.

My concealed vest is rated Level IIIA, heavy-duty, but not specced to stop a .223 round fired from twenty yards.

There's only one crazy thing I can think to do.

I accelerate as if preparing to ram the chain.

Tiff hesitates, the red light jerks upward as she dives for cover.

Seconds before impact I bring my good leg over the center of the machine and leap to the side into a cluster of baby pines. The steel chain scrapes the hood of the sled, pulls the windscreen off, catches the handlebars, and causes the Arctic Cat to complete a somersault.

I land on my right arm and shoulder in the saplings. Fortunately there are no big stones or stumps lurking beneath them.

The smashed sled provides a spectacular diversion. From my back, in the flattened conifers, I squeeze the shotgun trigger and blast a random hole in the night. I am not aiming at anything or anyone. I just want them all to duck and cover.

Panicked, Tiff lets off her own unaimed burst of semi-automatic fire.

Behind me on the hillside, Tori shouts at her sister to stop.

I push myself to my knees and grab a sapling with my gloved left hand to regain my footing. I expect to be shot before I can take a step toward the broken chain, the smoking, demolished sled.

But there are no more shots—not from above at least. Someone, behind me, down the hill, is trying to send bullets my way in vain. It sounds like a handgun. *Pop, pop, pop.*

I stagger around one of the steel posts to which the limp chain is hooked, looking for Tiff.

I don't want to shoot her, but I am prepared to do so.

The breeze has swirled the exhaust from her idling snowmobile into its headlights. The effect is eerie: a glowing blue vapor of snow and smoke. The air tastes of spilled gasoline.

I see Tiff Dillon sitting on her ass in the road, fiddling with her gun.

She's thrown off her helmet to deal with her malfunctioning rifle. She aims it at me, pulls the trigger, and nothing happens.

She keeps trying the trigger. Even the best guns are subject to misuse and misfires.

Has she bent the barrel?

Has she mistakenly engaged the safety?

Somehow ejected the magazine?

I don't have time to wait for her to figure out the problem. She is desperate, terrified, and under the mistaken belief that I am going to gun her down.

It must blow her mind when, instead, I steal her ride.

30

Outside Grambo's trailer, the dog with the curled tail was barking at my Jeep. He must have scented the wolf. I was half-tempted to open the kennel to see what would happen. Shadow was overdue for lunch.

"Hey!"

The yapper laid his ears flat against his skull and snarled at me. Then he recommenced his leaping attacks on my rear bumper.

The sun had become a pale yellow spot fading into clouds that weren't there when I entered Grambo's trailer. The wind had turned and was coming from the northwest, not steadily but in half-hearted gusts. For the first time all day, I tasted snow on the air. Emma Cronk's spell seemed to be working.

The little cur slunk off a few paces as I approached the Jeep, then rushed to the bumper after I'd climbed inside.

Shadow let out a yawn that ended in a growl.

I couldn't see the wolf inside the crate, but the Jeep smelled of his urine-soaked blanket.

"Did the barking wake you?"

He jabbed the cage door with his nose, then proceeded to gnaw at the metal. If he kept it up, he might break one of his shiny clean teeth.

"I know you've had a shitty day, brother. But we're finally going home. I just have to make one last stop."

He huffed.

"Yeah, I know I said that before."

I was so intent on the wolf that I was startled upright by a rapping at my window.

Tina Dillon—I assumed that was her surname since she wore no wedding ring—had come out of her grandmother's trailer and was looming beside the door in a black parka. I couldn't see her hands.

When I was a new graduate of the criminal justice academy, and for some years afterward, I had been prone to paranoia in these situations. Someone would approach my window, and I was positive they were going to shoot me through the glass. Our instructors had shown us dash-cam videos of law-enforcement officers being ambushed, overpowered, and assassinated during "routine" traffic stops. Out of a well-placed concern for our safety, they had cultivated a fear in us of the very people we would be policing.

Like everyone in the years since, I had seen the news stories of the cops who leapt out of cruisers with guns drawn: the stupid, life-ending mistakes. And I had endeavored to change my mind-set, to cultivate the bravery inside myself instead of the fear. Most people are good, after all.

Even so, I kept my hand on my sidearm as I powered down the window.

She had the parka hood up over her russet hair. The sunlight was dimming but still brighter than it had been inside the trailer, and I noticed she had a yellow half-moon beneath her left eye. Someone had punched her, some time ago. At six feet tall and two hundred pounds, she was a physically imposing person. Whoever had attacked her hadn't been afraid of being beaten to a pulp.

"Would you mind calling off your attack dog?" I said.

"He ain't mine," she said in that same smoke-strained voice.

"Whose is he?"

"Someone who died last year." She stepped clear of the Jeep and shouted at the dog. "Shut it, Waffles!"

The cur fell silent.

"What can I do for you, Tina?"

She coughed into her fist. "If I give you a name, you've got to promise you didn't hear it from me."

I hadn't taken Tina Dillon for a potential ally, the way she'd sneered at me inside Grambo's living room.

"Do you mean the man who found the life vest?"

"You're not going to find the guy from his fucking aura."

"Who is he?"

"Promise first."

"All right."

"His name is Vic Bazinet. He lives down at number two. He drives one of those septic trucks. If he's home, you can't miss it. Otherwise look for a blue Corolla. It belongs to his cunt daughter, Felice."

I had never appreciated that word used for a woman but wasn't about to lecture her on profanity.

"Bibi told me she had a friend named Felice," I said.

"A friend! That's one way to put it." She scissored the fingers of both her hands together. "You understand what I'm saying? Felice lives with her dad and her two brats, Levi and Noah."

I recognized the name of Levi. He had been the rude boy playing with Tina's daughter, Treasure.

"No offense, Tina, but you don't strike me as the neighborhood watch type. Why are you telling me this?"

Laughter brought on another coughing fit. "Felice took my man," she said, hoarsely. "It sounds like a cheesy country song, don't it? Anyway, he's not in the picture anymore."

"I thought you said—"

"That girl swings every which way. Jamal turned her lez again, is my guess."

"You're referring to the man Felice 'stole' from you?"

"Jamal Marquess."

"He's dead?"

She widened her tired eyes. "How the hell did you guess that?"

"You said this Jamal was out of the picture. You said that dog, Waffles, used to belong to someone who died. What happened to Mr. Marquess?"

She shook a Kool out of the pack. She brought up a lighter, sparked a flame, and took a long drag on the cigarette so that the end sizzled. Her gaze remained focused on mine the entire time. The calculation was plain for me to see.

"Jamal fell asleep with a bottle of Bombay gin and a blunt," she said, exhaling smoke. "He managed to light his carpet on fire, but he was too drunk to wake up. Waffles got out somehow. Now that dog sort of belongs to everyone—we feed him scraps. But sooner or later, someone's going to run over the little shit, probably on purpose. It might even be me."

The pitiless way she told the story made me question the accidental nature of Jamal's tragic end. I was under the impression that Tina Dillon had no problem with me jumping to a more nefarious conclusion. She enjoyed arousing my suspicions, in fact.

"The funny thing is, I didn't even like the asshole," she said, aware of my turn of mind.

"I knew Jamal was using me. I knew he was a player. Would've been fine if he hadn't knocked me up same time he was fucking Felice. The day I let a man disrespect me—I don't care how big his dick is. He got what he deserved."

"Is that a confession?"

For the first time, she showed me her tobacco-stained smile. "I have no idea what you mean."

I started to roll up the window, then stopped.

"The baby you had with Jamal—was it a boy or a girl?"

The smile vanished. "There was no baby."

The residents of Pill Hill were toying with me. I had zero doubts that Lynda Lynch had ordered her "granddaughter" to come after me. They were incriminating this Vic Bazinet for reasons I didn't yet understand.

Was it because they hated cops in general and game wardens in particular? And punking me was a low-cost way of getting kicks on a drab December afternoon? Or were their motives more sinister?

One thing I knew for certain was that Tina hated Felice. You don't fake that kind of contempt.

She hadn't radiated personal warmth toward me either. None of the Dillons had. Of all of them, Tori had been the most vicious. Her story about having an embittered friend on Maquoit Island might or might not be true. But there was no question that her animus toward me *felt* intensely personal.

"Don't get caught up there alone after dark."

A vision flashed through my memory of a septic truck passing me on the hill. I doubted I would find Bazinet at his trailer. Maybe that was why Tina had chased me down. They were worried about me leaving if my interviewee wasn't home from work.

I drove around the loop, looking for the green pumper. People who have trouble with the law tend not to use house numbers or put their names on their mailboxes. They don't want to make it easy for the police to find them.

The Bazinets' house was clearly numbered. And, as Tina had said, there was a Corolla parked out front.

I stopped a hundred feet up the street and took its measure through my binoculars.

In the minds of most middle- and upper-class people, trailer parks are places of generalized squalor. The prefab buildings are indistinguishable. The yards are littered with junked appliances and derelict autos.

Sometimes the stereotype holds true. I have driven through redneck slums, loud with barking dogs and crying babies.

But I have also visited mobile home developments that are as wholesome as an English country village.

Pill Hill seemed to run to both extremes.

Burch's double-wide had been over-the-top in its architectural invention. Its yard was an outdoor showroom for every motorized toy a man-child could want. Everything about it was extravagant.

Lynda Lynch's home, by contrast, had been frumpy outside and folksy inside. But not dirty in any sense. The word that came to mind was "grandmotherly."

Vic Bazinet's trailer was something altogether different. To use a four-letter word, the place was a dump.

Out front: a cigarette-burned armchair with a FREE sign on it, a smashed air conditioner on a wood pallet, a telephone-cable spool repurposed as a picnic table, a cord of firewood waiting to be stacked.

Nor could I overlook the vacant lot across the road. A burnt trailer had been torn down and trucked away for scrap metal. But the scorched foundation remained. Jamal Marquess, RIP.

It must've made for a hell of a view for Felice Bazinet: looking out your window at the place where your ex-lover burned to death.

While I was surveying the scene through my binos, the Bazinets' Christmas lights came on. Strings of green and red bulbs were nailed up and down the corners and along a roofline jagged with lengthening icicles. As holiday displays went, it was simultaneously tacky and heartbreaking.

The sight made me think of my own Christmas predicament. Where would I go? And more importantly, with whom? I had successfully dodged making a decision, but my time was up.

Aimee Cronk had once teased me, "It must be torture being loved by two women."

In fact it was. All the more so because I had always felt undeserving of love.

Without pausing to indulge in a bout of self-pity, I picked up my phone from the console and called Dani. I was legitimately curious about how her interview had gone. And sooner or later, we needed to discuss the rumor her mother was spreading around Pennacook.

To my surprise Dani picked up immediately.

"I was about to call you!" she said.

"Yeah?"

"I've got awesome news."

"What's happened?"

"Jemison wants me to come in for a sit-down. He said he'd been talking to people around the state, asking who he should recruit, and my name kept coming up. We really hit it off on the phone, too. I'm going in for an interview *tomorrow*. He didn't say it, Mike, but I think I'm going to get the job."

The feeling in me was of a bomb having dropped and yet failed to explode. The news was a dud. I registered the impact but nothing else. But at least the uncertainty was over.

"Congratulations."

"Aren't you happy for me?"

"I'm very happy for you." She worked so hard, and I was one of those old-fashioned people who liked to see virtue rewarded. "I guess the new job will mean you'll move to Greater Portland. You won't want to commute in from the boondocks."

Greater Portland was even farther from Ducktrap than her current rental.

"I haven't thought that far ahead. I mean, I don't even have an offer yet. I'm so excited, though. I've had trouble focusing all afternoon. This could be my best Christmas present ever, Mike."

"It puts the Nintendo I bought you to shame."

"You're upset."

"I was trying to make a joke. I'm thrilled for you, Dani. Really. I know how hard you've worked for this opportunity. You deserve it."

"You're upset," she said again.

"It's been a long day."

"Is Shadow all right?"

"He's healthier than me. But we're still not home yet."

"Where are you?"

"You ever hear of a charming place called Pill Hill in Stratford?"

"Vaguely," she said. "I'm guessing a few

dealers might live there. What have you been doing?"

"Wasting my time, mostly."

When I'd called, I'd thought of talking her through the events of my day, telling her about the crazy characters I had met. I'd had an idea of engaging her in the puzzle. But I found now that I didn't have the desire.

"Have you had Shadow with you this whole time?"

"He's been sedated until a little while ago."

"You shouldn't keep him cooped up like that."

"So he's been telling me."

"Jesus, Mike."

Any thought I'd had of confronting her with the rumor her mom was spreading around Pennacook was gone. We were past that now.

"I'll give you a call when I get home." I sounded tired in my own ears. "I want to hear more about what Jemison said."

"Maybe it would be better if we talked tomorrow, after the interview," she said. "I've got to study tonight, learn more about him and what he did in Indiana. I want to be the best-prepared job applicant he's ever met."

"Just be Dani Tate," I said. "If he doesn't recognize how great you are, then you don't want the job anyway."

"You've always been in my corner, Mike. You've been such a steppingstone in my life."

A steppingstone?

"You should head home soon, too," she said. "There's supposed to be snow tonight. The roads will be slick, and we're putting out extra troopers. I'm so glad I don't work the night shift anymore."

We said our goodbyes. Only later did I realize she never asked what had brought me to Pill Hill.

31

The new sled I have stolen lacks the raw power of Tori's. It is an older Yamaha, one of the base trail models, fireplug red, with a lower windshield than I am used to. It's a practical all-purpose snowmobile, not a flat-out suicide machine. I won't be outracing anyone on this nag.

Driving a sled at night in the snow is always a challenge. Without the benefit of a helmet or goggles, it constitutes cruel and unusual punishment. I find myself squinting through crusted eyelashes to lessen the sting. My ears are numb. My cheeks are burning.

But at least I'm on a road, albeit an unpaved one. The skis make a god-awful racket, and the lugs churn up buried gravel. This is as far from a joy ride as you can have on a snow machine, but I have no other choice.

I'm looking for a house, preferably inhabited. But the first one I encounter is a darkened ranch with an unplowed drive and a general air of vacancy. The vibe I get from the place isn't of snowbirds gone to Florida but of old people who have disappeared into a nursing home forever.

Lights appear as pinpoints in the mirror. I cast a glance over my shoulder and see that one of my pursuers has managed to avoid the pile-up. They are hundreds of yard behind, but gaining steadily.

When I turn back, I see another set of headlights—larger, brighter—approaching through the storm. Since we're on a collision course, it's hard for me to gauge the vehicle's speed, but I have the impression it's crawling. It doesn't seem to be traveling in a straight line either.

Chances are the driver will have a cell phone to call 9–1–1. And hopefully the presence of a witness will make the Dillons think twice about gunning down a law-enforcement officer. I flash my headlights.

Without warning, a cleared field opens to my right, a gentle hillside sloping into darkness.

When I refocus on the road, I see that the driver hasn't slowed, stopped, or pulled over. He has to see my lights. So what is he doing? Trying to engage me in a game of chicken I can only lose?

As I'm about to turn into the field, the strangest thing happens.

The vehicle—which I see now is a van—begins to sway as if blown by a tremendous gust of wind. It loses its grip on the road and goes sliding off into the field almost in slow motion and somehow without flipping over. While I watch, the errant van manages to find the single pile of fieldstones in the field. It plows into the ancient cairn, sends rocks tumbling, and stops dead.

A voice in my head that sounds a lot like my dead father's speaks to me.

"Keep going," it whispers. *"Don't be an idiot."*

Instead I brake and pull hard on the right handlebar. I almost spin 180 degrees around so that I am looking at the sled chasing me, a quarter of a mile behind and a closing.

I give the engine gas and leave the road, bouncing over icy ruts. The field is deeply furrowed beneath the deceptive blanket of snow. The sensation is like riding across a corrugated tin roof.

I come up to the crumpled, steaming van on the driver's side. It is a commercial vehicle: a Ford Transit Connect. The left door is ajar, and I see a man's leg hanging out. The foot, visible in my headlights, is wearing a rubber boot.

My first thought is I've killed the poor guy.

I hop off the idling Yamaha and glance up at the hill and see that my pursuer has stopped along the road. A nimbus of hazy light surrounds the sled. The rider stands silhouetted in the illuminated haze of exhaust and snow. Conscious of my shotgun, he or she must be waiting for reinforcements.

When I pull at the van's door handle, I expect a bloody corpse to tumble out, but instead I find the driver slumped away from me, into the passenger seat. He isn't wearing a seat belt. Under the dome light I see a leather bomber;

wide wale corduroys, a salt-and-pepper goatee; and a brimmed hat tilted forward over his brow as if he'd pulled it down to take a nap.

The bottle of rum he'd been sipping from has shattered on impact. Bright bits of glass sparkle. The sickly smell of distilled molasses rises from the vinyl and cloth upholstery.

"Sir? Can you hear me?"

He groans and flaps his left arm. I detect no blood on him whatsoever.

"Am I dead?"

Every cop has a story about a drunk who impossibly survived a crash because his body was as limp as a rag doll at the moment of collision. I've always thought these tales were bunk, until now. It's possible he has internal injuries, but I suspect a doctor would pronounce him in better shape than me were we admitted into an ER at the same time.

"You've been in a crash. You slid off the road and hit some rocks. Can you tell me your name?

"Reynolds."

This might be his first or last name, he gives no indication.

I sneak a peek at the ominous sled waiting atop the hill. "Where's your phone, Reynolds?"

"Why am I all wet? Did I piss myself?"

He means the rum. I have no doubt his urine would be close to eighty proof, too.

"Your phone. Do you have one? Where is it?"

"Somewhere."

His left hand finds the cigarette lighter in the dash and follows a spiral cord that disappears into the shadows beneath the passenger's seat. He lifts the end of the charging cable. Nothing is attached.

"I'm going to help you out of the vehicle," I said. "Do you think you can stand?"

"Of course!" His eyes are bloodshot, but he actually manages to flash some disdain at me.

"I'm a Maine game warden. My name is Mike Bowditch. I need to find your cell phone and call an ambulance."

"I've been drinking, but I'm not drunk."

"I'm not arresting you, sir. I'm just calling for help."

"That bottle wasn't open. You can see the glass broke."

"I'm going to take your arm, OK? I'll support your weight."

While I am busy with Reynolds, another snowmobile has appeared along the road. The first one is still there but it has shut off its headlights. Now the second one does, too. They don't want to give me easy targets.

I begin to pull on Reynolds's forearm as he steps gingerly down onto the snow, and for a second I think everything is going well, but he makes no effort to support his own weight, and the next thing I know, I have an overweight man, falling like a chopped-down tree on me.

I try to catch him around the torso as he topples, but my hands are still feeling the effects of frostbite, and he doesn't bother extending his arms to catch himself before he hits the ground.

"Oh!" he says, less in pain than in surprise.

At least he's out of the way. I dive headfirst into the vehicle, heady with rum fumes, and feel around under the seats. I touch aluminum cans, a crumpled snack bag, a roll of duct tape, and what feels like a forgotten sandwich before my gloved fingers feel a rectangular device made of metal and glass.

As I yank the phone out, my wrist trailing a ball of fishing line, the screen awakens with surprising brightness. And I see that it is cracked.

I push the home button, and nothing happens.

"Shit!"

The phone is the one thing I need above all others, and of course it broke during the crash. Meanwhile its owner lies, seemingly uninjured, beyond my outstretched boots.

Now I am pinned down, unable to call for help, and still bleeding out from the reopened wound on my leg. I managed to lose the bandanna and the clotted ice that had formed over the injury.

What to do? What to do? What to do?

The duct tape.

I don't have time for careful bandaging. But,

given the blood I've lost, I would be a fool not to make use of it. I have to be quick, and I am, wrapping the tape as tight as I dare around my upper leg—it's not quite a tourniquet, but close.

I tuck the roll in my pocket and raise the useless phone again. It glows at me mockingly. As I do, a hole appears in the passenger door. The driver's seat spits out stuffing where the bullet lodges above my head.

The next round, fired seconds later, misses by a wider margin, merely glances off the top of the van.

The third shatters the side window, throwing more glass down onto the already sparkling and booze-soaked floor.

I withdraw from the van and drop to my knees as the scattered shots become bursts of semi-automatic fire, punching through the sheet metal frame of the van.

My father speaks again from beyond the grave. *Idiot.*

Despite the proof of the past hours, I keep lulling myself into a false sense of superiority; I keep assuming that the Dillons aren't as intelligent as they have demonstrated themselves to be. Of course they've deduced I've been searching the van for a phone. Whatever else happens, I must not be allowed to call for help. The Dillons will abandon their plans to slow-roast me over a cookfire before I can identify them to a dispatcher.

Under normal circumstances, every attacker prefers the high ground, but because of the slope of the hill and with the van as an imperfect barrier, the shooters can't get the firing angles they need. Not unless they move, which I am sure they are already doing, flanking me on both sides. One or more will skirt the tree line while another will make a circle to come at me from behind.

The suppressing fire keeps me from poking my head up to locate a target of my own.

In movies people always take cover behind car doors and wheels. In real life, most parts of a car or truck offer no more protection than an aluminum can. Just about every rifle round in common use, especially those with a metal jacket, is capable of piercing the thin sheets of steel automakers wrap around their vehicles. The only reliable shelter is behind the axles, or even better, the engine block, and that is where I throw myself.

Drunk as he is, Reynolds wants no part of this jackpot. He is crawling toward the river like some stomach-dragging reptile.

"No! This way!"

But he keeps inching away from the cover of his ruined van.

I have to fight the urge to dart into the open and

pull him to safety. But if the Dillons have night-vision scopes, as they must, they'll spot me in a second. For the moment, Reynolds is probably safer the farther he gets from me.

I try the spiderwebbed phone again. The glowing screen enrages me. I feel like I'm being mocked by a malevolent gremlin.

I push the Home button and nothing happens. Touch the cracked screen and nothing happens.

But, of course, Tori and the others don't know the phone is broken. They have to presume that I am using these precious seconds to call dispatch for help and identify my attackers. Their one imperative is to shut me up.

Out of desperation I shout at the fractured phone, "Hey, Siri, call 9–1–1."

To my shock, a mechanized voice answers. "Calling emergency services."

Out of my peripheral vision I spot Reynolds. He has managed to worm his way further into the open. Two red dots quiver along his shoulders and skull. The lasers, I see, are coming from different directions.

Through the broken phone screen, I see numbers counting down, presumably to give a caller time to reconsider before they are patched through to emergency services.

Three, two, one—

"Throw out the phone," a female voice shouts from my left. I recognize it as Tiff's.

"Throw it out!" says a man.

Then, to prove they mean business, one of the red dots veers to Reynolds's right boot. There is a sharp crack. The crawling man screams as a high-powered bullet pierces rubber and flesh and pulverizes the bones in his ankle.

32

The woman who opened the door for me had skin the color of caramel. She was somewhere between stocky and shapely, with a buzzcut that on anyone else would have been her defining physical attribute. But Bazinet's daughter, Felice, had beguiling eyes. They were extraordinarily large, and the irises were a mixture of greenish bronze and copper brown.

"Hello?"

She addressed me through the storm door. The glass was covered with enough small handprints to tell me at least one child resided inside.

Her severe haircut gave her a military vibe. She'd gone all in on the bootcamp look with a white tee and green cargo pants. Her arms were toned and tatted.

"You wouldn't happen to be Felice?"

"I think you know I am. What I can do for you, *officer?*"

I sometimes fancied that, because of the middling length of my hair and the fact that I didn't use a razor every morning, there wasn't a sign above my head announcing to the world that I was law enforcement.

I produced my badge. She squinted at it like

someone who wore or would soon wear reading glasses.

"I'm Mike Bowditch. I'm an investigator with the Maine Warden Service. Does Vic Bazinet live here?"

"I think you know that, too."

"Is he at home?"

"No."

"Do you expect him home soon?"

"Why? What's this about?"

Inside a television was going. I saw the flickers of a screen and heard the tail end of a commercial warning that a certain prescription drug shouldn't be used by women who were pregnant or planned on becoming pregnant.

"I've been assigned to take another look into a case we investigated several years ago. A duck hunter drowned in the river above Gulf Island Pond. You knew him, I think. Eben Chamberlain."

"What is there to look into exactly?"

"Could I come in? It's not easy having a conversation through this door."

She glanced over her shoulder, considering.

Now that I was looking at the side of her face, rather than head-on, I realized that she wasn't as young as I'd first assumed. Late thirties. Maybe even forty.

"I'll come out," she said finally.

"It's pretty cold out here."

I'd been hoping to warm up, as well as get a

look inside the home of the mysterious Vic Bazinet. As if Chamberlain's life vest would be hanging on display on a wall.

"I've been cooped up inside all day and need some air," said Felice. "My youngest has been sick. I didn't know you could get Montezuma's Revenge if you were three years old and had never set foot outside Androscoggin County."

"The truth is, I was hoping to use your bathroom."

"For real?"

"Too much coffee."

"If you come inside, I can't be responsible for whatever germs you pick up." She undid the lock on the storm door.

Unlike everyone I'd met on Pill Hill, with the possible exception of Arlo Burch, she seemed relatively at ease. She was alert, of course. That is the natural reaction to a strange man showing up on your doorstep with a badge and a gun, asking questions.

The layout of the single-wide was cookie cutter. The door opened onto a living room, carpeted from wall to wall with a green rug that yielded beneath my boots like ancient moss. The floor was littered with school papers, discarded coats and mittens, boyish toys. Wheeled stuff, mostly, as well as figurines of superheroes and space warriors. An artificial Christmas tree, heaped with tinsel and wrapped with lights that flashed in a kaleidoscope of colors, asserted itself from the corner.

The boy I'd met earlier, the companion of Tina's daughter, Treasure, lay sprawled in front of a flat-screen TV, staring vacantly at the same wrestling show that the Cronk boys found so fascinating when they snuck over to my house to watch television. I was always disturbed by their obsession with steroid freaks yelling into microphones. It made me worried for their generation.

"Say hello, Levi," said Felice.

"Hey, cop."

"Levi!"

"It's OK," I said.

"It's not OK." She didn't sigh, but she might as well have. "Through the kitchen, second door on your right."

I passed a refrigerator decorated with paintings done by kids not destined for careers in the visual arts. The air smelled of soup cooking in a crockpot. Chicken or maybe turkey. As always happened when I was engrossed in my work, I had forgotten to eat. If Felice Bazinet had offered me a bowl, I wouldn't have refused.

I passed what I guessed was the sick child's room, door closed, and entered the bathroom.

I did my business without peeking inside the medicine cabinet because I try not to be that kind of person. My late mother used to say, "Integrity is doing the right thing when nobody is watching." She attributed the quote to C. S. Lewis, but in the age of memes, when words float around social media detached from their authors, God only knows who said it.

When I returned from the bathroom, I found Felice waiting for me wearing an expensive Canada Goose parka, pack boots, and a skeptical expression. I was taken aback by the fancy coat. It didn't match the surroundings.

"Find everything you were looking for?" she asked.

She assumed I had pried.

"Thank you, yes. But while we're here, I understand your dad was the one who found Eben Chamberlain's life vest."

"Who told you *that?* The Dillons?"

"You wouldn't happen to know if he still has it?"

"He never had it. That's just a lie the Dillons fed you. Which one of them told you? It was Tina, right?"

"I'm not at liberty to say."

She laughed without any humor showing in her metallic eyes. "I figured as much. Never mind. I don't want to continue this conversation here. Can you wait outside while I talk to Levi?"

"Absolutely."

Felice closed the inner door behind me, but it

was thin enough that I could hear everything she told her son:

"Don't open the door for anyone while I'm out. I don't care who it is. Do you hear me? I'm just going to walk around the loop with this man. I won't be long. Text me if someone comes to the door, and I'll run back here. Are you listening to me, Levi? Did you hear what I said about texting me?"

The welcome mat, I noticed, was upside down. I wasn't sure what to make of that. Maybe they'd worn out the top side.

Felice emerged from the house and locked the door behind her. She must not have trusted her son to bolt it.

Our breath showed in the cold air beneath the outdoor light.

"How old is he?" I asked.

"Levi is nine. Noah, the sick one, is three." She found a knit cap in her pocket and pulled it over her shaved skull. "Do you have kids?"

"Not yet."

"*Don't* is my advice."

If we were normal people, and this was a casual, friendly conversation, I might have asked how she'd come to hold that opinion. But the sky was growing darker every second and I needed to get down to business.

"I realize I don't know your last name," I said. "What should I call you?"

"Felice is fine. I'm married technically. But I haven't used my husband's name in a long time. Sometimes I go by Bazinet. I heard you were up here. On the hill I mean. Levi told me how Treasure held you up for five dollars."

"That little girl is the first Treasure I've met."

"It's like Tina wants her to grow up to be a stripper. Well, she's got the hustle down already, I'll give her that. Fortunately, she takes after Tori and Tiffany in the looks department."

"Actually, she only held me up for two dollars," I said.

Felice walked with her head bowed, but I could see she was smiling. "Would you have paid five?"

"Probably. When do you expect your father to be home?"

"Tomorrow. He's on a bus trip with his buddies to Atlantic City."

This was a lie. Lynda Lynch had said that Bazinet ran a septic business. Who else's pumper truck could I have passed earlier?

Felice had seemed so forthright that my instinct had been to trust her. Knowing that I was dealing with a liar disappointed me. She seemed clever and good-humored, and I had wanted to like her.

"Why go all the way to Atlantic City to gamble when there's a casino half an hour from here in Oxford?"

"The hookers. My dad doesn't get sex anymore

without paying. I feel sorry for him, but the pickings around here are slim."

As she'd intended, that remark shut me up for a minute.

We began following the loop counterclockwise, past the blackened ruins of Jamal Marquess's trailer.

"Your father has lived here a while, I understand," I said at last. "How about you?"

"I thought you wanted to talk about Professor Chamberlain."

"I do."

"We never actually met, but he seemed like a piece of work. I've always been biased against eccentric people, though. They're performance artists and scammers, in my experience."

Again, her response intrigued me, but I had to remind myself to stay on topic.

"How did he and your father get along?"

"They disliked each other, as I'm sure you already know."

"Why?"

"It's not the gay thing, if that's what you're thinking. My dad is open-minded for a man of his generation. He doesn't believe in casting stones. Unlike Chamberlain who judged everyone and everything. Humans were a disappointment to him, I've heard."

"Did they get into arguments?"

"I know where you're going with that. My dad

was hunting on the river the same morning the professor went overboard. But they didn't have any interaction—my father kept his distance from the professor to preserve his peace of mind—and the wardens cleared him of any involvement."

To me it sounded like a well-prepared story, which didn't necessarily make it a lie.

"Were you living with him at the time?"

"I was still with my ex down in Savannah. I had learned I was pregnant when he ran off. It seems a lifetime ago." She gazed up at me with an embarrassed smile. "We were supposed to be talking about my dad."

"We're just talking."

"No, offense, but I dated a cop once. Police never just talk, whether they're on duty or off."

"Ouch."

"Not that you had to work too hard to get me going. So many of my conversations are with kids, it's a novel experience to talk to an adult. Anyway, I moved back up here two and half years ago, with my belly about to burst. It wasn't my plan, coming back to Maine. Nothing in my life has ever gone according to plan."

"Whose does?"

"Bibi Chamberlain's. You were about to ask me about her, right? You know we're friends."

"How well would you say you know her?"

"What does that mean?" she asked with sudden sharpness. "You've been talking with Tina Dillon, haven't you? Because Bibi's gay, everyone up here assumes I am, too. I think there may be a little projection going on. Did you know that the most popular porn watched by women is girl-on-girl?"

Felice Bazinet had a talent for shocking me into silence.

"What else did the Dillons have to say about me?" she asked.

I cleared my throat. "That you're Bibi's drug dealer."

"You've found me out. Now you understand how I pay for this lavish lifestyle. The Porsche is in the shop being detailed, by the way. And you didn't see the cases of Cristal I got hidden behind the trailer."

The jokes were funny, but they didn't add up to a denial.

"Can I ask you a personal question?"

"If that isn't what you've been doing, I'm eager to hear what you consider an actual invasion of my privacy."

"How'd you end up here, Felice?"

"On the hill? I already told you. Pregnant. Bankrupt. A couple of bench warrants out for me in Georgia. *Not* drug-related. My hubby forgot to pay certain taxes on our business. I should've taken the hint. When you marry a snake, he's bound to turn on you, too, eventually."

"Where is he now? Your husband?"

"Somewhere in the Caribbean would be my guess. One of those islands where his income can't be garnisheed for child support. I picture him on a boat with a twenty-two-year-old in a bikini. Meanwhile I'm back home, waiting tables, living in a rat trap. I thought I'd seen the last of Maine after I left college. The day I graduated from Bates, I loaded a van and never looked back—until I ran out of money and chances."

"You went to Bates? I went to Colby."

"Good for you."

I waited for an apology, but none was forthcoming.

"Colby, huh," she said. "That explains a few things. The other wardens I've met have trouble speaking in complete sentences. Yeah, I majored in theater, but my thing was dance. A lot of good that did me in the working world."

"For some reason, I thought you'd been in the military."

"For some reason? I've got a buzzed head. The truth is Noah came home from daycare with lice, and I had to chop it off. Then I decided I liked the look." She pointed at a well-trampled path that led off through a cleared area, a vacant lot that was waiting for a new mobile home to be deposited there. "You want to see a view?"

"A view of what?"

"The river. The fields. Everything below."

Normally, I would have, but the bleary sun had descended into the skeletal treetops to the west.

She didn't give me a chance to object, though. She dug her hands into her pockets and began to trudge along the well-beaten footpath. Among the boot tracks were paw prints and the occasional urine stain. The route was favored by dog walkers.

"Watch your step," Felice said as she skipped over a crusted turd.

The trail entered some scrubby underbrush—sumac, willows, and speckled alder—the usual bushes that spring up at the edges of fields. A thorny sprig of multiflora rose tried to snag my arm as I pushed it aside.

When we came to the edge, we had a view down the winding road that led to the summit, past some of Jewett's land, and all the way to the professor's experimental orchard.

It wasn't a cliff, per se. But it was a place where you wanted to watch your step. Neither the drop nor the rocks below had stopped the neighborhood kids from sledding down the slope.

"Levi comes here to play," Felice said. The breeze tore the breath from her mouth. "I tell him he's going to kill himself, but Treasure Dillon eggs him on—that girl is as mean as Tina."

"What's your connection to the Dillon family?"

"None, thank God."

"I'd heard everyone here is related."

"My dad isn't, and I'm not. Arlo isn't. There's also—"

"Who?"

"Some others."

In the blue-gray light I could see fissures running down the Androscoggin where the river hadn't yet frozen over. There were patches along the edges of these open channels that looked like they'd melted when the sun had hit them but were hardening again in the twilight.

Beside me Felice put a hand to her mouth. "Oh, God."

She had fixed her attention on Jewett's land. The devastation caused by the skidder was even more horrifying when viewed from above. The three young loggers had left for the evening, gone drinking probably, abandoning their savage machine in the wasteland.

"They totally destroyed those lovely woods," she said.

"I met the guys with the saws on the way up," I said. "I don't think they knew what they were doing."

"You're wrong there. They knew exactly what they were doing."

"What do you mean?"

"That they're assholes like the rest of them."

"You mean the Dillons?"

She extended her arm toward the edge of the

clearcut where the stone wall followed the road. "Is that a deer down there?"

My father hadn't been blessed with much in life, but he'd always had spectacular eyesight. He could make a headshot on a buck, without a fixed scope, from a distance of half a mile. I'd inherited his blue eyes and his 20/10 vision.

"It's a man," I said.

He was too distant for me to make out beyond his form (short and wiry) and the color of his clothing (navy blue), but those details were all I needed to make an identification.

"It's Bruce Jewett."

"I shouldn't say this," Felice said, "but I'm almost glad they made a mess of his land. The racist piece of shit. I tell Levi not to go down there because he's probably got it landmined. That's not legal, is it? To booby-trap your property?"

"No, it isn't."

Not that it didn't happen. Years earlier, I had been present when a fellow warden tripped a wire strung along the perimeter of a marijuana grow and set off an improvised explosive device. The horrific memory—of a man torn in half—still visited me on bad nights.

The nightmarish image stuck in my mind now. Earlier I had been reminded of that botched raid on the dealers' compound. It must have been the horror stories people had been telling me about Pill Hill. There was something of the same hateful vibe here as I'd encountered in those trip-wired woods.

From the top of the bluff, Felice and I watched the solitary figure standing amid the stumps and waste. In Jewett's stillness I saw the posture of a man trying to process a sight that defied belief.

He didn't want this to happen.

"What else do you know about Jewett?" I asked.

"His crazy mother lives with him. She got out once and was running around naked. People still laugh about it. Misfortune is cause for great merriment among the Dillons."

"You disapprove?"

"Of course I disapprove. I'm not a monster."

Jewett wandered out of view. A minute later, I heard a four-stroke engine roar to life. A yellowish snowmobile appeared and disappeared where the road curved below the woodlot.

"I'm surprised he dared leave her alone again," Felice said. "Although maybe it would have been for the best if she'd frozen to death."

"You don't mean that."

"My worst fear is that my dad becomes like that—although maybe it's not the worst thing, to forget the pain of your life."

I was having a hard time taking the measure of this woman. On the one hand, I enjoyed our conversation. She was witty and intelligent, and although she was more cynical than I was, her life story made a compelling case for her worldview.

On the other hand, Felice had deceived me about her father being in Atlantic City. And knowing she had lied had colored everything else she'd told me. I suspected she might indeed deal drugs, as Tori and Tiff claimed. She'd said something about waiting tables, but that parka she was wearing had easily cost a thousand dollars. So if she had a sideline selling candy, why was she living in her father's dumpy trailer and not a home fit for human habitation?

"There's Bibi's house," she said.

At the bottom of the hill, the Chamberlain house twinkled with tasteful lights. I wondered if Mariëtte had given up waiting for me to return. I had no intention of giving her a "report" of my day, in any case.

"One last question about Professor Chamberlain," I said. "I'm trying to determine who might have wanted him dead."

"Some people are easy to dislike."

"But you said you'd never even met him."

"I heard the stories, though. Like how he'd be out in his orchard plucking apples by lantern light until midnight, and then before dawn, my dad would see him, walking *backward* up the hill for exercise."

"Backward?"

"Bibi told me he alternated each day, backward

324

and forward, in order to exercise all the muscles in his legs. What kind of asshole does that? And that tired old dog of his struggling to keep up."

"He might have been an odd man," I said. "But it's clear Bibi really loved him."

She seemed puzzled. "Loved him? No, I wouldn't put it that way."

"How would you put it?"

"Bibi hated his guts."

33

Reynolds was feeling no pain when he ran off the road. Now he lies in the snow, beating his fists against the ground and screaming questions at God.

"I don't understand, I don't understand. Why is this happening? Why are you doing this?"

Meanwhile the glowing laser dots have moved to his head. One of the shooters has steady hands. The red spot never quivers more than an inch from Reynolds's hairline. The other is shaky.

A man's voice speaks from the phone. "What's the nature of your emergency?"

"This is 2154 Augusta. I'm a Maine game warden, taking fire from multiple assailants. My name is Mike Bowditch. One bystander has been shot. Situation is 10–74. Send help."

"2154 Augusta, what is your location?"

"Leeds? Greene? Ping the phone for God's sake!"

"Say again, 2154," says the dispatcher. "I'm not receiving you well."

Then a woman's voice calls from the darkness, "Throw out the phone, Mike!"

Even if I don't say another word, the dispatcher is required to ping my location. He'll send a nearby unit to check it out, possibly a state trooper, possibly a deputy sheriff. Either of those officers would be driving into a turkey shoot.

Steady Hands very deliberately moves her red dot a foot from Reynolds's thrashing head and fires into the ground. The shot echoes across the field.

What choice do I have?

"Send every available unit," I shout into the phone.

And because I am afraid for Reynolds, I softly toss the cell at him. My aim is too good. It bounces off the poor guy's chest and lies glowing on the snow beside his flailing elbow.

The red laser finds the screen and a second later the phone disintegrates in a small explosion of glass, metal, and lead fragments.

The state police will have at least three cruisers roaming northern Androscoggin and western Kennebec counties, more with the bad weather. I can also count on at least two sheriff's deputies in the vicinity. Maybe a warden on patrol. Lewiston and Auburn have patrol officers working their streets, but the Twin Cities are half an hour away on these slick roads. Everyone else will need to be called out of their homes.

Can I stall for five minutes?
Maybe.
What about ten?
Not a chance.

"Now, throw out the shotgun," shouts a woman. I think it's Tori.

Law-enforcement officers are told *never* to give up your gun. The idea is drummed into our heads so hard it leaves a permanent scar on the cerebellum. Our first week at the academy, we're taught about the famous Onion Field incident where two LAPD detectives made that mistake and found themselves transported to a farm outside Bakersfield for summary execution.

I have only one card to play.

Tori, whom I am imagining as the leader, is betting I will comply with her demand rather than watch helplessly while they execute poor Reynolds. But if they kill their only hostage, they will have lost their leverage over me. I can hunker down, return fire, and wait until I hear sirens approaching. They'll be the ones fighting the clock, not me.

Those same thoughts must be going through her mind, too, because she locates the significant flaw in my logic.

Steady Hands fires another shot, into Reynolds's collarbone.

His scream tears a hole in me.

"Throw out the gun or the next one's through his face," Tori says, and her voice sounds even nearer. Thirty yards at most. She's left the cover of the trees, darted into the field.

Reynolds's cries are no longer even words.

My throat burns with acid that I can taste in my mouth.

I want to scream obscenities. But I can't let them know they're weakening my resolve. I have to remain dead silent for Reynolds's sake as much as mine.

They can't risk killing him, I tell myself. But I am not sure I believe my own reassurances.

Tori's strategy isn't working. She knows they're running out of time.

I hear a radio squawk to my left. Then her voice again: "Finish it!"

Now comes the hailstorm.

Bullets tear through the sheet metal and smash the windshield and the windows. They skip off the steel axles and puncture the tires. They whine and thud and crash. They dislodge snow that has settled on the roof. I make myself as small as possible behind the engine block.

There is a pause in the shooting, and I raise my head. Snow and broken glass fall from my shoulders.

I look over at Reynolds and the twitching of his ruined foot has stopped. I doubt anyone deliberately tried to kill him. They simply didn't care enough to avoid hitting him.

I will make them pay for that.

The Dillons are going to wait to see if they got me before they close in on the van. Maybe I'm as dead as Reynolds. But they won't wait long because they can't be sure what I told dispatch. Dozens of cops may be on the way. If I identified them to the dispatcher, Pill Hill might soon be under siege by the State Police Tactical Team and the Violent Crimes Task Force.

Did I give their name to the dispatcher?

Just then, I hear a war whoop, then footsteps coming toward me. Some foolhardy gunman plans on ending the stand-off single-handedly.

A fast-moving figure in Carhartt coveralls slides past the end of the van and, from his side, brings a black carbine up to the ready position, the sights searching for me in the shadows.

I pull the trigger. Double-ought buckshot punches a hole through his chest, shredding his heart and lungs. Lifeless, his body continues its slide, among the bits and pieces of the dismantled van.

"Todd!" a female voice screams.

My young attacker comes to rest so that only half his face is visible in the beam of the tactical flashlight. I see milk-white skin, a half-grown goatee.

It's the kid I spoke with earlier. The logger who was cutting down Jewett's woods.

What happens next happens fast.

A big-engined vehicle comes roaring along the road, and my heart rises with the hope that it's a state trooper. But if it's a cruiser, why don't I hear a siren? Where are the blue strobes?

I hear but don't see the over-powered truck leave the road and come skidding and sliding down the hill, and I understand that it is about to ram Reynolds's van and crush me in the process. The realization comes almost too late. There is not enough time to throw myself clear. When the moving vehicle hits the stationary one, the best I can do is fall in the direction of the cairn, where my head strikes stone, and in an instant, everything becomes nothing.

34

Felice led me back to the darkening playground. The crows I'd noticed before were still hanging around, and more were flying in by the minute. The growing mob reminded me of the scene from *The Birds* where crows gather ominously on a jungle gym while the oblivious heroine smokes a cigarette. I had never seen the entire movie, but I knew the sequence, and I suspected that if I watched the whole film, my sympathies would lie entirely with the birds.

Felice perched her butt on a swing. She gripped the chains holding the seat to the crossbar and began to rock back and forth.

"I'm sure Bibi told you she adored her grandfather," she said at last. "That's been her line since he went missing. She didn't tell you he was changing his will, leaving most of his estate to the college he used to run."

I tried to keep disbelief out of my tone. "He was rewriting his will?"

"It sounds like Miss Marple, I know."

"Did Bibi tell you why he was doing this?"

"The current president of Bollingbrook—that's the college where he was dean—had flown to Maine with an appeal. They were going to name a new library in his honor if he made a big enough donation. Chamberlain was too much of an egomaniac to resist. He wasn't going to disinherit Bibi completely or anything. He knew she makes decent royalties off her books, and she'll get money when her mom dies—if she dies. Lady Mariëtte told you she's *Rhodesian,* right? That woman counts herself as part of the master race. She plans on living to 120."

"Bibi told you this?"

"She was high at the time. I am sure she's regretted it every day since. We're not as close friends as people think. We never hooked up, because that ain't my bag. I'm only telling you this in case I'm found shot someday. Bibi Chamberlain is quite a markswoman."

Again I sensed that Felice was lying to me, not about Bibi's proficiency with firearms, but this story about a new will was outlandish. All I had to do was call the president of Bollingbrook to ask if he'd made an appeal to the professor. So why was Felice wasting my time spinning a transparently ridiculous story? She must have known I would see through it.

I didn't hear a beep, but Felice pulled her phone from her pocket, glanced at the screen, then tucked it away without a word of explanation. Evidently it wasn't the text she was dreading from Levi.

"What were you saying?" she asked.

"I wasn't saying anything. You were telling me

a story in which an old man is murdered before he can rewrite his will."

She began to swing faster so that her feet left the ground. "Make fun of me if you want, but it's the truth."

"You're suggesting Bibi Chamberlain killed her grandfather?"

"I didn't say that." Her smile was coy. The expression didn't suit her face. "I only meant that, whatever happened, Bibi didn't grieve for the old guy. He probably fell out of his boat, like everyone says. And it was lucky timing for Bibi. What's that term for when someone dies by getting crushed by a car while they're changing a tire or knocking an electric radio into a bathtub?"

"Death by misadventure. It's a legal term that describes a situation where someone does something to contribute to their demise."

"Like threatening to cut their granddaughter out of their will."

When I didn't respond, she laughed. "I'm joking!"

"A few minutes ago, you called Bibi Chamberlain your friend. Now you're going out of your way to cast aspersions on her. You're even suggesting she might kill you because you know her secrets."

"Forgive me for having fun," she said, swinging high. "I've been stuck inside the house with a sick kid all day."

"In that case, I'll let you get back to him."

She leaped off the swing in midair and landed with the agility of a teenager. "Wait! I'm sorry. What else do you want to know? I promise not to be a wiseass."

I had to consider whether she was worth another question.

"I want to know about Arlo Burch," I said.

"The eyewitness!"

"What can you tell me about him?"

"He's sweet and goofy, not to mention easy on the eyes. If he didn't have such lousy taste in women—anyway, he wasn't living the high life when it was just him and my dad up here. Then he fell into some easy money, starting with the reward. Arlo's circumstances changed overnight. And the hill's did, too."

"How?"

"He hooked up with those nasty girls. Tiff, or maybe Tori, met Arlo at the Brass Monkey, and they got their claws in him. My dad said it was only a few weeks later that trucks were hauling trailers to the top. Suddenly, the hill was teeming with Dillons."

"Your father didn't find that strange? One family taking over a housing development en masse?"

"Bruce Jewett thought they must be gypsies. He tried to scare them off at first by shooting in the woods below the hilltop. As if anyone could ever scare off the Dillons! By then, my dad had no use for Bruce anyway. My mom was half-black, and my father didn't like it when the fucker started going on about the 'dindoos.' "

"Dindoos?"

" 'Didn't do nothings.' Black people." The phone beeped in her pocket, but this time she didn't bother to look at it. "So what are you going to do?"

"Are you asking if I plan on reopening this investigation?"

"Yes."

Now it was my turn to lie. "I haven't decided."

She removed one of her mittens to nibble on a hangnail. She worked on the skin tag in silence for the better part of a minute. But she only succeeded in drawing blood.

"What I said about Arlo before," she said, pulling her mitten on, "about him coming forward with a made-up story in order to collect a reward? You get that I was joking, right? My dad always says, 'Arlo Burch is as sharp as a marble.' But he wouldn't have lied to the investigators about what he saw."

"What if someone prodded him?"

"Like I said, Tori and Tiff didn't live here then."

I hadn't mentioned the Dillons.

One of the crows started cawing at us, and the others joined in. Crows, in my experience, are as easily annoyed as they are annoying.

"How does you dad get along with the Dillons?" I asked.

"Fine," she said in a flat tone. "He plays cards with them."

Someone—was it Rivard?—had mentioned that Vic Bazinet had a gambling addiction.

"What about you?"

"You heard Tina's lies about me. If you think I enjoy having that family as neighbors, you've missed the point I've tried to get across. Those people are scary as fuck."

"I've met scarier."

"If you're not frightened of the Dillons, you're a fool."

"Is there something you're not telling me, Felice? About what's going on up here?"

It took me a moment to realize she was staring down the road at her father's house, its windows glowing warmly in the deepening cold. She was thinking about her children inside.

"I wouldn't be helping my family if I snitched on my neighbors, would I?"

"That's pretty close to a tacit admission that the Dillons are running a criminal enterprise."

"I didn't say that. But even if I did, what does it have to do with Professor Chamberlain?" Her body grew rigid and her voice became louder. "Why are you even asking these questions? You didn't need to come up here today. It's so . . . senseless."

"I'm asking questions because it's my job."

"I don't understand why you're still here. If I were you, I'd leave and never look back."

"If you hate it so much, why do you stay?"

"I can't abandon my dad. I can't leave him alone with them." She jammed her fists into the pockets of her parka. "What business is it of yours, anyway?"

"None."

"If you don't think I spend every waking hour trying to figure a way out of this trap."

"What do you mean 'trap'?"

"Desperation drives you to do things. Things you might hate doing. It takes away all your choices. Please understand, please remember, that everything I've done, I've done for my family."

This time I finally heard the message beneath her words.

Everything I've done, I've done for my family.

She wasn't talking about the past few years. She was talking about the past few minutes.

35

How long am I out? Long enough that by the time I can refocus my eyes, I am stretched flat on my stomach with my arms extended before me. My wrists are being tied together, and when I lift my face from the snow, I see a stooped figure lashing the ropes to an idling snowmobile.

The sound of revving engines reverberates inside my skull. Ice adheres to my lips. My mouth tastes of blood and exhaust fumes.

In my life I have incurred as many concussions as an All Pro tight end. But I don't feel like I'm going to vomit. Bells aren't ringing in my ears. Aside from the double vision and the localized headache, I am not experiencing any of the familiar symptoms of traumatic brain injury.

Even my confusion passes. I blink and squint and realize that the person tying the ropes is a woman. She has a scoped AR-15 rifle slung over her shoulder. The machine she climbs aboard is ruby red, which means the woman is probably Tiff, reclaiming her ride.

And the torture she has planned for me is obvious even before she casts a glance at my trussed body.

"He's awake!" she shouts, and there's no missing the joy in her voice.

"We've got to go!" shouts a man.

I get a glimpse of the big vehicle that rammed Reynolds's pickup. It is an ancient Chevy Suburban with a push bumper grill guard on the front, and it is the first to peel out. The sleds take off, one after another. At least three of them, maybe four. Tiff waits. She wants a clear lane ahead so she can open the throttle.

I have lost my gloves or had them removed. I close my hands around the rope above my wrists before she accelerates because I don't want the sudden force to snap bones or tear ligaments in my wrists. I don't know if it will help. But I know I don't have the strength to hold on for more than a couple of minutes.

When the sled takes off, there is an instant that seems elastic when I don't budge. It feels like a miracle has occurred. The knots have somehow slipped free. Then a barrage of powder and ice hits me and I feel a jerk, like my arms are being pulled from their sockets. The rope goes taut, and I am being dragged on my chest and thighs across the field.

The ground looks so smooth beneath its blanket of snow, but the sensation is of being pulled bodily across a cheese grater. My hidden ballistic vest absorbs a lot of the punishment. If they'd taken a moment to search me, they would have stripped me to the waist. But the Dillons are in too big of a rush.

Still, the pain—head, arms, torso, and especially my bad leg—is so intense my left hand loses its grip on the rope, and now my wrist is being squeezed as the cords tighten. How long before the rope severs my hand?

I struggle to keep my chin raised despite the projectiles being churned up by the sled's tracks. I am having trouble breathing. It's not just the pressure on my chest. The engine smoke is displacing the air from my lungs.

My legs start fishtailing as Tiff accelerates.

I pull hard with my right hand, straining the muscles in my arm to gain a few precious inches. I'm not sure how I manage it—adrenaline is said to give you extra strength—but I get hold of the rope again with my left hand. I throw back my head and puff out my chest. Skidding along on my forearms and chest, I reach ahead with my right hand, trying to *climb* the rope.

Tiff must be watching me over her shoulder. She doesn't like what she sees.

She begins to switchback across the road, moving from one snowbank to the next in a sine wave pattern. Being jerked around like this is about as pleasant on the spinal column as you might imagine. But the maneuver has the unintended consequence of introducing slack into the line that I can use to continue climbing toward the rear of her sled.

Tiff's attempt to dislocate my shoulders and

flay the skin from my body isn't working out the way she planned.

She tries something new. She veers off the road. I feel the bounce as she goes up and over a snowbank. When my body hits the plowed ridge, I go airborne. If I flip onto my back, I will be dead in seconds; there will be no way to protect my head in an upside-down position.

Maybe I imagine the sound of Tiff laughing.

But it comes moments before a terrific crash.

I feel a sudden slack in the rope while my own forward momentum continues. The next thing I know I am rolling on my side. The line catches around a tree and I am whipped halfway around its trunk.

I find myself lying on my back, gasping for air. I have no idea what has happened. The agony is so all-encompassing, I can't move.

A red glow rises around me to the black branches above. Except for the hissing of snow against hot metal and a steady, bomblike ticking, the engine of the Yamaha has gone quiet. The air tastes of burned plastic and hot petroleum.

I seem to have bit my tongue. With a great effort, I roll onto my side to spit blood. My wrists are still tied, but the rope lies in a loose S on the forest floor. I feel like a medieval prisoner removed from the rack.

Then I hear the whine of a returning snowmobile.

The approaching sled pushes me to try harder, and I end up on my knees with my bloody wrists limp before me. The left one is sprained. Maybe even broken.

I have trouble assessing the scene because, among other things, the headlights of Tiff's sled have been smashed. The only illumination comes from the two red taillights perpendicular to the ground. The machine has come to rest on its side.

One of my jobs, as a warden, is to reconstruct snowmobile crashes. Every winter I am called out to a dozen or more sites like this in the woods. Many of them are death scenes. I have seen this before.

When Tiff left the road, she must have caught one of her upturned skis under a log hidden beneath the snow. The jolt caused the sled to tumble as it broke apart. The spindle connecting the skeg to the chassis snapped. The shock-absorbing spring came loose. The front end crumpled while the machine, still moving forward, tilted onto its side, then came to an abrupt stop when it collided with an ancient birch tree. Birches will bend very far before they break, but the sudden impact caused this one to snap like a pencil.

I don't see Tiff beyond the faint glow of the dying machine. I don't hear anything at all except the engine of the sled speeding toward us.

You've got to get up.

But I can't. My body is too bruised, too battered. It needs time to recover from the damage done.

The snow is coming down lightly now, a few lazy flakes. The storm might have stopped in fact, and what I am seeing isn't falling snow but windblown bits dislodged from the boughs and branches above.

The returning snowmobile slides to a stop with its headlights trained on the wreckage. The rider leaps clear of the machine and throws aside her helmet and goggles. It is Tori, and I notice she has "my" shotgun slung over her shoulder again.

Her gaze is fixed on something beyond my field of vision, beyond the crashed sled.

She takes a step forward, then stumbles. Her mouth opens but nothing comes out. No words, no screams, not even a moan.

She drops to her knees and disappears from view.

Now is my chance.

Move, God damn it.

I pull my wrist against the knot, but it won't yield. Even if I get loose, I don't have the energy to outrace Tori on foot, let alone on her snow machine. There seems to be no escape, but my mind refuses to accept the inevitability of death after what I've already survived.

Maybe the dispatcher pinged Reynolds's phone.

Maybe responding units are on the way.

But it's not sirens that I hear next. It's the recognizable chugging of a V8 engine racing down the forest road.

My frost-damaged fingers are useless. There is no untangling this knot.

A white light finds me. I blink into its source. Tori Dillon has the shotgun aimed at me again.

I spit blood onto the snow and take a few rasping breaths. My tongue is beginning to swell. Not that I have anything to say to her.

Tori's face is contorted. It looks like a mask some ancient craftsman carved to represent the mortal sin of wrath. Her hands tremble. Her sister's were steadier.

A vehicle door opens somewhere behind me and a man says, "Jesus!"

"No," cries a woman with a hoarse voice.

Two new flashlights find the wrecked sled.

I don't recognize the man, but he's broad across the chest, with a strawberry blond beard and a mullet, and a 1911 semi-automatic holstered on his belt, which means he's another Dillon. The hair color and the guns are the family's field marks.

Tina, tall beneath her black coat, trains her light on an area beyond Tiff's sled. The man bends down and is gone for what seems like a minute. When he straightens up, he has a limp form in his arms. Held that way, Tiff Dillon appears as small as a child. Something is wrong with her neck.

"What did you say?" Tori hisses.

I hadn't realized I'd spoken. I feel her finger curling around the cold metal trigger of the Benelli. I don't dare open my mouth again.

Instead I repeat the words to myself.

Death by misadventure.

36

I watched Felice Bazinet set off down the road into the purple twilight. She had her head bent and her hands in her pockets. The swing she'd been sitting on came to rest.

There was not a breath of air. The stillness was eerie and ominous.

I had spent the better part of an hour in Felice's company and still had no idea what to make of her. She was a proven liar and an admitted tax cheat. Almost certainly she dealt drugs or served as an accomplice to people who did. There had been moments when I'd felt she'd been toying with me, and yet I'd never sensed malice in her, the way I had in some of the people I'd met that day. She seemed to have a conscience, or she made a good show of having one. I had no question she cared for her father, the elusive Vic Bazinet, who seemed to have run up gambling debts with the Dillons, if I read the situation correctly. And I did not doubt Felice's love for her boys. I found that I liked her, pitied her, and mistrusted her all once.

If her intent had been to overwhelm me with information, she had succeeded. She had stalled me long enough for the sun to vanish. I was to blame for that, as well, though. I had hoped to linger long enough for Vic to return from work in his septic truck.

A black cloud passed, or what I thought was a cloud until I realized the wind had died.

Thousands of crows were flapping overhead, moving in a great flock across the Androscoggin toward the city limits of Lewiston.

When Charley had told me about the roost, I hadn't expected anything this vast. The image that entered my mind now was of John James Audubon dismounting from his horse as a multitude of passenger pigeons darkened the sky from horizon to horizon—a living storm of wingbeats instead of thunder.

I do not consider myself a superstitious person. I reject the primitive thinking that tempts us to see ill omens in the behavior of birds and other animals. I never use the term "murder of crows," even in jest. But the pall cast by the flock touched some ancient part of my soul. And a shiver passed through me that had nothing to do with the fast-plunging temperature. I was overcome by the spectacle of these carrion birds so numerous as to be beyond counting.

I doubted I could capture their flight in a photo, but I dug out my phone, even so. I had turned it off while I'd been interviewing Felice. Now I found the usual texts and emails, but only one voice message.

It was from Stacey Stevens of all people.

Seeing her name made me catch my breath.

I pressed Start and held the cold glass to my ear.

"Hey, you. I heard my folks invited you and Dani to the house for Christmas supper. And I wanted to let know you I'm bowing out. I don't want to create a problem or make her uncomfortable. I'll be there Christmas Eve, anyway, and I have another invitation for Christmas supper, so it's no big deal."

She'd always been a lousy liar. There was no other invitation for Christmas supper. Stacey had friends in Maine, but not many. She had always been hard to know and blunt with her opinions. Before she'd left the state for Florida, she had been written off by most of the people we worked with as difficult and arrogant. And because she was a woman who did not defer automatically to men or use charm to win them over, she was described in the ugliest of terms. I'd never heard a woman called a bitch as often as Stacey Stevens.

Remembering this, I missed the second half of her message and had to play it again.

"Dani must think I came back to Maine to cause trouble," Stacey said. "But I didn't, and I'm sorry if my being here has been a problem. It's just that I realized Maine is where I belong, where my heart is." She paused. "That came out wrong. Maine is where I belong, is what I meant to say. The one favor I have to ask you, Mike, is not to avoid my parents. Please don't punish them on my account. They love you like a son, and it breaks their hearts not to see you."

For the past six months, ever since Stacey had returned, I'd known I needed to make a decision. Not choosing becomes a choice. Not acting becomes an action.

The last crows passed over.

Again I had to remind myself that nature was not sending me a message.

I watched the stragglers dwindle over the half-frozen river, and then I returned to my Jeep and the caged animal inside.

I wasn't sure if wolves held grudges, but I had a feeling mine did. No expensive cut of meat would make up for being trapped in a box with a piss-stained blanket. The series of growls he let loose as I raised the lift gate made his resentments clear.

"I know, I know."

Through the metal bars in the kennel door he glared at me with eyes the color of embers.

But when he saw me bring out the Nalgene bottle, he submitted to the drill. Even before I started squirting water, he opened his mouth wide. His muzzle always seemed longer with his jaws apart. His enormous fangs seemed more prominent, too, now that they had been brushed.

He caught the liquid on his tongue and used the tip to curl it into his gullet.

"Your breath isn't exactly minty fresh," I said, opening the Ziploc bag of moose jerky.

Charley had made this dried, smoked meat. The retired warden was locally famous for his secret blend of herbs and spices. Hunters would trade him meat in exchange for his dried delicacies. At Christmas he always presented me with pounds of moose jerky, turkey jerky, salmon jerky, even bear jerky. Stacey liked to joke that there wasn't a game animal in Maine's North Woods her dad hadn't jerked.

I thought again of Stacey as I slid sticks of dried meat into the cage for Shadow to swallow.

"What do you think I should do?" I said to him. "You've had better luck in love than me."

In the years he'd run wild in the Boundary Mountains, Shadow had somehow managed to pair up against all odds with a she-wolf, despite wolves having been declared extirpated in Maine for more than a century. Now, only a few lonely wanderers were ever sighted. And Shadow had managed to find a female who wasn't put off by him having been neutered as a pup. Evidently the need of the two canines to form a pack, even a pack of two, outweighed his problematic lack of hormones.

As a wildlife biologist, it pained Stacey that she had never met Shadow. Nor had she seen my house in Ducktrap, I realized. She had respected my relationship with Dani and stayed away.

To what end though? Dani was in line for a job that would keep us apart more than ever.

"So you don't have any advice for the love-lorn?" I asked the wolf.

His reply was a belch.

Painful as it was to give her credit, Mariëtte Chamberlain had been right about me. I was like a dog—or a wolf—when I got hold of a bone. The strongest man on earth couldn't tear it loose from my jaws.

Had Eben Chamberlain's death been a tragic accident or something else?

The question resonated inside me with the clarity of a struck chord. Everything else that had happened that day was mere noise.

I had started out thinking Mariëtte was one of those desperate people who require closure at all costs and must find meaning in tragic circumstances. Then I had met Jewett who was, if anything, more scurrilous than she had described. Lynda Lynch had seemed positively eager to cast suspicion on Vic Bazinet. And Felice, maybe out of some perverse humor, had sought to incriminate her "friend," Bibi Chamberlain.

Magicians rely on misdirection to perform their tricks. Con artists use obfuscation to conceal their crimes. In the course of the afternoon I had been subjected to both devious devices, and the same question kept bouncing around my skull.

Why?

To divert me from the truth under my nose?

To use my growing obsession with the Chamberlain case to keep me knocking on doors?

To stop me from leaving?

"I wouldn't get caught up there after nightfall if I were you," Bibi had told me.

It was too late for that. It wasn't even four o'clock and darkness had already fallen.

37

They throw me into the rear of the SUV, atop a bed of crushed beer cans. I have a container of gasoline for a pillow. The sloshing sound it makes is oddly soothing.

They've refastened my wrists behind my back, this time with plastic cables. These aren't the zip-ties you can buy at any home improvement store; they're specially designed for cops to use in place of steel handcuffs. I don't know the proper name for these restraints; I've only heard them referred to as "cobra cuffs." None of the methods one can find online about how to escape conventional flex cuffs work with these heavier pieces of plastic.

I honestly expected Tori to shoot me. God knows she wanted to pull the trigger. Fear of her grandmother must have stopped her. Or maybe she knows that the punishment Grambo has planned for me will be torturous. Where I am being transported is a mystery beyond the powers of my exhausted brain to solve.

To keep me quiet for the trip they did some tenderizing first. The bearded man had held me up, arms pinned behind my back, while Tori jabbed the butt of her shotgun in my shoulder, my solar plexus, my bleeding thigh. It didn't escape my notice that she was wearing an Israeli bandage taped to her leg where I'd slashed it.

I'd wanted to roll my eyes when she and Tiff had said they were home health aides (although what better job to rob old and ill people of their pain meds). But Tori knows about human anatomy. There are nerve bundles that, when pressed, can reduce tough guys to whimpering babies. She is a natural born torturer, this one.

Fortunately for me, they hadn't had more time. They had two bodies to collect—Tiff and the young logger who'd tried to shoot me behind Reynolds's van—and reason to believe that cops were on the way. I'd watched them carefully place their beloved dead in the cab-covered back of a Ford truck that rolled late onto the scene.

I didn't see what they did with poor Reynolds.

Now I am lying on my side with my knees raised. The bed liner under my cheek smells of stale beer and another foul smell I recognize. Someone shot a deer recently and threw it here, probably under a tarp so that the local warden wouldn't see. From the amount of half-dried blood and the overpowering musk, it might have been multiple animals. I'm riding in a deer hearse.

The surface is tacky from the blood and beer. My face sticks to it, and there is a peeling sound when I lift my head. Bristles of hair adhere to my skin.

The bearded man is at the wheel, and Tina rides in the passenger seat. The vehicle is large enough that there is a second unoccupied row behind them. At least they've got the heat jacked. It's the first time I've been truly warm since I went into the river.

Someone up front has a two-way radio. I hear the hissing of an open channel.

Then Tina says: "See you at the gravel pit."

The response is fuzzed, but I am guessing it's an affirmative.

The countdown to my execution has begun. The one consolation is knowing that Shadow escaped. The last sight I had of him, rushing into the forest, brings tears to my eyes. Maybe he'll find his way north to the mountains.

Why can't my last thought be a sentimental fantasy about the wolf reuniting with his lady love?

Inevitably I find myself picturing the faces of everyone who cares about me: Charley and Ora, Kathy Frost, Billy and Aimee and the Cronklets, Dani, and Stacey. The thought that they'll never know what became of me hurts almost as much as the physical punishment my body has endured. Because I have a strong certainty that mine won't be the first corpse the Dillon clan has successfully disposed of.

I try pulling my hands through the cobra cuffs, but they're too tight, and even if my left wrist weren't sprained, and both of them bleeding from the tow rope, it would all be for naught.

The road is rough, definitely unpaved, and was probably last plowed two and half storms ago. Sand and gravel rattle around the wheel wells. The muffler has a hole in it that causes it to emit a continuous farting noise.

My captors are making no effort to keep their voices down: another bad sign.

"Tiff was always careless," Tina says in her smoke-strained voice. "Just like her old man. I was thinking they practically died the same way."

"What are you talking about? It was totally different. Tiff wasn't riding an ATV. She didn't hit a moose."

"Both of them ran into things because they were going too fast, Tanner. They both deserve Darwin Awards."

"Show some fucking respect, Tina."

"My dad deserves one, too," she argues, before succumbing to a coughing fit. "I went to see him in prison the week before he died. And do you know what he said? That I should be putting more money into his canteen account. Nothing about missing me or his granddaughter."

Suddenly, I realize there's another noxious odor circulating in the vehicle, beyond the spilled beer and the deer stench. It is coming from the bench seat in front of me. Like someone emptied a chamber pot.

"Christ!" Tina says. "Do you smell that?"

"I think he shit himself," says Tanner.

"Bowditch?"

"No, the other one. People do that when they die. The muscles in your ass loosen and out comes the crap."

"Gross!"

Reynolds is in here with me. They've thrown his body into the SUV, too.

This really is a hearse.

That's going to complicate matters for the crime scene investigators back in the field. From the blood, they'll know someone died, and not from the crash. There will be footprints and drag marks showing a body was removed. And the license plate of the wrecked van will lead them to Reynolds. But they won't be 100 percent sure his is the missing corpse, not without first processing the physical evidence they collect.

Tina has rolled down a window and lit a menthol cigarette to obscure some of the stench inside the cab, but the smoke, from my perspective, only makes the miasma even more stomach-turning.

"We're going to have to burn this vehicle anyway," says Tanner. "We can't just drop it in a quarry like we did that other one. Those CSI guys can pick a fiber off a body and match it to a blanket that's only for sale at Marden's."

"Half that stuff is made up for TV," she says.

"Gram won't take that chance. I'm glad we didn't take my Toyota. I love that 4Runner. I couldn't have torched it."

"You would have done it if Gram told you to."

He actually laughed, the son of a bitch. "Hell yeah, I would. I saw what she did to Lynda for being cute with the warden."

But I'm thinking about what Tina and Tanner said before how the twins' father died. He crashed into a moose.

It's not an exotic way to die in Maine. I've stood over a dozen of those fatals.

But Tina mentioned that her own father had perished in prison.

All day I have walked around with a vague discomfort, haunted by shadowy thoughts that refused to take shape into suspicions. I knew I was being played but I was too blind to understand why. The "Dillons" were batting me around like a cat with a stunned mouse.

In my mind now their names began to stream downward like credits at the end of a movie.

Tori.

Tiff.

Tina.

Tanner.

The kid I'd met in Jewett's woodlot, the one I'd shot when he rushed Reynolds's van, his name began with a T, too.

Todd.

Now the realization passes through me like a hot flash.

These people aren't who they are pretending be. In an effort to escape their criminal history and start anew, they have changed their last name since our paths last crossed.

These people aren't Dillons.

They are Dows.

And suddenly I understood the reason behind the family's hatred for me.

When I'd first met the Dows, they were a clan of drug dealers, blackmailers, camp burglars, extortionists, and insurance cheats who lived in a heavily guarded compound outside the North Woods town of Monson. I was in the area searching for two hikers who'd disappeared from the Appalachian Trail. In the process I'd stumbled on a criminal dynasty.

To the world at large, two brothers had seemed to head up the outlaw gang. Troy and Trevor Dow had bullied and menaced the communities around Lake Hebron for decades until the Maine Warden Service ended their reign of terror.

Both were dead now. Because of me.

Troy Dow, fleeing the raid in which I'd taken part, had crashed his ATV into a moose. He had been Tori and Tiff's father.

Trevor Dow, I'd arrested. Less than three years later, he lay dead on the floor of the Maine State Prison laundry room. Tina, his daughter, had said she'd visited him the week before he was stabbed through the neck.

We'd thought the Dows were finished. But we had forgotten the rumors that surrounded the family before their fall.

Troy and Trevor were never the ones calling the shots. It had always been their mother, a little old lady who looked like anyone's grandma. Her name wasn't Lynda Lynch. It was Tempest Dow.

I should have recognized the danger she posed, but after Troy died and most of the male Dows went to jail, I hadn't considered the females a threat. I hadn't even encountered most of them the day I'd been in their compound. Meanwhile the matriarch had begun plotting her revenge.

When chance brought me to Pill Hill, she had seized her opportunity. She had sent out her granddaughters—none of whom were known to me—to string me along. And then used her friend Lynda as a mouthpiece, all the while staying out of my sight.

That morning Rivard had asked me, "How much time do you spend looking over your shoulder? . . . You've made a lot of enemies over your career. . . . And even the dead ones have brothers and sons eager for payback. . . . I always said your cockiness was going to get you killed."

And how had I responded? "It hasn't yet."

"Just wait," he'd said, as if he knew what was coming.

I wandered into their hyenas' den without a clue. Fortune had delivered one of their most-hated enemies onto their doorsteps. I'm surprised Tori didn't shoot me the moment she read my name on the ID card.

I know now why Lynda Lynch had been so attentive to her phone during our conversation. She'd been receiving texts the whole time. Tempest must've had fun sending out her dim-witted friend in her place. She was probably in the next room, barely suppressing a cackle while she listened through the wall to her ventriloquist's dummy.

When I left Pill Hill, I had been so cocky about having figured out the mystery of Eben Chamberlain's death. Even if I couldn't be sure of the motive, I was confident I knew who had done it. I even had an idea how Tori and Tiff were tangled up in the conspiracy.

But it was the crucial thing I had missed—the true identities of the Dillons—that was going to get me killed.

I roll onto my back and my head knocks the gas can. Not hard enough to hurt, but hard enough that Tina hears.

"Don't make us stop the car, Mike!"

I remain quiet. I know that Tanner won't be

stopping the Suburban until they're well clear of the cops.

As if she's reading my mind, Tina tunes the radio to the police band.

A dispatcher says: "419 Augusta. Last words came in broken."

Call numbers beginning with four are state troopers.

This one responds: "419 Augusta. There's a van in the field, but everyone who was here has cleared out. Tire prints and snowmobile tracks all over the area. I don't want to disturb them. I'm going to try to get my spotlight on the van from here."

The radio snapped silent.

"Why'd you turn it off?"

"I don't want him hearing that," Tina says, between hacks. "I don't want him knowing what's happening."

"Yeah, but—"

"Just drive, Tanner."

"It's not like he can do anything, Tina."

"I don't want him getting his hopes up."

38

Darkness had come to Pill Hill, but despite the hour, I wasn't ready to leave. I pulled a U-turn in what had been Jamal Marquess's dooryard and drove clockwise around the loop.

Light peered from Felice's front windows. A silvery thread of smoke swirled from the chimney pipe. Her father still hadn't returned home.

The next householder had crowded their small lot with inflatables. A waving Santa Claus, ten feet tall. A giant snow globe that contained a nuclear family of geographically confused penguins. I continued on, past glowing reindeer on rooftops, one lonely crêche. The grotesque figurines and Technicolor lights gave the neighborhood all the class of a carnival row.

Despite her fondness for Sugar Plum Fairies, Lynda Lynch had forgone all decoration.

As I idled past, I saw a curtain part and a wrinkled face peek out of the frosted window. My fleeting impression, before the drapes closed, was of pale hair and skin like an apple dried in the sun.

Maybe this was the real Grambo, the woman who had hidden in another room while her friend pretended to be Tina Dillon's grandmother.

As I continued around the circle, more blinds parted and curtains opened. Maybe they were all on the phone with each other, passing word along. The warden was finally leaving.

The last house belonged to Arlo Burch. Red candles glowed in its windows, but they looked less like Christmas decorations than lamps in a brothel. The Rubicon was gone—maybe the mixologist really had left for work—but the two Monte Carlos remained.

As my headlights lit up the trailer, the door opened, and the twins stepped onto the porch. Someone had called or texted to them I was coming. Tiff gave me both middle fingers. Tori did something more disconcerting: She blew a kiss.

Now that I'd seen the entire development, a question loomed in my mind.

Why was Burch's place the biggest, grandest place on the hill?

The reward Arlo had collected wouldn't have paid for this architectural showplace or the motor toys displayed in its yard. From the outset, I had assumed that drug money must have funded this monstrosity. Lots of bartenders had a sideline selling narcotics.

But Arlo was too dumb to run a successful criminal enterprise. The Dillon twins definitely had the smarts for that line of work, and it was possible they were setting Burch up as a potential fall guy if the DEA ever paid a midnight visit to Pill Hill.

The theory held up—but it felt incomplete.

Then, as I was nearing the end of the loop road, I passed the trail where Felice had led me to the overlook. And I remembered the lonely figure of Bruce Jewett standing in the dusk. And I saw clearly what I had missed all day. I stopped short and put the Jeep into park.

Shadow whined in his crate. He must have believed me when I said we were heading home. Here I was delaying again.

I grabbed my phone and brought up my list of recent calls. I hit the top name.

"Mike?" said Stacey.

There was no missing the surprise in her voice, or the delight.

My words came out in a cascade. "I got your message about Christmas, but that's not why I'm calling. I'm working on a case and need to bounce something off you."

"Off me?"

"If you had dirt on someone and wanted to squeeze money out of them, what would you do?"

She'd always had a musical laugh. "You have a question about committing extortion, and I'm the first person who came to mind?"

"I know this must sound strange."

"No, it sounds like *you*. But wouldn't Dani be

the better person to ask? She's the state trooper."

"But you understand how my mind works, Stace."

"Oh."

She paused, probably fighting the urge to ask why I'd doubted Dani's ability to understand my thought process. But part of knowing how my mind worked was knowing not to ask me that question.

"After I squeezed the cash out of them, I guess I'd make them give me things," Stacey said at last. "But I'd draw up fake bills of sale because I'd want a paper trail. Everything would need to look legitimate from a legal perspective. But really they'd just be handing over whatever I demanded. Now you've got me thinking like a gangster. I guess the trick would be doing it gradually, so as not to kill the golden goose. Squeeze somebody too hard, and they'll say, 'fuck it,' and go to the cops. Or they'll show up at my house with a gun because they no longer care if they die, as long as they take me with them."

The liquidated rooms inside Jewett's ancestral house made sense now.

"What if you owned a woodlot?"

"Easy," Stacey said. "I'd cut the hell out of it and sell off the wood. Eventually I might get them to transfer the property to me for development or resale, but only after there was nothing else left."

When I'd told her she understood my thought

process, I hadn't expected this tour de force of criminal thinking.

"How *do* you know this stuff?" I asked.

"The same way you do. My dad always says a good warden needs to have some poacher's blood in his veins."

"That describes me. I'm not sure it describes you."

"Because I don't have a dark side? You must have different memories of our years together than I do. What's this about anyway? What have you gotten yourself into? Because it doesn't sound like a typical warden investigation."

"Bruce Jewett."

"What?"

"Remember that name, OK?"

She brought her phone closer to her mouth. "Are you in some kind of danger?"

"I *was* in danger a few minutes ago. I'll be all right when I'm back on the road."

Her end of the line went very quiet. I thought I had lost the signal. But then she spoke again.

"No, you're not all right."

Stacey and Ora both had powerful intuitions. Charley and I joked about the mother and daughter being clairvoyant. But their perceptions were often uncanny in their accuracy.

"I'm going down a hill, and there's black ice. Maybe that's what you're picking up with your ESP."

"It's not ESP. It's me knowing you and sensing you're afraid."

That was why I hadn't called Dani, I realized. I hadn't wanted to show that side of myself to her. Even after everything she and I had been through, I hadn't been able to share my fears with my girlfriend.

"I'll call you to explain when I'm safely home."

If I had predicted what she would say next, it might've been something about taking care. Instead she blew my doors off.

"Mike, I love you."

One of my wheels hit a slick spot. When I'd regained traction I said, "I'll call you back, Stacey. I promise."

And with that, I hung up.

Her unsolicited declaration had filled me with so much excitement every nerve in my body was tingling.

But I needed to focus. The road was steep, and there was a sharp curve ahead.

39

They never searched me.

Because they'd only seen me using the shotgun I'd taken from Tori, they assumed I was unarmed. And because she'd beaten the snot out of me, they assumed I was too exhausted to fight. But no one thought to rummage through my pockets.

None of them know about Billy's knife.

There is no room for error in this. I will only get one chance.

I roll onto my left side, putting as much weight as I can onto my shoulder, and lifting my knees as if trying to touch my chest with them. Even if I were uninjured and had spent half an hour stretching, this contortion would hurt. As it is, I have to crunch my molars together to keep from making a noise.

I move my conjoined wrists around my lower back, feeling the edged cobra cuffs cutting into the skin under my wristwatch. I am trying to reach around my torso to slide my fingers into my front pocket. I hold briefly onto my belt, but as soon as I release my grip, my hands slide back again.

"Those lights up there," Tina says from the front seat. "That's them."

"I see it."

The SUV slows and the engine groans as Tanner downshifts. Then the vehicle begins to really bounce. We're going off road again, and it's almost more than the shocks and struts can bear. Whatever our destination, it's well off the beaten path. Tempest Dow wouldn't have gone through the trouble of bringing me to her alive if she was worried about some luckless deputy spoiling her long-awaited revenge.

I'm almost out of time. It's not enough to get hold of the blade. I also need an opening that'll allow me to use it.

Again I contort my arms behind my pelvis. My right hand inches along the still-wet pants fabric until I feel the copper rivet at the seam. Making an extra effort, I hook my index finger in the coin pocket.

I roll onto my back again, keeping my finger snagged, pulling the whole pocket open. The Suburban jostles as it goes up and over a rock or frost heave. The movement causes the knife to slide out an inch. I feel metal touch my finger.

Better not to hesitate. I make one final effort to pry open the pocket. The pain is excruciating.

When the knife falls onto the blanket beneath me, I almost can't believe it. The sound it makes, this big block of metal, seems so loud I can't believe Tina and Tanner don't hear it. As a distraction, I knock my head against the gas can again.

"That must have hurt," says Tanner.

He has no idea.

I close my right hand around the grip of the automatic knife. I can feel the raised button that will release the lock and free the blade. All I have to do is push it, and the spring inside will do the work for me. But cutting myself loose *now* is the dumb play, I realize. When they haul me out of the Suburban, they're sure to have multiple guns pointed at me. Even if I surprise Tanner with a stab in the stomach, someone will put a bullet in my head.

I have to be patient. And my luck has to hold.

I slide the knife up under my shirt sleeve, bending my wrist and cupping my hand to hold it in place.

I'm going to drop this when they lift me.

But it's too late to change plans because we've come to a halt.

The lights outside the frosted window have the quality of cheap strobes. I hear high-pitched snowmobile engines and voices raised to be heard above the whining machines. Someone knocks a fist against Tanner's window. He rolls it down.

It's Tori. "He better be alive," she says. "After what he did to my sister—"

"Have a look for yourself."

A moment later, the power gate opens seemingly of its own accord. I am blinded by a white sunburst. Even with my eyes shut, I know it's the light mounted on the barrel of her Benelli shotgun.

"I want you to know," Tori says. "After we're done with you, I'm going hunting, and I'm going to find that big black dog of yours, and I'm going to make a rug from his skin."

"He's not a dog."

Frankly, I'm surprised I am able to speak, given how swollen my tongue is.

The light wavers. "What the fuck are you talking about?"

"He's a wild wolf I was transporting. You'll never catch him. He's already twenty miles from here."

"My cousin saw it by the river half an hour ago."

God damn it, Shadow. Why haven't you run?

The next thing I know I feel strong hands close around my ankles. Tanner pulls me across the steel gate with no regard for my head. I fall and hit the ground hard. There's not enough snow to cushion the impact.

Miraculously, I don't lose hold of the knife. It's still there, pinned under the sleeve by my bent wrist.

Blurred faces surround me, their heads glow as if with halos from the lights of the vehicles. I hear another trigger being cocked. In the background an idling diesel engine rumbles.

Then a thin voice speaks to me from a half-remembered past. "Never thought I'd see you again."

It's an old woman, her face red from the tail-lights of the idling Suburban. Even bent over me, Tempest Dow seems as small as a child. Maybe she has shrunk as she's aged, as people tend to do. More likely, the matriarch of that criminal clan had grown in my imagination over time. Seeing her again in the flesh has reduced the woman to her proper size.

She's wearing the same man's leather jacket I remember from our last encounter, but she's added a scarf against the night chill. Underneath, she has on a pair of denim overalls she must have found in the kid's section of Walmart. The hems are tucked into a pair of snow boots likely purchased in the shoe department of the same store.

"Mrs. Dow," I manage.

"Missus! I ain't never been married. Besides, I'm Dillon now. All of us are, legally."

"I preferred Dow."

Her curls are the bone-yellow of someone who was once a red-head. Her skin is extraordinarily wrinkled.

"You and your warden friends put a stain on our good name," she says. "We couldn't use it no more without someone Googling us. My lawyer in Dover-Foxcroft did the paperwork for us. Cost me three thousand dollars. But what else am I going to spend money on at my age? There ain't nothing more important in life than family. And there ain't nothing worse than being alone." Then she adds, "Like you are right now."

There has always been something at once terrifying and ridiculous about Tempest Dow. The people around Monson called her a witch, and it wasn't entirely a joke. She'd actively conjured an aura of supernatural menace by placing the head of a steer on a pike at the edge of her property. Those tarot cards Lynda Lynch had used for a parlor trick were hers, no doubt.

I make an effort to speak clearly, despite my swollen tongue. "It doesn't matter what your legal name is. I told the dispatcher who you are. Where to find you."

"Except we ain't there. We're here."

Through the legs of the people around me I expect to see a gravel pit. Isn't that where Tina said they were taking me?

Instead I see a long weathered building with a saddle-backed roof, and walls scaled with wooden shingles. Decades ago, this low-slung barn must have housed thousands upon thousands of chickens.

Tina's mention of a gravel pit over an open radio channel had been another act of misdirection.

Tempest has another subject on her mind. "So you say that was a wolf with you before? I thought I felt an unusual vibration coming from your vehicle. Every species of creature gives off a different one. Speaking of vibrators—" She casts a glance over her shoulder. "Where's Lynda? Get up here, you walking dildo."

The dozen Dows around me—I don't care that they're calling themselves Dillons now—make way for the stout, dark-haired woman. Someone has beaten her bloody since last we met. Both eyes are ringed with bruises. She wears a bandage taped over her broken nose.

"Hey, Tempie," she says, sounding congested.

Tempest Dow bends over me again.

"You really thought this stupid cow was me? I knew you were dumb, but—"

"If you're going to shoot me," I say, "can you just get on with it?"

She straightens. "Oh, I am not going to shoot you, although I considered it before. When my granddaughter said it was you at her house, I got out my Smith and Wesson. I told her to send you over to my place with some tale. I was going to plink you the second you walked through the door. Then, I figured let's see if I can have some fun with him."

"I knew she wasn't you," I say. "I knew she wasn't Tori and Tiff's grandmother."

Tempest nods. "You might just be saying that, but I guess you're telling the truth."

"It was the way she kept checking her phone."

She turns her head toward Lynda, and it's enough to make the other woman shiver.

"And here I thought it was that dumb card trick she pulled," says Tempest. "I was sure you were onto us after that stupid stunt. Hell! I almost shot you through the drywall."

"Why didn't you?"

"Because I couldn't believe you didn't recognize us—Tina and the twins I mean. In your place, I would have seen the resemblance in a minute. I wanted to make sure you were a fool and not faking being ignorant."

"And you needed time to plan a better revenge."

She squats down so I can gaze into her evil eyes. My fingers feel for the automatic knife. She's less than three feet from me, but I'm being watched by her armed relatives. I won't have time to cut my bonds, let alone drive the blade into her neck. I have no choice but to keep waiting for a moment that might never come.

"People think I'm dumb because I never went to school above eighth grade," she says. "I can still hear their voices, all these years later. 'Tempest Dow is so little. Tempest Dow is just a stupid girl. Tempest Dow is nothing but trash.' I made them pay later, oh, yes, I did. Most of them never even knew it was Tempest Dow who turned their lives to shit."

She extends her small hand and pinches my ear like one of her misbehaving offspring.

"I've always been patient. That's what's got me where I am in life."

"You've done well for yourself, all right."

"Don't embarrass yourself trying to act tough. I told you I was patient. Your insults won't hurry me to shoot you and be done. We're going to take our time here. Especially after what you did to my grandbabies Tiffany and Todd, we're going to make your worst nightmare come true."

"It'll give the police more time to find this place."

For the first time, I seem to get under her skin. "That ain't going to happen. I already know I won't be arrested tonight."

"And how's that?"

"Because I have intimations of the future. I always knew you'd cross my path eventually—maybe in a parking lot, maybe at a rest stop along some country road—and you wouldn't see me coming. All I would have to do is push this into your side and squeeze."

She removes a small revolver, a .38 snub nose, from her coat pocket. She presses the barrel against my hidden body armor. She feels the resistance of the ceramic plate.

"Now what's this?" she says, then raises her scornful eyes at her family. "Didn't any of you numbskulls think he might be wearing a bulletproof vest? He's a game warden."

If they strip me, they'll find the knife. I have to divert her.

"Maybe you really can see the future."

She thinks I'm mocking her. She jams the gun hard under my chin.

"What's that?"

"Maybe all your wishing is what brought me to Stratford today. Maybe you made it happen."

She takes half a minute to process what I've said.

"I know you think you're mocking me, but that's what happened. It was my intentions that blinded you to my presence. There was calculation, too. That Bazinet girl stalled you even longer than I wanted. I only said to keep you around till sundown. Instead she talked your ear off. I guess I'll have to pay her a visit later and ask what she was trying to pull."

"She did everything you asked," says a deep-voiced man I can't see. "You have no reason to be upset with her."

"Don't give me lip, Vic Bazinet," Tempest says. "I won't tolerate lip from you or your friend."

"Can we get on with this?" says a familiar male voice. I'm guessing it's the man she'd called Bazinet's friend.

She waves her revolver in the air. "Are you really going to test my patience tonight after what happened to my grandbabies?"

I crane my neck. Bruce Jewett stands in his navy snowsuit behind an obese man in coveralls who must be Vic Bazinet.

Jewett looks drained; as bloodless as if he'd spent the night in a cave full of vampire bats.

Of course Tempest would bring Jewett here. She needed to keep the pressure on him.

It was Stacey, of all people, who had made me see the pattern in the scattered puzzle pieces.

Ever since the Dows learned that Burch had seen Chamberlain and Jewett arguing in the boat, they'd been blackmailing the Navy vet. It must have been Tori or Tiff's idea, to convince their new boyfriend to give Jewett an alibi. After he was in Arlo's debt, but still facing the possibility of a murder charge, they could steal him out of house and home.

"You can't go back to the hill," I say. "Not any of you. Jewett included."

Tempest laughs. "Sure, we can."

"I gave the dispatcher your names."

"I know you're lying," she says. "But even if it's true, it won't matter. We'll tell the police you visited us all and asked us questions. What happened after you left, we have no idea. My family knows how to keep a secret. Dows don't ever crack—"

"What about Jewett, though? Or Lynda?"

This gives the old woman pause. She presses her thin lips together. Then rises creakily to her full height of four and a half feet.

My last-ditch hope is to provoke a confrontation between Tempest Dow and Bruce Jewett. The paranoid gun-sniffer has to be armed. If I can find some way to encourage him to draw down on the woman who has destroyed his life. . . .

But Lynda Lynch foils my plan.

"Tempie," she says, almost whining, "You know I would never—"

Tempest swings on her as if to administer another pistol-whipping. "Shut up, you!"

Lynda recoils like a dog used to being kicked.

Tempest turns to Jewett next. "Make yourself useful, Bruce. Help Tanner drag the warden over there. And be careful. We're going to have to go over all this ground with Oxy-Clean. There can't be any trace of his DNA here. And we're going to need to torch the Chevy to be on the safe side."

She stands aside as Tanner and Jewett take me under their arms. God knows I am not going to make it easy for them. I refuse to take a single step toward my own execution. They drag me through the new-fallen snow to an enormous blue tarp spread out across it.

The whole time I am praying that I don't lose the knife in all this jostling.

I spent the time Tempest was talking counting

my enemies. There are only four men, Tanner, Jewett, Bazinet, and a guy on crutches, missing his lower left leg.

I can't fathom why Felice's dad is here until I see the truck.

A diesel pumper that is essentially one enormous tank chugs away beside the chicken coop. Black soot smokes from exhaust pipes that rise like dual chimneys behind the cab. Painted on the backside of the enormous machine are words I remember:

YESTERDAY'S MEALS ON WHEELS

It's harder to dispose of a body than what you see on television. It takes weeks for most acids to turn bones to jelly. Not just any fire is hot enough to burn away DNA. You need a potter's kiln or a blacksmith's forge to pull off an impromptu cremation. Pigs are reliable dispose-alls, if you have enough of them and give them time to digest.

The method the Dows have chosen is to dump me, probably alive, more likely in pieces, into a tank filled with shit, piss, and every imaginable bodily fluid. To any K-9, even an experienced dog, my distinct odor will be lost in the miasma of scents. All that is uniquely me will decay, dissolve, and disappear into raw sewage in the tank of some treatment plant.

"Tori, you want to do the honors?" Tempest asks with new merriment.

"You bet, Gram."

Behind me, I hear a chainsaw roar to life. I knew this was going to be bad. But this is worse than anything I imagined.

"Throw him there," orders Tempest.

Tanner heaves me into the tarp behind the idling truck. I land on my chest but roll onto my back quickly. I don't want them seeing the knife.

No one points a gun on me. Some of them have opened cans of beer. Tina has a fifth of Fireball. Others are passing around a gallon milk jug into which they've added coffee brandy. They're getting ready for their show of shows.

"Please, please." I put a weepy desperation into my voice. "Not this."

What they don't realize, as they're howling with laughter at my pathetic display, is that they can't see my hands. Behind my back I pull out the knife, push the button, and feel the high-carbon blade swing out of the handle. The edge of the Gerber 06 Automatic Knife is partially serrated above the finger guards. I saw through the plastic cable tie with quick strokes.

Tempest refuses an offered beer. "Tori, baby, I assume you want to take his leg first."

"I'd rather take his dick, but it's too small." She advances fast on me with the upraised saw. The jagged chain whirs, smoke rises from the vents.

"I'm going to make this slow, motherfucker. I'm going to cut off your legs and then your arms and then I'm going to make you wriggle on your stumps."

Tempest says to Jewett, "Bruce, help Tanner hold him down."

Jewett doesn't budge. He seems on the verge of catatonia.

"You afraid of getting blood on you?" she snarls. "Don't think you're getting out of this without taking part."

His voice comes out quieter than I've heard. "No, Tempest."

She levels her revolver at the bridge of his eyeglasses. "What did you say?"

"I said, 'No.' I won't help you kill him. I'm done."

It's the chance I have waited for. Distracted by Jewett, Tempest has stepped within reach. I jerk my arm out from under me, grab her ankle, and pull her off her feet. She goes down hard beside me on the tarp.

Tanner, nearby, is caught entirely off guard and doesn't know what to do.

Some of the Dows drop their bottles, others fumble for their guns. Tori lifts the screaming saw above her head and holds it there.

But none of them move because I have a knife pressed against their grandmother's carotid artery.

It figures that the only Dow with the presence of mind to act is Tempest herself. She casts around for the .38 special she dropped. But the gun has fallen beyond her reach—beyond my reach—bounced off the tarp and into the snow.

It is Lynda Lynch, of all people, who retrieves the revolver. Her hands shake as she points it in my direction.

Tanner stands like a tree. Out of the corner of my eye, I see Tori toss away the saw as she goes for the shotgun over her shoulder.

I'm on my backside, holding Tempest Dow around the waist, using her tiny body for cover, while I press the blade of Billy's knife against the skin beneath her ear.

One of the less drunk Dows, a woman whose name I don't know, has managed to get an AR-15 aimed. The laser activates when she closes her hand around the pistol grip. The red dot burns a hole in my forehead.

"Back off," I say.

"Shoot him!" says Tempest, kicking my shins with her boots. It's like trying to hold onto a starved bobcat. "Remember he's wearing a vest. Shoot him in the head, you stupid—"

She breaks off in mid-sentence because she's heard something. I have, too.

Then everyone does. Sirens, approaching fast.

How do they know where we are?

Even I don't know where we are.

I can feel the moment building. The Dows, increasingly panicked, are all waiting for a sign from Tempest, telling them what to do. Vic runs off as fast as his fat legs will carry him. Jewett collapses to the ground like a marionette whose strings have been cut.

"Shoot him, I said, you miserable—"

The gunshot has a snapping sound, typical of a .38. All at once, the old woman goes limp in my arms.

More than one person screams.

"Oh God!" says Lynda Lynch. She drops the Saturday Night Special as if it burned her hands.

I push Tempest's lifeless body aside and scramble across the tarp for the dropped gun. The roar of a shotgun tears through the night. Out of my peripheral vision I see blood spatter and Lynda crumple. She is missing part of her head.

The night has turned blue as the wailing cruisers pull up behind Tanner's Suburban, bathing the scene in their pulsing lights. A sled whines as someone takes off into the trees.

My hand closes around the grip of the Smith and Wesson revolver. I raise my arm.

Tori swings the semi-automatic shotgun around. The flashlight attached to the barrel finds me in the darkness.

We pull our triggers simultaneously.

If you go into a gun store and tell the clerk you

want a gun for personal protection, nine times out of ten they will try to sell you a revolver.

"The advantage of revolvers over semi-autos," they will say, "is they almost never jam."

The Benelli jams.

My Smith and Wesson doesn't.

40

At the hospital I refused all visitors, but I couldn't keep out the detectives.

The doctors had needed twelve stitches to close the gunshot wound in my leg and two pints of blood to replace what I had lost overnight. My toes were pale and swollen with second-degree frostbite, as were my ears. Ice crystals had formed beneath the skin, but I was unlikely to lose any body parts, the docs said. I had sustained multiple contusions, as well as abrasions to my thighs, shins, and chin from my Nantucket sleigh ride behind Tiff's Yamaha. My ballistic vest had minimized injuries to my torso although my ribs were most certainly bruised. To no one's surprise, my left wrist and elbow were sprained. To everyone's surprise, I had sustained no broken bones.

"It's because I drink so much milk," I told my physician, a towering, long-faced man with a high forehead. He had a mossy gray beard and reminded me of a giant tree creature out of J. R. R. Tolkien, an Ent.

Somehow, too, I had not received a concussion from having my head slammed against the rock when Tanner's Suburban nearly ran over me.

"Antibiotics are fine, but don't shoot me full of

painkillers," I told the doctor when I heard him discussing the specific medications he planned on injecting into my veins.

"You need to sleep." He had a deep, slow, Entish way of speaking.

"I can do that without being pumped full of opiates. Besides I need to be alert to give my statements. I want to get patched up and get out of here."

He stared at me with deep-set eyes that had seen everything. "Is there somewhere you need to be?"

"Yes, as a matter of fact."

I was thinking of Shadow.

The doctor said patiently and kindly something about how my body had suffered multiple traumas, including what sounded like hypovolemic shock, that I had lost a lot of blood, that my injuries would only become more painful as inflammation set in, et cetera, et cetera.

But I was already making plans to check myself out after they'd completed their sewing and wrapping and had refilled my circulatory system with O negative. I had no intention of spending a day and a night in the ICU.

"No one's giving you a medal for suffering," the giant doctor said, finally showing exasperation. "It's not weakness to admit you're in pain."

I wasn't playing the tough guy. I just hated hospitals.

The attorney general's chief investigator stopped by first. Because I was a law-enforcement officer who had used deadly force in self-defense, he was required to open an inquiry to determine if my actions were legally justified. Our union had hammered into us that we should answer as many of the AG's questions as we could with monosyllables. Otherwise we risked talking ourselves into serious criminal and civil jeopardy.

I couldn't have cared less. I treated the investigator to paragraph-long responses. My attitude seemed to worry him since he'd never encountered it after one of these police-involved homicides.

"Are you sure you want to do this now?" he said.

"I've got a hot date in an hour."

My near-death experience had left me giddy, but I knew from past experience, that the emotion would be fleeting and darkness waited.

The investigator asked me to hand over my service weapon. I had to explain he was welcome to my SIG if he could find it in the river.

He then said I was on paid administrative leave as of that moment while the attorney general completed his investigation into my shooting of Todd Wayne Dillon (formerly Dow) and Tori Anne Dillon (formerly Dow).

The warden colonel and captain stopped by next. Because they had listened to the wise counsel of our union attorneys, they didn't ask me for details of the shooting. The captain, however, teased me about not entering any beauty pageants in the near future. But I could see the colonel was deeply concerned for my well-being. Jock DeFord was a good man, and it was no less than what I'd expected of him. He said I should use my time off to heal. And he recommended I speak with the warden chaplain as soon as possible.

"Sorry about losing the Jeep," I said.

"Knowing you," Colonel DeFord said, "I'm sure it was just a ploy to get a better ride."

It was the best he could do by way of a joke. But I appreciated it.

Next were the state police detectives who had come straight from the crime scene. They also needed to hear from the doctor that I wasn't impaired by medications or suffering mental side-effects from my injuries, that I was capable of delivering a statement that would hold up if it was entered as evidence in a courtroom. They couldn't believe I had refused opioids. They brought in the doctor to vouch for my refusal.

The state police detectives were people I knew well, Ellen Pomerleau and her jerkwater partner Roger Finch. I was glad Ellen had caught the case. She had been a mentor to Dani and would no doubt take the news of her job change hard.

As usual, Detective Pomerleau was dressed entirely in black—car coat, turtleneck, and slacks—which made the milkiness of her complexion all the more pronounced. Her eyelashes and eyebrows were so faint you needed to squint. Her shoulder-length hair, a little wet from the snow, was the color of old ivory.

"I know this isn't the best time, Mike."

"You need to know what you're up against with the Dows. I heard some of them got away, but with Tempest and the Twisted Sisters dead, you shouldn't have trouble rounding up the rest. Tina was the smartest of the survivors, and you've got her, I heard. You want to hear my story? Take a seat and grab some popcorn."

"If I didn't already know your sense of humor, I would think you're not in your right mind," Ellen Pomerleau said. "But I want to start at the beginning. Tell me what brought you to Stratford yesterday."

What can I say? I told my tale, and by the end, the inflammation the doctor had warned me about was burning me up, and I was reconsidering my refusal of narcotics.

"Maybe we should stop for now?" Finch said, reaching for his herringbone topcoat.

"Not yet," I said. "Now it's time for you to answer my questions."

"Such as?"

He was a man of late middle age who dressed like detectives had forty years ago when his father had been on the job. The cleft in his chin looked like it had been drawn by a comic book artist. Finch had never approved of my methods, such as they were.

"Let's start with Jewett," I said. "You need to send a unit to his house to look after his mother. She has Alzheimer's and shouldn't be left alone."

"Already done," said Finch.

"A little bird told me he confessed to killing Chamberlain."

When her colleague failed to answer, Pomerleau stepped in. "He claims it was an accident. He and Chamberlain were arguing, and the professor fell out of the boat."

"Arguing about what?"

"Money Chamberlain had loaned him and wanted back."

"That's it? He didn't mention any other reasons?"

"His motive doesn't matter if he said he did it," she observed. "And there's no way he'll get off with manslaughter since he refused to admit this for four years. Plus whatever other charges the AG decides to bring. Jewett's going away for the rest of his life, Mike."

That was true, but it didn't satisfy my curiosity.

"I hope one of those other charges will be setting those spikes in the road for me to run over."

"He claims he was ordered to do it by Tempest Dow. Her plan was to delay you on the hill until dark so you wouldn't see the spikes until it was too late. From what you've said, I'm surprised she considered drowning an acceptably gruesome death for you."

"You didn't have to fight your way out of that river."

"True."

"What about Arlo Burch? Are you going to arrest him for blackmail?"

"He doesn't strike me as the brightest bulb," said Finch, who'd grown tired of my grilling and was making a show of putting on his coat over his blazer. "I don't think he ever really understood that he was involved in a criminal conspiracy."

Pomerleau had practice ignoring her partner's rude gestures. "The prosecutor has a busy day ahead. I don't think Arlo is going anywhere, and I'd lay down money that he'll come quietly when we put the cuffs on. He broke into tears when we gave him the news of his girlfriends' deaths. He really seemed to care for those pieces of shit. He kind of reminds me of a lost puppy."

"Ellen has a thing for the guy," said her partner.

I remembered something Dani had told me about Finch: how he smirked through every state-mandated sexual harassment video.

Pomerleau acted as if she hadn't heard him now. She hadn't gotten where she was in the state police by rising to every bait dangled before her. Maybe Dani was right to jump ship.

"Any other questions for us?" she asked me.

"Yeah. The big one. How did you find us?"

"That woman you spoke with, Felice Bazinet—"

"That's her maiden name."

Ellen ignored my hair-splitting. "She called 9–1–1 when she saw the Dows hauling out the heavy weapons. I don't think she wanted your murder on her conscience."

"But how did she know where we were?"

"Her father. She called and got him to tell her. I think her alerting us was as much about saving her old man as about saving you."

I pictured again the sad woman with the shaved head and the exotic eyes. "What's going to happen to her?"

"That's another conversation we'll be having with the prosecutor," said Finch curtly.

"And her dad, Vic?"

"Right now he's in lock-up as an accomplice to criminal conduct," said Pomerleau. "I'm sure we'll be adding charges. Conspiracy, felony murder, there will be no shortage of them. But my gut tells me you wouldn't have been the first of Tempest Dow's enemies to be chopped into pieces and trucked away as raw sewage."

Finch very much wanted to make a sewage joke at my expense—I could see it on his face—but he restrained himself.

"The prosecutor will offer him a deal for flipping on the Dows," I predicted.

"Will it bother you if he does?" she asked.

"No."

I had put off the hardest question for last because I hadn't wanted to hear the answer.

"The man they tortured to death, Reynolds—did he have a family?"

Pomerleau opened her notebook. "Reynolds Pedersen, age sixty-one. Resided at 252 River Road in Strickland. The van was registered to Carpet-Clean in Lewiston. We spoke with his employer who said Pedersen's wife died unexpectedly last spring, and he'd been having trouble coping. They had no children, the employer said. So far, we've been unable to locate any next of kin. It happens sometimes. A person dies and there's no one to inform."

"Is that better or worse?" I said.

Finch looked at me as if I'd asked the question in Cantonese.

I'd instructed Colonel DeFord to send a strongly worded message to my friends telling them I was "fine," whatever they might hear or read online, and that I would be in touch when I was ready to receive visitors.

"I don't want them rushing here," I'd said.

I feared Charley would be unable to help himself. He'd be gassing up his new Cessna 185 to fly down-state no matter what I said unless I escaped the hospital first. Stacey was right about her dad's feelings for me. I was the son he'd never had.

I heard from my doctor that wardens and other police had come by and been turned away as per my instructions.

The one person who managed to slip in to see me came as no surprise.

Danielle Tate peeked around the edge of my screen while I was drifting in and out of sleep. She was dressed in her powder blue trooper's uniform and holding her campaign hat. No doubt she had convinced the security guards and attending nurses that she'd been charged with keeping out unapproved visitors.

Dani was the shortest trooper the state police had ever hired, but she was sturdily built. The uniform hadn't been designed for female officers, but underneath the ill-fitting clothes she had the body of a former gymnast. Her face was square; her eyes a stony gray. She wore her dark-blond hair pinned up with barrettes. Most men considered her plain. But the longer I had known her, the lovelier she had become to me. She had more grit than any of the men in her barracks and a heart twice the size of mine.

"Jesus Christ!"

"Hey."

"What did those SOBs do to you?"

"Everything they could. At the end, I managed

to avoid losing my leg to a chainsaw, but it was a close call."

She came over and lightly took my hand, the one that didn't have an IV needle threaded into a vein. "Why didn't you tell me what you were up to when we were on the phone? I had to hear about you nearly dying from Ellen Pomerleau."

"I thought I had everything in hand. Besides, you were so excited about your interview with Jemison."

"I should be pissed at you, but you look so damn pathetic I can't do it. What happened, Mike? What did those people put you through?"

"Later," I said. "I went through it all with Pomerleau and Finch, and I don't have it in me. Ellen can fill you in on the details."

"I don't want the official version," she said, showing the frustration she'd tried to suppress. "Oh, Mike, why do you have to be so fucking reckless?"

"That's who I am, Dani. You should know that by now."

She set her broad-brimmed hat down on the wheeled cart beside the bed. "I guess I should. I guess I do."

"There you go then."

She let her gaze drift around the room with all its pumping, blinking medical wonders. "I used to think it was cool. I remember watching you jump thirty feet into a quarry to pull a girl out of a sinking car and I thought, *Holy shit!* But it's been exhausting being in a relationship with someone who risks everything all the time."

"You have to be willing to die to do the job."

Her cheeks flushed as she turned to me. "Don't give me that. You enjoy taking risks. You live for the danger."

"I can't apologize for being who I am."

"I used to think you'd grow out of it, but now I know you won't."

" 'Women think men will change, and men think women won't.' That was one of my mom's favorite quotes."

"I wish I'd met her."

"She would have liked you. She would have thought you were good for me."

She released my hand and patted it almost the way one would a small child's. "I tried to be good for you," she said with resignation.

I attempted to raise myself up and must have made a pained face. She helped me by sliding another pillow under my head.

"The last time we were in a hospital together I was the one visiting you," I said.

"But I didn't put myself there. It was a random virus. You played an active part in landing in this bed."

"True."

"I almost died from that virus, Mike. It's still unreal how close I came."

"The first near-death experience is always the hardest."

"I wish you wouldn't joke."

She was right, of course. Ever since I'd arrived at the hospital, I'd tried to use humor to ward off the emotions that would soon be busting down my door.

"Do you remember what I asked you?" I said. "When I visited you in the hospital, I suggested we should move in together. You said I wasn't ready for happily ever after. You told me to take care of my wolf first and see how it went. I didn't do a very good job of that, it seems."

"I'm so sorry about Shadow, but you'll find him. I know you will."

She hadn't offered her help, and I took that for what it was.

We both became quiet. I let the silence stretch on until I couldn't take it anymore.

"You have your interview today," I said.

"At ten o'clock."

"You deserve to get the job. You're one of the best cops I know."

She smiled, showing her killer dimples. "One of the best?"

"The best. Good luck, Dani."

"Thanks, but I won't need it." She took her hat from the cart, put it on at the forward angle troopers preferred, and fastened the chin strap.

She looked very official. "I'll swing by afterward and see how you're doing."

"If I get my way, I'll be long gone by then."

She leaned down and kissed me on the forehead.

41

On Christmas morning, I awaken before dawn, as I have the previous three days, and drive my Scout west to the Androscoggin. We have had consecutive subzero nights after the weather event I nicknamed "Emma Cronk's Magic Snow," and now the river is frozen solid from bank to bank. I drive up and down the road along both shores looking for signs of Shadow.

The day can't be more beautiful. The skies are blue all the way to the heavens. Fresh snow glistens from the boughs of the evergreens. And the bracingly cold air reminds me with each new breath of my continuing existence as a living creature on this planet. An eagle passes downstream, heading south to hunt ducks and gulls on the open water below the dams, and my soul rises to meet it. Even the slopes of Pill Hill, glimpsed across the frozen river, shine like hammered gold in the light of the newly risen sun.

My friends don't like me coming here, not like this. I might tear my stitches if I move awkwardly, they say. I shouldn't be driving at all while on pain medication (they don't know I've ditched the Vicodin the doctor pushed into my hand). After what I endured on the night of the solstice, they say, I shouldn't be alone.

They assume I must be suffering from post-traumatic stress syndrome because what person wouldn't be suffering from PTSD who was nearly drowned, frozen, shot, battered, and then threatened with dismemberment and disposal in a tank full of shit? Surely, too, the night's dead must haunt me. And it's true that new souls have joined the parade of ghosts that follow me silently in my dreams. After everything I endured, how can I not be a wreck?

But I have had post-traumatic stress syndrome before, in the fall and winter following my father's death. I hadn't recognized it at the time, but I remember the symptoms vividly: the paranoia, the edginess, the increasingly self-destructive behavior. Most of all, I recall the guilt. None of which I am experiencing now.

Instead of breaking my spirit, the ordeal seems to have strengthened me. Every day since I left the hospital, I have awakened in severe physical pain but with a serenity that doesn't require an hour of meditation to attain. This calmness puzzled me at first. Even troubled me a little because I kept expecting the demons to arrive.

Then I found a metaphor.

There is a word that blacksmiths use, *annealing,* to describe the process a blade undergoes when it is allowed to cool slowly. Tempering makes metal harder, sometimes so hard it risks shattering.

Annealing makes steel ductile: capable of withstanding tremendous stress without breaking.

I have been annealed.

Only my friends who are combat veterans understand this.

Charley was a prisoner of war in Vietnam where he endured unimaginable tortures, and yet he'd somehow come home a functional human being. More than functional. He is the best man I've been privileged to know.

Billy Cronk was not so lucky. His tours with the 10th Mountain Division in Iraq and Afghanistan left his body unscarred but his spirit shattered. With the help of his family and counselors, he is gluing himself together. But I suspect he will never be fully intact again; there will always be sharp edges not safe to touch.

When Billy came to the hospital to take me home, he looked into my bloodshot eyes and went quiet.

"I look that pretty?" I said.

"No."

"What then?"

"Have I ever told you you're my hero?"

"Isn't that a song?"

I was joking because I could see he was sincere, and it embarrassed me.

"I'm serious, man. You've gone through shit in your life that would've broken the toughest guys in my brigade."

"It was your knife that saved me, Billy."

"The blade is just an extension of the man."

"Now you sound like a samurai movie."

But it was those words—that uncomfortably admiring sentiment—that gave me the analogy of the annealing process.

Two nights after returning to my empty house, I celebrated Christmas Eve at the Cronks' place.

"You sure you won't let me go with you tomorrow?" he said.

"It's Christmas morning, Billy! Your first since you got out of prison. You can't not be here with your family."

"I've already received my gifts." He smiled at Aimee who was seated with Emma in her lap while the girl read aloud from the new Harry Potter book she'd unwrapped, my present to her. "I don't deserve the blessings I've been given."

He'd had a few glasses of eggnog and his emotions were running high.

I sipped my own (unspiked) eggnog. The Cronk boys were passing back and forth the personalized jackknives I'd bought (with their mother's permission) from L.L.Bean. The gifts seemed appropriate after the crucial role Billy's blade had played in saving my life.

"Is your phone still ringing?" my friend asked.

"I've unplugged it."

The national media had gotten wind of my torment at the hands of the Dows and wanted to interview me. I'd kept silent at the advice of counsel (and my own common sense), but that hadn't stopped a few online outlets from flailing me for having shot and killed a woman half my weight, ignoring the fact that she'd nearly murdered me. The polemicists wanted Tori Dow to be in death someone she had never been in life. They wanted her to stand for a cause she would have found laughable.

"I still can't get over it, Mike," Billy said, lowering his bearish voice. "How you managed to survive everything you did."

I had worried he might return to the subject of my heroism the deeper he got in his cups. "It was Emma's magic. Remember she cast protection spells on Shadow and me that morning?"

"It was more than that."

"If I had to credit anyone, I guess it would be Felice Bazinet—or whatever her married name is. She called the police to tell them where the Dows were going to take me. I don't know how she got the information out of her dad. But I'm glad she did."

"You said she was in on the plan, though. It was her job to delay you until dark. The Dows needed time to plant those spikes in the road and alert everyone in their network."

"It wasn't the Dows who planted them—it was Jewett. Tempest liked nothing better than manipulating people into doing her dirty work for her. She had Bruce Jewett under her thumb for years because of what Arlo Burch had seen. Now Jewett is probably going to prison for the rest of his life. But after years of being bled dry, I think he's relieved it's finally over."

"But he still won't say *why* he did it?"

"Just that he and the professor got into a heated argument and the boat began to rock and Chamberlain fell over. Jewett claims that life vest came off when he tried to haul the old man onboard, which can happen. He says the professor went under because the river was fast and cold, and there was nothing he could do."

"Not a lover's quarrel?"

"That's what Mariëtte Chamberlain thinks. I have no idea. But it's interesting that Jewett gets so enraged at the implication that he and the professor had a sexual relationship. He doesn't mind being branded a murderer, but he considers being outed as gay as the worst stigma a man can suffer."

Billy had finished his eggnog and poured some straight rum from the bottle into his mug. He was secretive, turned his broad back, not wanting his wife to see. He only thought he got away with it. Aimee Cronk missed nothing.

"You sure you don't want some?" he whispered. "Oh, right. You're on those meds. Be careful with that stuff. I've lost too many of my army friends to opiates."

"You don't have to worry about me."

"That's what they all say." But even drunk, he seemed to sense I was telling the truth. "One thing I've been wondering about. Who left the note on your windshield?"

"Beats me."

"Don't you want to—?"

"It doesn't matter, Billy. You're never going to solve every little mystery in life. So forget the unimportant ones."

He brooded on this, and I could see he was far from satisfied. "And you never explained about that Felicia."

"Felice."

"Why she'd do it? Why did she inform on the Dows after helping them?"

"Felice kept me talking because Tempest ordered it, but she didn't know why. She should have suspected it was more than a mean prank. But I never got the feeling she was an evil person. She might not have liked me, or maybe she did, but she didn't want me to die. Sometimes people become brave when they're more afraid for others than they are for themselves."

I didn't mention to Billy that Felice had confessed that everything she'd told me about Bibi Chamberlain had been a lie. The granddaughter loved her grandfather and vice versa. There had been no changes in the will. It was all bullshit meant to string me along until darkness fell.

"What's going to happen to her?" Billy asked.

"To Felice? Nothing, if I have any say in the matter. I'm not sure what crime the prosecutor could even charge her with. But I'm guessing her friendship with Bibi Chamberlain is over."

"Has the mother been in contact with you?"

"Mariëtte sent me a thank-you note."

It was an actual stationery card, the kind you mail someone who's given you a present off your wedding registry. There was a letter folded inside.

Dear Warden Bowditch,
Thank you for helping me bring Bruce Jewett to justice. It is no compensation for the loss of Professor Chamberlain, both to his family and the world. I have heard that you were injured by his accomplices. For your suffering and the good work you did, I have made a five thousand dollar donation in your name to _____."

The beneficiary of *my* largess was an animal rights organization that was engaged in a strategic campaign to outlaw hunting in Maine, piece by piece. I could only imagine how wardens would react if they saw my name on its list of donors, among the Hollywood stars and Manhattan socialites.

Billy and I spent a quiet minute watching his

family. The room was toasty from the wood stove, and the entire house smelled of the pumpkin pie Aimee was baking for the next day's supper.

"You sure I can't come with you to the river?" my friend asked again.

"No, but thank you. Maybe another morning. I am not going to rest until I find him, Billy."

"He's a survivor. Like you."

"Once maybe, but he suffered a lot of damage from that crossbow bolt. I saw how awkwardly he ran across the ice. He might be able to fend for himself for a while. But his days of chasing deer are over. He won't make it out there alone."

"I'm thinking of getting a dog," said Billy, out of nowhere.

"Because there's not enough chaos in your life?"

"I've always had them. I'm thinking of a Chessie I could use sea-duck hunting. It would be good for the kids to have a dog again." He sipped some rum. "You need to find that wolf, Mike. He's depending on you."

"I know."

Later, as I was bundling up to limp the mile home—the exercise would hurt, but I wanted to keep my joints loose—Billy said, "Are you ever going to get around to decorating your house for Christmas?"

"It's too late for that," I said. "Besides, it's only going to be me there tomorrow."

"No Dani?"

"No Dani."

The house was dark and cold when I got home. I couldn't sleep.

Now I carry a frozen deer haunch down to the river.

Since the morning of the 23rd, I have been putting out food on both sides of the river: venison quarters, hog's heads, beef bones red with marrow. My offerings have been greatly appreciated by the resident coyotes, foxes, eagles, and especially the omnipresent crows. The black birds watch me from the pines while I search in vain for wolf prints, waiting to swoop down the moment I leave.

I trudge on snowshoes up and down the banks and even across the channel to the island where I ambushed Tori. I make a pilgrimage to the ice fishing shack where I regained my life, then almost lost it again.

The snow is a map of the past. I see where a flock of turkeys crossed after the storm, followed by a bobcat. Later, shrews tunneled beneath the surface. Everywhere are the tiny, busy feet of mice, always moving from cover to cover.

But I find no trace of the wolf.

The day is short and passes quickly. As the sun sets, the western sky glows with colors so beautiful I feel a lump form in my throat: butter yellow, blush red, and a streak of salmon orange that you only see in winter. Against this radiant backdrop, the crows begin to gather and move in ragged clouds to their roost.

I nearly fail to notice the raven. He is bigger than his cousins, with a ruffed throat and a wedge-shaped tail, and he beats his wings in a rowing motion. This one is strangely quiet for his kind.

Ravens and wolves have evolved to have a symbiotic relationship. The birds alert the canines to injured animals or carcasses not yet scavenged. Then they wait until the wolves make their kills or finish their meals. The bills of ravens are not sharp enough to open the thick skins of deer and moose, and so they rely on their furry partners to do the butchering.

As I have said, I try not to locate signs and omens in the natural world, but the unexpected appearance of the raven intrigues me—as a naturalist.

I grow more excited when I realize he is soaring over the beaver lodge where I'd last seen Shadow.

In the purple dusk I tramp up the channel, and it is here that I finally find his tracks.

He must have ventured out of the woods in the vain hope he would find beavers inside the abandoned house. But he lacked the strength to open a hole between the logs, and even if he had, it would have done him no good. Two of his paws were bleeding, probably from ice chunks like broken glass between his toes.

Standing there, in the failing light, I call his name. My voice doesn't echo. The raven, however, responds with an inscrutable, *"Quork!"*

The breeze whips up little clouds of powder from the surface of the snow. I listen to the trembling of the dead leaves still attached to the oaks. Brown prayer flags in the wind.

I call again, louder.

Still no response.

I decided to trudge back to my personal vehicle, the International Harvester Scout, to fetch the grocery store turkey. It's the last item left in the cooler. I plan on placing the frozen bird atop the lodge where, hopefully, Shadow's sensitive nose will locate its scent on the wind.

But as I limp my way up the boat launch a feeling comes over me. Tempest Dow might have called it a vibration.

I turn slowly, and there he is, fifty feet down the ramp, looking gaunt and ragged. The hairs on his muzzle are white with frost. He shows no sign of aggression; he hasn't raised the hackles along his neck. But his sulfur eyes are as unknowable as ever.

"Hey, big guy."

He remains so motionless he might as well be

a stuffed exhibit in a diorama at a natural history museum.

"I hate it to break it to you, but you look terrible. I know you're hungry. You might even be thinking of eating me at the moment. I'd rather you didn't, but to be honest, it would be a fitting end to the week we've both had."

His tail twitches. A plume rises from his panting mouth into the bitter air.

"I've got food for you in the truck. I know turkey's not your favorite, but it's better than the mice or whatever you've been catching."

He lowers his head to sniff an odor blowing past.

"I'll come back with the turkey. If you feel like taking off, I'll leave it for you. I promise it's not a trick."

And with that, I turn slowly and keep walking on scraping snowshoes to my parked truck. I don't pause or glance over my shoulder. I am sincerely afraid to look in case he's vanished.

When I arrive at the Scout, I raise the door on the cap over the bed, then lower the gate. I wrestle out the massive Yeti cooler that weighs a ton and pull the rubber latches free. Even wrapped in a brace my sprained wrist complains. I reach inside with both hands to lift out the thawing Butterball.

Shadow has followed me halfway up the ramp. He freezes as I turn, watching me with that same hyper-alert posture: front legs spread, ears pointed, eyes on mine.

It hurts like hell, but I squat to place the turkey on the frozen gravel. "I'll leave this here."

He doesn't trust me. He gives a glance in the direction of the woods. I am afraid he's about to bolt.

Slowly, I straighten up again, feeling the effort in my thighs, especially the left one, and my back.

"Or we can go home," I say.

His gaze reveals nothing.

"I haven't had a chance to buy another kennel. I bet you'll never get inside one of those again. I wouldn't either if I were you. So you'd have to ride in back. I don't mind if you want to eat while I drive."

He takes a tentative step forward. My heart begins to swell.

"I'll let you hang your head out the window if you want to pretend you're a golden retriever. We might scare a few drivers off the road, but what the hell." I retrieve the turkey and place it in the rear of the Scout.

Wolves and dogs are closely related, but humans have spent millennia learning to communicate with our so-called best friends. I can yammer at this big, black creature all I want. Maybe he understands me; maybe he doesn't. He is and always will be a wild animal.

"Take your time. I need to get these snowshoes off."

I take a big-footed step toward the driver's door, worried again that I am moving too fast for him.

But as I approach the side mirror, I see his reflection, trotting forward, tail wagging.

Without another word from me, he vaults into the rear of the truck.

By the time I circle around, he is lying on his stomach, beside the cooler. He gnaws the frozen turkey, taking scraping bites. I hesitate to close the gate on him, but I take the chance. He keeps right on eating.

The drive home is surreal. Despite the turkey being a block of ice, Shadow manages to polish it off. I resort to tossing him granola bars from my personal stash in the glove compartment. These, he swallows whole.

I am dying to call someone, anyone, with the good news. But the situation inside the moving vehicle seems too delicate. I don't want to speak, let alone stop in case it unnerves the wolf. That's all I need: him going haywire.

I have lost so many things in my life that I have forgotten what it's like to receive a gift this precious.

After half an hour on the road, Shadow clambers into the backseat, ripping my leather upholstery with his claws in the process, but so what? His big body stretches from door to door. He lets out a sigh and seems to fall asleep. But when I tilt the rearview mirror to get an angle on him, one brimstone eye opens.

Despite my misgivings about stopping, I slow down as I pass the Cronk place. I expect to see a line of vehicles from Aimee's visiting family, but the windows are dark, and the Tahoe isn't in the driveway. Aimee's parents and sister live Down East. Maybe the Cronks changed their plans and drove to Washington County instead of hosting supper here?

When I turn down the drive to my house, Shadow rouses himself.

"I'm assuming you want to stay at your place. But you're welcome to crash with me. It'll be a lot warmer."

Through the hemlocks I see lights coming from the house. It is unlike me to leave lamps on by mistake. Then I see that my entire trim is strung with Christmas lights. There are electric candles glowing in the windows, and a big wreath on the door.

The Cronks must have come by while I was away and decorated the place. No doubt this was at Emma's insistence. I find myself wishing they had stayed. The occasion of Shadow's return calls for celebration.

Unsure whether to drive into his enclosure

or attempt to lure him indoors, I stop the truck outside my front steps. The key to the gate is hanging on a hook in my kitchen.

"I'll be right back," I tell him.

He answers with a growl which I interpret, without evidence, as a sign that he wants to come inside rather than sleep another night in the cold.

"Let me pick up a few things first."

I slip out of the Scout and drag myself up the steps and turn the key in the lock.

Suddenly there is a choral shout. "Surprise!"

Emma Cronk runs toward me, nearly tripping over her wizard robe, while the Cronklet boys emerge, grinning, from the living room, with Billy and Aimee behind them. Charley and Ora are next, followed by a slim woman with brown hair and jade-green eyes. I wrap my arms around Emma and some of the younger boys, and shake hands with the older ones. I give Billy a bro hug and have the air squeezed out of me by his wife. Charley claps his hand against my shoulderblade, as he always does, and I manage not to wince. I lean down to kiss Ora on the cheek, only to have her pull me down for a real hug.

Last is Stacey. She seems to hang in the middle of the room as if suspended. When I am finally free, she rushes forward, throws her arms around my waist and buries her face in my neck for the first time in three years.

"Merry Christmas, Mike Bowditch," she says.

AUTHOR'S NOTE

There's no one I am indebted to more for this book and all the others I have written than my wife and teammate Kristen Lindquist.

I am grateful as ever to my wonderful agent Ann Rittenberg and my insightful editor Charles Spicer who collaborate so well together to bring out the best in my writing—and in me. As always, my team at Minotaur Books—Andy Martin, Kelley Ragland, Sarah Melnyk, Paul Hochman, Joe Brosnan, and Sarah Grill—has been a delight to work with. David Rotstein, this might be my favorite of all the excellent covers you have done for my novels.

Certain people and certain books were of special importance to the writing of *Dead by Dawn*. Corporal John MacDonald of the Maine Warden Service is always my first call when I have an idea that promises to become the next chapter in the Mike Bowditch saga. Matt Weber, author of *Making Tracks: How I Learned to Love Snowmobiling in Maine*, provided invaluable assistance in educating me in the finer points of sledding. Maine artist and authority Eric Hopkins provided generous feedback. Mat and Nancy McConnel encouraged me and caught errors in the manuscript. My reading in preparation for writing this book included first and foremost *Deep Survival: Who Lives, Who Dies, and Why* by Laurence Gonzalez; *Winter World: The Ingenuity of Animal Survival* by Bernd Heinrich; *Gunshot Wounds: Practical Aspects of Firearms, Ballistics, and Forensic Techniques* by Vincent J. M. DiMaio, MD (always good for a little light reading); *Snowmobile and ATV Accident Investigation and Reconstruction* by Richard Hermance (same).

Lastly, I send my love and gratitude to my parents, Richard and Judy Doiron, my siblings, nieces, and nephews, and to the rest of my wicked bitchin' family. You, too, Rooney.

Center Point Large Print
600 Brooks Road / PO Box 1
Thorndike, ME 04986-0001 USA

(207) 568-3717

US & Canada:
1 800 929-9108
www.centerpointlargeprint.com